THE HIGHLANDER'S TEMPTATION

PREQUEL TO THE STOLEN BRIDE SERIES

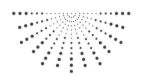

ELIZA KNIGHT

~

FIRST EDITION
February 2014

Copyright 2014 © Eliza Knight

Cover Design: Kimberly Killion @ The Killion Group, Inc.

ABOUT THE BOOK

Desire tempted them, but love conquered all...

Laird Jamie Montgomery is a warrior with a mission. When he travels to the northern Highlands on the orders of William Wallace, temptation in the form of an alluring lass, could be his undoing.

Lady Lorna Sutherland can't resist the charms of one irresistible Highlander. Though she's been forbidden, she breaks every rule for the pleasure of his intoxicating embrace.

When their love is discovered, Jamie is tossed from Sutherland lands under threat of death. But danger can't keep the two of them apart. No matter what perils may try to separate them—Lorna and Jamie swear they'll find a way to be together.

Praise for **The Stolen Bride Series**...

"For fans of Highlander romance, this series is a must read!" ~Night Owl Romance

The Highlander's Reward – winner of InD'Tale Magazine's Best Historical Novel 2012

The Highlander's Reward – *"The powerful yet sensitive Magnus and the saucy and beautiful Arbella are a winning pair in this Scottish themed romance that even boasts cameos from William Wallace himself."* ~Publisher's Weekly Reviewer for the Amazon Breakthrough Novel Contest

To Mel, my dearest friend in all the world.

ACKNOWLEDGMENTS

Many special thanks to my wonderful readers! Without you, I'd not be able to create these exciting stories. And also, much appreciation to my beta readers! Vonda, Lizzie, Andrea and Gwyn!

PROLOGUE

Spring, 1282
Highlands, Scotland

They galloped through the eerie moonlit night. Warriors cloaked by darkness. Blending in with the forest, only the occasional glint of the moon off their weapons made their presence seem out of place.

'Twas chilly for spring, and yet, they rode hard enough the horses were lathered with sweat and foaming at the mouth. But the Montgomery clan wasn't going to be pushed out of yet another meeting of the clans, not when their future depended on it. This meeting would put their clan on the map, make them an asset to their king and country. As it was, years before King Alexander III had lost one son and his wife. He'd not remarried and the fate of the country now relied on one son who didn't feel the need to marry. The prince toyed with his life as though he had a death wish, fighting, drinking, and carrying on without a care in the world. The king's only other chance at a succession was his daughter who'd married but had not yet shown any signs of a bairn filling her womb. If something were to happen to the king, the country would erupt into chaos. Every precaution needed to be taken.

Young Jamie sat tall and proud upon his horse. Even prouder was he, that his da, the fearsome Montgomery laird, had allowed him to accompany the group of a half dozen seasoned warriors—the men who sat on his own clan council—to the meeting. The fact that his father had involved him in matters of state truly made his chest puff five times its size.

After being fostered out the last seven years, Jamie had just returned to his father's home. At age fourteen, he was ready to take on the duties of eldest son, for one day he would be laird. This was the perfect opportunity to show his da all he'd learned. To prove he was worthy.

Laird Montgomery held up his hand and all the riders stopped short. Puffs of steam blew out in miniature clouds from the horses' noses. Jamie's heart slammed against his chest and he looked from side to side to make sure no one could hear it. He was a man after all, and men shouldn't be scared of the dark. No matter how frightening the sounds were.

Carried on the wind were the deep tones of men shouting and the shrill of a woman's screams. Prickles rose on Jamie's arms and legs. They must have happened upon a robbery or an ambush. When he'd set out to attend his father, he'd not counted on a fight. Nay, Jamie merely thought to stand beside his father and demand a place within the Bruce's High Council.

Swallowing hard, he glanced at his father, trying to assess his thoughts, but as usual, the man sat stoic, not a hint of emotion on his face.

The laird glanced at his second in command and jutted his chin in silent communication. The second returned the nod. Jamie's father made a circling motion with his fingers, and several of the men fanned out.

Jamie observed the exchange, his throat near to bursting with questions. What was happening?

Finally, his father motioned Jamie forward. Keeping his

emotions at bay, Jamie urged his mount closer. His father bent toward him, indicating for Jamie to do the same, then spoke in a hushed tone.

"We're nearly to Sutherland lands. Just on the outskirts, son. 'Tis an attack, I'm certain. We mean to help."

Jamie swallowed past the lump in his throat and nodded. The meeting was to take place at Dunrobin Castle. Why that particular castle was chosen, Jamie had not been privy to. Though he speculated 'twas because of how far north it was. Well away from Stirling where the king resided.

"Are ye up to it?" his father asked.

Tightening his grip on the reins, Jamie nodded. Fear cascaded along his spine, but he'd never show any weakness in front of his father, especially now that he'd been invited on this very important journey.

"Good. 'Twill give ye a chance to show me what ye've learned."

Again, Jamie nodded, though he disagreed. Saving people wasn't a chance to show off what he'd learned. He could never look at protecting another as an opportunity to prove his skill, only as a chance to make a difference. But he kept that to himself. His da would never understand. If making a difference proved something to his father, then so be it.

An owl screeched from somewhere in the distance as it caught onto its prey, almost in unison with the blood curdling scream of a woman.

His father made a few more hand motions and the rest of their party followed him as they crept forward at a quickened pace on their mounts, avoiding making any noise.

The road ended on a clearing, and some thirty horse-lengths away a band of outlaws circled a trio—a lady, one warrior, and a lad close to his own age.

The outlaws caught sight of their approach, shouting and pointing. His father's men couldn't seem to move quickly enough and Jamie watched in horror as the man, woman and child were hacked down. All three of them on the ground, the outlaws turned on the Montgomery warriors and rushed forward as though they'd not a care in the world.

Jamie shook. He'd never been so scared in his life. His throat had long since closed up and yet his stomach was threatening to purge everything he'd consumed that day. Even though he felt like vomiting, a sense of urgency, and power flooded his veins. Battle-rush, he'd heard it called by the seasoned warriors. And it was surging through his body, making him tingle all over.

The laird and his men raised their swords in the air, roaring out their battle cries. Jamie raised his sword to do the same, but a flash of gold behind a large lichen-covered boulder caught his attention. He eased his knees on his mount's middle.

What was that?

Another flash of gold — was that blonde hair? He'd never seen hair like that before.

Jamie turned to his father, intent to point it out, but his sire was several horse-lengths ahead and ready to engage the outlaws, leaving it up to Jamie to investigate.

After all, if there was another threat lying in wait, was it not up to someone in the group to seek them out? The rest of the warriors were intent on the outlaws which left Jamie to discover the identity of the thief.

He veered his horse to the right, galloping toward the boulder. A wee lass darted out, lifting her skirts and running full force in the opposite direction. Jamie loosened his knees on his horse and slowed. That was not what he'd expected. At all. Jamie anticipated a warrior, not a tiny little girl whose legs were no match for his mount. As he neared, despite his slowed pace, he feared he'd trample the little imp.

He leapt from his horse and chased after her on foot. The lass kept turning around, seeing him chasing her. The look of horror on her face nearly broke his heart. Och, he was no one to fear. But how would she know that? She probably thought he was after her like the outlaws had been after the man, woman and lad.

"'Tis all right!" he called. "I will nay harm ye!"

4

But she kept on running, and then was suddenly flying through the air, landing flat on her face.

Jamie ran toward her, dropping to his knees as he reached her side and she pushed herself up.

Her back shook with cries he was sure she tried hard to keep silent. He gathered her up onto his knees and she pressed her face to his *leine* shirt, wiping away tears, dirt and snot as she sobbed.

"Momma," she said. "Da!"

"Hush, now," Jamie crooned, unsure of what else he could say. She must have just watched her parents and brother get cut to the ground. Och, what an awful sight for any child to witness. Jamie shivered, at a loss for words.

"Blaney!" she wailed, gripping onto his shirt and yanking. "They hurt!"

Jamie dried her tears with the cuff of his sleeve. "Your family?" he asked.

She nodded, her lower lip trembling, green-blue eyes wide with fear and glistening with tears. His chest swelled with emotion for the little imp and he gripped her tighter.

"Do ye know who the men were?"

"Bad people," she mumbled.

Jamie nodded. "What's your name?"

She chewed her lip as if trying to figure out if she should tell him. "Lorna. What are ye called?"

"Jamie." He flashed her what he hoped wasn't a strained smile. "How old are ye, Lorna?"

"Four." She held up three of her fingers, then second guessed herself and held up four. "I'm four. How old are ye?"

"Fourteen."

"Ye're four, too?" she asked, her mouth dropping wide as she forgot the horror of the last few minutes of her life for a moment.

"Fourteen. 'Tis four plus ten."

"I want to be fourteen, too." She swiped at the mangled mop of blonde hair around her face, making more of a mess than anything else.

5

"Then we'd best get ye home. Have ye any other family?"

"A whole big one."

"Where?"

"Dunrobin," she said. "My da is laird."

"Laird Sutherland?" Jamie asked, trying to keep the surprise from his face. Did his father understand just how deep and unsettling this attack had been? A laird had been murdered. Was it an ambush? Was there more to it than just a band of outlaws? Were they men trying to stop the secret meeting from being held?

There would be no meeting, if the laird who'd called the meeting was dead.

"I'll take ye home," Jamie said, putting the girl on her feet and standing.

"Will ye carry me?" she said, her lip trembling again. She'd lost a shoe and her yellow gown was stained and torn. "I'm scared."

"Aye. I'll carry ye."

"Are ye my hero?" she asked, batting tear moistened lashes at him.

Jamie rolled his eyes and picked her up. "I'm no hero, lass."

"Hmm... Ye seem like a hero to me."

Jamie didn't answer. He tossed her on his horse and climbed up behind her. A glance behind showed that his father and his men had dispatched of most of the men, and a few others gave chase into the forest. They'd likely meet him at the castle as that had been their destination all along.

Squeezing his mount's sides, Jamie urged the horse into a gallop, intent on getting the girl to the safety of Dunrobin's walls, and then returning to his father.

Spotting Jamie with the lass, the guards threw open the gate. A nursemaid rushed over and grabbed Lorna from him, chiding her for sneaking away.

"What's happened?" A lad his own age approached. "Why did ye have my sister?"

Jamie swallowed, dismounted and held out his arm to the other young man. "I found her behind a boulder." Jamie took a deep breath, then looked the boy in the eye, hating the words he would have to say. "There was an ambush."

"My family?"

Jamie shook his head. He opened his mouth to tell the dreadful news, but the way the boy's face hardened, and eyes glistened, it didn't seem necessary. As it happened, he was given a reprieve from saying more when his father and men came barreling through the gate a moment later.

"Where's the laird?" Jamie's father bellowed.

"If what this lad said is true, then I may be right here," the boy said, straightening his shoulders.

Laird Montgomery's eyes narrowed, jaw tightened with understanding. "Aye, lad, ye are."

He leapt from his horse, his eyes lighting on Jamie "Where've ye been, lad? Ye scared the shite out of us." His father looked pale, shaken. Had he truly scared him so much?

"There was a lass," Jamie said, "at the ambush. I brought her home."

His father snorted. "Always a lass. Mark my words, lad. Think here." His father tapped Jamie's forehead hard with the tip of his finger. "The mind always knows better than the sword."

Jamie frowned and his father walked back toward the young laird. It was the second time that day that he'd not agreed with his father. For if a lass was in need of rescuing, by God, he was going to be her rescuer.

CHAPTER ONE

Dunrobin Castle, Scottish Highlands
   Early Spring, 1297

"*I*'ve arranged a meeting between Chief MacOwen and myself."

Lorna Sutherland lifted her eyes from her noon meal, the stew heavy as a bag of rocks in her belly as she met her older brother, Magnus', gaze.

"Why are ye telling me this?" she asked.

He raised dark brows as though he was surprised at her asking. What was he up to?

"I thought it important for ye to know."

She raised a brow and struggled to swallow the bit of pulverized carrot in her mouth. Her jaw hurt from clenching it, and she thought she might choke. There could only be one reason he felt the need to tell her this and she was certain she didn't want to know the answer. Gingerly, she set down her knife on her trencher and took a rather large gulp of watered wine, hoping it would help open her suddenly seized throat.

A moment later, she cocked her head innocently, and said, "Does not a laird and chief of his clan keep such talk to himself and his trusted council?" The haughty tone that took over could not be helped.

After nineteen summers, this conversation had been a long time coming. It was Aunt Fiona's fault. She'd arrived the week before, returning Heather, the youngest and wildest of the Sutherland siblings, and happened to see Lorna riding like the wind. Disgusted, her aunt marched straight to Magnus and demanded that he marry her off. Tame her, she'd said.

Lorna didn't see the problem with riding and why that meant she had to marry. So what if she liked to ride her horse standing on the saddle? She was good at it. Wasn't it important for a lass to excel in areas that she had skill?

Now granted, Lorna did admit that having her arms up in the air and eyes closed was borderline dangerous, but she'd done it a thousand times without mishap.

Even still, picturing her aunt's look of horror and how it had made Lorna laugh, didn't soften the blow of Magnus listening to their aunt's advice.

Magnus set down the leg of fowl he'd been eating and leaned forward on the table, his elbows pressing into the wood. Lorna found it hard to look him in the eye when he got like that. All serious and laird-like. He was her brother first, and chief second. Or at least, that's how she saw it. Judging from the anger simmering just beneath the surface of his clenched jaw and narrowed eyes, she was about to catch wind.

The room suddenly grew still, as if they were all wondering what he'd say—even the dogs.

He bared his teeth in something that was probably supposed to resemble a smile. A few of the inhabitants picked up superficial conversations again, trying as best they could to pretend they weren't paying attention. Others blatantly stared in curiosity.

"That is the case, save for when it involves deciding *your* future."

Oh, she was going to bait the bear. Lorna drew in a deep breath, crossed her arms over her chest and leaned away from the table. She could hardly look at him as she spoke. "Seems ye've already done just that."

Magnus' lips thinned into a grimace. "I see ye'll fight me on it."

"I dinna wish to marry." Emotion carried on every word. Didn't he realize what he was doing to her? The thought of marrying made her physically ill.

"Ye dinna wish to marry or ye dinna wish to marry MacOwen?"

By now the entire trestle table had quieted once more, and all eyes were riveted on the two of them. However she answered was going to determine the mood set in the room.

Och, she hated it when the lot of nosy bodies couldn't get enough of the family drama. Granted at least fifty percent of the time she was involved in said drama.

Lorna studied her brother, who, despite his grimace, waited patiently for her to answer.

The truth was, she did wish to marry—at some point. Having lost her mother when she was only four years old, she longed to have a child of her own, someone she could nurture and love. But that didn't mean she expected to marry *now*. And especially not the burly MacOwen who was easily twice her age, and had already married once or twice before. When she was a child she'd determined he had a nest of birds residing in his beard—and her thoughts hadn't changed much since.

She cocked her head trying to read Magnus' mind. Was it possible he was joking? He could not possibly believe she would ever agree to marry MacOwen.

Nay, Lorna wished to marry a man she could relate to. A man she could love, who might love her in return.

"I dinna wish to marry a man whose not seen a bath this side of a decade." Lorna spoke with a reasonable tone, not condescending, nor shrill, but just as she would have said the flowers looked lovely that morning. It was her way. Her subtlety often left people second guessing what they'd heard her say.

Magnus' lip twitched and she could tell he was trying to hold in his laughter. She dared not look down the table to see what the rest of her family and clan thought. In the past when she'd checked, gloated really, over their responses it had only made Magnus angrier.

Taming a bear meant not baiting him. And already she was doing just that. She flicked her gaze toward her plate, hoping the glance would appear meek, but in reality she was counting how many legumes were left on her trencher.

"Och, lass, I'm sure MacOwen has bathed at least once in the last year." Magnus' voice rumbled, filled with humor.

Lorna gritted her teeth. Of course Magnus would try and bait her in return. She should have seen that coming.

"And I'm sure there's another willing lass who'll scrape the filth from his back, but ye willna find her here. Not where I'm sitting."

Magnus squinted a moment as if trying to read into her mind. "But ye will agree to marry?"

Lorna crossed her arms over her chest. Lord, was her brother ever stubborn. "Not him."

"Shall we parade the eligible bachelors of the Highlands through the great hall and let ye take your pick?"

Lorna rolled her eyes, imagining just such a scene. It was horrifying, embarrassing. How many would there be in various states of dress and countenance? Some unkempt and others impeccable. Men who were pompous and arrogant or shy or annoying. Nay, thank you. She was about to spit a retort that was likely to burn her Aunt Fiona's ears when the matron broke in.

"My laird, 'haps after the meal I could speak with Lorna about marriage…in a somewhat more private arena?" Aunt Fiona was using that tone she oft used when trying to reason with one of them, that of a matron who knew better. It annoyed the peas out of Lorna and she was about to say just that, when her brother gave a slight wave of his hand, drawing her attention.

Perhaps his way of ceasing whatever words were on her tongue.

Magnus flicked his gaze from Lorna to Fiona. Why did the old bat always have to stick her nose into everything? Speaking to her in private only meant the woman would try to convince Lorna to take the marriage proposition her brother suggested. And that, she absolutely wouldn't do.

"'Tis not necessary, Aunt Fiona," Lorna said, at the exact same time Magnus stated, "Verra well."

Lorna jerked her gaze back to her brother, glaring daggers at him, but he only raised his brows in such an irritating way, a slight curve on his lips, that she was certain if she didn't excuse herself that moment she'd end up dumping her stew on his head. He had agreed on purpose—to annoy her. A horrible grinding sound came from her mouth as she gritted her teeth. Like she'd thought—brother first, chief second.

"Excuse me," she said, standing abruptly, the bench hitting hard on the back of her knees as so many people held it steady in place.

"Sit down," Magnus drawled out. "And finish your supper."

Lorna glared down at him. "I've lost my appetite."

Magnus grunted and smiled. "Och, we all know that's not true."

That only made her madder. So what if she ate just as much as the warriors? The food never seemed to go anywhere. She could eat all day long and still harbor the same lad's body she'd always had. Thick thighs, no hips, flat chest and arms to rival a squire's. If only she'd had the height of a man, then she could well and truly pummel her brother like he deserved.

She sat back down slowly and stared up at Magnus, eyes wide. Was that the reason he'd suggested MacOwen? Would no other man have her?

Nestling her hands in her lap she wrung them until her knuckles turned white.

Magnus clunked down his wooden spoon. "What is it, now?"

"Why did ye choose MacOwen?" she whispered, not wishing the rest of the table to be involved in this particular conversation. Not when she felt so vulnerable.

He shrugged, avoiding her gaze. "The man asked."

"Oh." She chewed her lip, appetite truly gone. 'Twas as she thought. No one would have her.

"Lorna..."

She flicked her gaze back up to her brother. "I but wonder if any other man would have me?"

Magnus' eyes popped and he gazed on her like she'd grown a second head and then that head grew a head. "Why would ye ask that?"

She shrugged.

By now everyone had gone back to talking and eating, knowing there'd be no more juicy gossip and Lorna was grateful for that.

"Lorna, lass, ye're beautiful, talented, spirited. Ye've taken the clan by storm. I've had to challenge more than one of my warriors for staring too long."

"More than one?" She couldn't help but glance down the table wondering which men it had been. They all slobbered like dogs over their chicken.

"None of the bastards deserve ye."

She turned back to Magnus. "And yet, ye picked the MacOwen?" She raised a skeptical brow. Ugh, of all men, he was by far the worst choice for her.

Magnus winked and picked up another scoop full of stew, shoveling into his grinning mouth.

Lorna groaned, shoulders sinking. "Ye told him nay, didna ye? Ye were baiting me."

Magnus laughed around a mouth full of stew. "Ye're too easy. I'd see ye married, but not to a man older than Uncle Artair," he said, referring to their uncle who had to be nearing seventy.

"Ugh." Lorna growled and punched her brother in the arm. "How could ye do that? Ye made every bit of my hunger go away and ye know how much I love Cook's stew."

Magnus laughed. The sound boomed off the rafters and even pulled a smile from Lorna. She loved to hear him laugh, and he didn't do it often enough. When their parents died, he'd only been fourteen, and he'd been forced to take over the whole of the clan—including raising her, and her siblings. Raising her two brothers, Ronan and Blane, and then the youngest of their brood, Heather was a feat in itself, one only Magnus could have accomplished so well. In fact, the

14

clan had prospered. She couldn't be more proud. If anyone deserved a good match, it was Magnus.

Her heart swelled with pride. "Ye're a good man, Magnus. And an amazing brother."

He reached toward her and gave her a reassuring squeeze on her shoulder. "I'll remember that the next time ye wail at me about nonsense."

Lorna jutted her chin forward. "I do not wail—and nothing I say is nonsense."

"A true Sutherland ye are. I see your appetite has returned."

Lorna hadn't even realized she'd begun eating again. She smiled and wrapped her lips around her spoon. Resisting Cook's stew was futile. The succulent bits of venison and stewed vegetables with hints of thyme and rosemary played blissfully over her tongue.

"My laird." Aunt Fiona's voice pierced the noise of the great hall.

Magnus stiffened slightly, and glanced up. Their aunt was a gem, a tremendous help, but Lorna had heard her brother comment on more than one occasion that the woman was also a grand pain in the arse. Lorna dipped her head to keep from laughing.

"Aye?" he said, focusing his attention on their aunt.

"I'd be happy to have Lorna return home with me upon my departure. Visits with me have helped Heather so much."

Lorna's head shot up, mouth falling open as she glanced from her brother to her aunt. Good God, no! Beside her on the bench, Heather kicked Lorna in the shin and made a slight gesture with her knife as though she were slitting her wrist. Lorna pressed her lips together to keep from laughing.

"I'm sure that's not necessary, Aunt," Lorna said, giving the woman her sweetest smile. At least she'd not told her there was no way in hell she'd step foot outside of this castle for a journey unless it was on some adventure she chose for herself. She'd heard enough horror stories about the etiquette lessons Heather had to endure.

"Magnus?" Fiona urged.

There was a flash of irritation in his eyes. Magnus didn't mind his siblings calling him by his name, but all others were to address him formally. Lorna agreed that should be the case with the clan, but with family, Lorna thought he ought to be more lenient, especially where their aunt was concerned.

Aye, she was a thorn in his arse, but she was also very helpful.

Before her brother could say something he'd regret, Lorna pressed her hand to his forearm and chimed in. "Haps we can plan on me accompanying Heather on her next visit."

That seemed to pacify their aunt. She nodded and returned to her dinner.

Ronan, who sat beside Magnus on the opposite side of the table, leaned close to their brother and smirked as he said something. Probably crude. Lorna rolled her eyes. If Blane was here, he'd have joined in their bawdy drivel. Or maybe even saved her from having to invite herself to stay at their aunt's house.

As it was, Blane was gallivanting about the countryside and the borders dressed as an Englishman selling wool. Sutherland wool. Their prized product. Superior to all others in texture, softness, thickness, and ability to hold dye.

She stirred her stew, frowning. Blane always came home safe and sound, but she still worried. There was a lot of unrest throughout the country, and the blasted English king, Longshanks, was determined to be rid of them all. It would only take one wrong move and her beloved brother would be forever taken away.

Lorna glanced up. She gazed from one sibling to the next. She loved them. All of them. They loved each other more than most, maybe because they'd lost their parents so young and only had each other to rely on. Whatever the case was, they'd a bond not even steel could cut through.

Magnus raised his mug of ale. "A toast!" he boomed.

Every mug lifted into the air, ale sloshing over the sides and cheers filled the room.

"Clan Sutherland!" he bellowed.

And the room erupted in uproarious calls and clinks of mugs. A smile split her face and she was overcome with joy.

She'd be perfectly happy never to leave here. And perfectly ecstatic to never marry MacOwen.

Even still, as she clinked her mug and took a mighty gulp, she couldn't help but wonder if there was a man out there she could love, and one who just might love her in return.

CHAPTER TWO

Glasgow Castle

*L*aird Jamie Montgomery leaned against the stone wall at the back of the great hall filled with at least a half dozen chiefs and two score warriors. Thousands more waited beyond the castle walls and in the courtyard. Their shouts and cheers a low din beyond the thick stone walls of Glasgow.

At the head of the men packed into the great hall, standing atop Jamie's trestle table upon the dais, was William Wallace.

The man was covered in weapons, his face painted and blood spattered. Long hair, once strung back in a queue but now floated about his face in wild, plaited strands. He'd not even bothered to seek out the healer before calling this emergency meeting. Not that a healer would have done more than clean out his wounds, 'haps give him a few stitches.

Thank goodness Jamie's servants had swept away the embroidered table runner his mother had created from the center of the table as the men barreled into the great hall. As it was, Wallace's muddy boots left marks on the table Jamie was certain his housekeeper would scoff at.

But what was he to do when Wallace was so obviously filled with passionate anger?

And so Jamie had taken up residence against the wall. Watching not only their country's freedom fighter rave, but the men in the crowd enticing him. Their fists pumped into the air, and ale flowed freely as though the amber liquid poured liberally from the springs.

They were all out for blood. Revenge against the dreaded English. And the lot of them would end up dead if they didn't start relying on their instincts and using their minds instead of their foolhardy hearts.

Wallace was the only man he'd ever met who fought with passion and strategy. But the men who followed him weren't all the same. Most were riled up by their leader, the cause, by their hate, and they rushed headlong into action with little thought as to how they should truly proceed. They played a dangerous game. And without Wallace's strategy, they'd have suffered much more loss. He might look uncivilized, with his wild hair and war paint, but the man was a military mastermind. And he'd gained everyone's trust, support and respect. Scotland's fight for freedom would never have gotten this far without him. That was a fact.

"We must fight! We must go now. Invade England!" Wallace was shouting, the skin beneath the paint reddening to match the splatters of blood on his cheeks. His white teeth flashed as he bared them, seeing whatever demons haunted him off in the distance.

The men raised their swords, daggers and fists into the air, sending battle cries echoing off the stone walls of the great hall. The other chiefs seated before a feast on the dais paused in their bites to stare not at Wallace but at Jamie.

The council members trusted Jamie's opinion. He was not a man who normally led with his heart, but rather tactical logic. A trait he'd learned from his father. God rest his soul.

Jamie kept his expression blank, flicked his eyes back to Wallace and waited for what else he'd have to say. He'd not let the man be pushed aside as some on the council wanted. They thought Wallace rash, ruled by emotion. Aye, part of that was true, but Jamie trusted the man all the same. He was intelligent and creative in the ways of war. In truth, Jamie respected him all the more for his passion. Not many a man was able to lead by such a thirst to see their cause reign triumphant.

"We'll take a force of Scots across the borders and crush them all!" The way the man was shouting, he was likely to be hoarse within the hour.

Wallace turned around, bent toward the table and grabbed a mug out of Chief MacArran's hands, gulping the contents and wiping the dribble on his sleeve before handing the mug back. MacArran grimaced as he took hold of the mug and set it on the table as though a dog had just slurped out of it.

Jamie repressed the urge to roll his eyes. Sometimes he felt like he was dealing with a crowd of green lads.

Wallace faced those in the great hall with blazing, angry eyes. And why shouldn't he? The man had just endured a battle against the bloody Sassenachs. And one he'd not planned. He'd been attacked, ambushed, he and his men just south of Glasgow.

Rather than going to Stirling where the council resided, Wallace had called half the council members to Glasgow, in fear the English were headed straight for Stirling, currently held by the Bruce's men, though not easily. Not even a year had passed since John Baliol had been stripped of his reign over Scotland. The northern English maggot, had been recruited by Longshanks—the English king, named so for his great height—to rule over Scotland because of his distant relation to King David who'd not ruled in over a hundred years. More distant was Baliol than their future king, Robert the Bruce—but Robert was not Longshanks' choice and while England feigned occupation of their country, they'd put a pretender on the throne. Now Baliol resided where he should, in the Tower of London.

A rat bastard he was. Toom Tabbard. The nickname, meaning Empty Coat, made Jamie snicker. Should have named him Empty Sac. Bastard had no ballocks.

Toom Tabbard never gave a fig for the Scottish people, and allowed the Sassenachs to traipse all over the countryside, raping, pillaging, burning. The reminder only made Jamie's gut rot with shame to have been acquainted with the man. Not that he'd been closely acquainted. When Jamie's father had passed, knowing the imposter was ruling, and his own seat so close to Jamie's father offered up his allegiance, if only to keep an eye on the man.

Keeping his enemy close kept him apprised of, and able to foil, so many plans Baliol and Longshanks had contrived for the Scottish people. And his father had been able to keep the Bruce informed. Because of that, Jamie had been well acquainted with their plans, and able to offer more than just his leadership and fighting skills to the country.

Jamie was damn proud that he'd been chosen as one of the twelve to reside within the Bruce's council—even if he was slightly annoyed that Wallace was clunking his gut-covered boots on the place he ate every night.

"What say ye, Montgomery? Will ye invade with me?" Wallace had stopped pacing, placed his hands on his hips and looked at Jamie with expectation.

Every eye in the grand hall whipped around to face him. Jamie kept his arms crossed but pushed off the wall, rocking slowly on his feet as he thought about a response that would be both diplomatic and diffusing.

"I would refer to the council. I am but a member of a voting assembly." He kept his voice even, meeting each of the council members' gazes and then Wallace's.

"Och, Montgomery, your opinion then," Wallace said. "Dinna give us another vague answer, but your thoughts, my laird."

Jamie tilted his head from side to side, cracking the tension away from his neck. "I have always been of the opinion that any action taken in haste is foolish."

Wallace bared his teeth, glaring daggers at Jamie. For a moment, Jamie wondered if the man would leap off the table and demand he battle it out with swords right there in the middle of the great hall. He kind of liked the idea. His sword was bigger than Wallace's by at least six inches.

But Wallace did not leap off the table. Instead he cracked his knuckles. "What would ye propose then?"

The five other council members present, leaned closer, over the table and the group standing between him and the table pressed nearer. The very air crackled with stale ale, sweat, meat, blood and rage lust.

Jamie did not hesitate in answering, for 'twas a thought he'd had for quite some time. "We need to gather more forces."

"More forces?" Wallace pursed his lips, crossed his arms over his chest. "Aye. We need more."

"We need to garner alliances with the north. Right now only half the country is fighting against the English. Of the other half, they've suffered, aye, but they've not had the battles in their courtyards as yet." Jamie stayed where he was, not stepping forward into the room. His voice reverberated through the great hall.

"And how do ye propose we seek them out?" Chief MacArran asked, peering from behind Wallace's legs.

"We speak to them. Let us leave enough forces here to protect our people, but let us recruit more warriors and clans from the north. We need more warriors, more supplies, more coin. We canna continue to do this as we are, else we'll end up defeated on the battlefield with lame horses and no boots, our ribs protruding enough to count."

Wallace nodded, and the men at the trestle table turned and discussed with each other.

Jamie leaned back against the wall, glad he was able to diffuse the situation and get across a point he'd been trying to make for the last eight months—they couldn't achieve Scottish freedom with only half the country fully invested.

After several moments of the men conferring, Wallace raised his hand, calling for silence from those in the great hall. He looked straight a Jamie when he said, "Ye'll be the one to go."

Jamie pushed back off the wall, taking a steady step forward. He must not have heard correctly. "What?" he questioned. The hint of menace in his voice could not be helped.

"'Twas your idea." Wallace shrugged as though he spoke of something simple. "Ye'll head north. Take your men with ye. We'll need as many clans on our side as ye can muster."

"Nay." Jamie clenched his jaw. "I'm needed here. A journey such as that would last months."

"Aye, ye're right. Would not Malcolm do well in your stead, keeping the clan and castle in order?"

Jamie glanced toward the hearth where his younger brother Malcolm leaned against the mantle. Only two years younger, Malcolm was just as well versed in the workings of the castle and lands as Jamie. Hell, he was his only heir since Jamie had yet to marry, though at twenty-nine it was nearing time he did so. Malcolm gave a curt, confident nod.

Jamie didn't feel any relief at the prospect.

"All right. I'll go, but I shall return within three months."

Wallace shrugged. "Suit yourself, my laird. As long as ye dinna take overlong. The English are likely to chew off their own feet in eagerness to cross the borders."

Jamie raised a brow. "They'd not be making it across too well, then."

Wallace chuckled. "Aye, but wouldn't it be a sight to see them crawling in the mud?"

A few of the men dropped to the ground and pretended to crawl the way they envisioned the English would, bleeding from their stumps.

"Seek out the Sutherlands first. Their chief has a large army and quite a fair amount of clans allied to him. If ye talk to him, he could send out messengers and ye might find yourself back at Glasgow a lot sooner."

Jamie was unsure of which council member spoke. As soon as he heard the name Sutherland he was tunneled back in time to fifteen years prior. He recalled every minute detail, even the scent of fresh spring flowers and grass. The blonde haired cherub who'd smiled up at him. Her parents slaughtered. Thank God her brother had only been injured, and not murdered as Jamie had originally thought.

He'd not had contact with the Sutherlands since, as his father was given Glasgow below the Highland mountains. They'd been keeping the English from crossing over into the north for as long as he could remember.

And yet, he had an intense curiosity. What had happened to them all? Had their brother, the laird, about his age, been able to gain control? Respect? And the girl… She'd be about nineteen now. Would her hair glisten as golden in the sun as it had back then?

Jamie frowned. Why the hell was he thinking about the lassie's hair?

"I'll leave at first light," he growled.

The men in the great hall all nodded, murmurs rippling through the crowd. His two childhood friends and the men he refused to fight without, Toby and Donald, stepped forward. Their fathers had been warriors within Jamie's father's army, and so they'd spent much time together. They'd even accompanied him to Clan Fraser's for his fostering.

"We'll go with ye, my laird," Toby said.

"Aye, Montgomery, we've got your back."

Jamie nodded. He wouldn't have gone without them.

Wallace grabbed a mug from the table, lifting it into the air. "To Montgomery!"

"Montgomery!" The great hall boomed with the clinking of pewter mugs, the chugging of ale, before shouts rang out for more.

Jamie took the mug thrust into his fist, raised it and gulped, his eyes locked on Wallace, who jovially slammed a fist on the table before the council.

No doubt, the man was very passionate about Scotland and its freedom. Just what the country needed. A man who wasn't willing to give up. A man who got what he wanted. For that was the case, was it not?

Jamie had never had any intention of leaving Glasgow in the hands of his younger brother in order to do a messenger's work. But here he was, planning to leave in less than twelve hours.

He tilted his head back and drank down the contents of his cup, visions of a little blonde cherub running on the moor, slowly tran-spiring into a full grown woman.

One thing was certain, he wasn't heading north for a woman. He was headed north to gain allies, forces and supplies. And he'd not let thoughts of some lass get in the way. Hell, the likelihood of her having survived was only fifty percent.

And yet, the name Sutherland could make any man shake in his boots. If anyone were to survive it would be one of them.

Wallace called for music and the pipers blared their horns as the leader of the freedom fighters took up a jig in the middle of the great hall. Even a couple of the council members joined in as they all celebrated.

But not Jamie. He frowned at the display. They'd nothing to cele-brate yet. Wallace had lost a battle that morning and there were many more battles to come before they were free of Longshanks' grip.

Malcolm trudged over to Jamie's side, nudging him with his shoulder.

"Dinna worry brother, Glasgow will be in good hands while ye're away."

"I've no fear that ye wouldn't take care of our people."

"Why the grim face? 'Tis not as if Wallace has sentenced ye to death."

Jamie grunted. "Nay, but he has sent me on a lesser man's errand."

"Och, nay. I say the opposite. Ye are the one he trusts most with such an important mission."

Toby and Donald nodded. "Aye," they said in unison.

"There's none other who would do the deed justice as ye would," Donald said.

Toby slapped Jamie on the back, a wide grin on his face. Of both his friends, Toby loved a good adventure more than Donald, who preferred a bonfire and a willing wench.

Jamie took another gulp of ale and glanced at his brother, who looked at him with a great deal of respect in his gaze. "What gives ye that impression?"

"As ye stated, we canna fight the English with only half the country on our side. We need more forces, supplies, men. We need the High-landers. They're the fiercest of all fighters."

"We are Highlanders."

"Aye, but the majority of Wallace's men now come from the south, since they've been most affected by that bastard English king."

Jamie nodded, watching as Wallace jumped back up onto the table and continued to dance, kicking a bowl of stew over onto the floor which was promptly set upon by the dogs. 'Twas hard for Jamie to refrain from grabbing Wallace by the throat and tossing him out for disrespecting his home. But resist he did all the same.

"The sooner I gain our cause more forces, the sooner I can have my table back."

Malcolm, Toby and Donald laughed.

"Aye, brother. There is much that would change." Malcolm grabbed a jug of ale a passing servant carried and refilled Jamie's mug.

"Aye, much," Jamie answered.

Another annoying flash of golden curls assaulted his mind.

Damn, Sutherlands.

CHAPTER THREE

Dunrobin Castle

luebells danced in the wind like a myriad of pretty court ladies swaying to music only the truly favored could hear. Lorna lay in the grass, staring at a thatch of flowers as they shimmied in the breeze. The spring sun warmed her skin, making her feel alive and renewed. She was nearly certain if she ended up with cheeks pinkened from the sun, Aunt Fiona was going to raise hell.

Precisely the reason she'd escaped this morning, riding her mare, Angel, across the moors and to the crest of the grassy knoll, where she could look down at the village and keep. It was a peaceful place. Only the sounds of birds calling, the gentle sea breeze wafting up the hill and blowing against the blades of grass. The scent of wildflowers calmed her, and she could lay in the grass all day and stare up at the clouds.

No brothers to argue with. No little sister demanding her attention, and no Aunt Fiona fussing over her every move. Out here, all was quiet. Calm. Just Lorna and Mother Earth. She could be herself. Could ride her horse any way she pleased, or lounge on the beach or moors as she was, not concerned for sitting properly nor for the grains of sand or blades of grass stuck in her hair.

Lorna gazed up at the tranquil sky. A few white puffs of clouds filled the blue, and in the distance a clash of gray clouds advanced. In her estimation, she had about an hour left of peace before a storm broke loose, drenching her in nature's tears—a situation she would never hear the end of from her aunt, and then from her brothers who would also be pestered by the woman. No lady of consequence would frolic in the rain, nor comport herself in a way that would be considered shameful to her family. Aunt Fiona was filled with ladylike rules of decorum that she expected all the female relations to follow. Lorna tried to follow them most of the time, but then there were those days where she just didn't care. She wanted to be happy. Being outside made her happy.

Now, the one thing that she didn't have in unlimited quantities was patience, and Fiona had already tried her enough on this visit.

Heather would blame Lorna for no longer being able to go outside unless the sky were free of clouds altogether, and would make certain Lorna paid for not following the rules in Fiona's presence, for it would mean that they'd both be under more strict scrutiny.

With a heavy sigh, Lorna sat up and gazed down at the keep, fingers absently toying with the bluebells. To avoid the entire stress one storm could cause her, it would probably be best to vacate the hill now and make way for home. She grabbed a cluster of bluebells and tucked them into the basket she'd brought with her—her excuse for leaving the walls.

Lorna whistled for Angel, who munched on grass some forty feet away. The dappled white and iron-colored mare's head bobbed up from the cluster of sweet clover she'd being dining on, to stare at Lorna as if she hoped to have not heard the whistle.

"The grass here is most sweet, is it not, Angel?" Lorna said with a laugh.

Her horse nickered, took a few more nibbles, then made her way over. The ground beneath Lorna's rear rumbled, vibrating. Glancing up at Angel, who was taking her sweet time, fear trickled like ice over her spine. She flattened her hands to ground, feeling the earth tremble. There were only two reasons the ground would pulse as it did—thunder from a storm and thunder from a horse.

And Angel wasn't running. In fact, her horse had stopped walking, ears perked as she, too, heard the oncoming rider. Lorna jumped to her feet, basket spilling from her lap. Ignoring the lost flowers, she flicked her gaze all around, trying to pinpoint the riders who had to be gaining on her, but there didn't appear to be anyone in sight.

A quick glance at the guards on top of the battlements showed they, too, seemed to see someone approaching. They waved frantically toward her. Zounds! They'd be giving her an earful, for convincing them yet again to let her leave without an escort—no matter how many sweet, buttered buns she brought them.

Not wasting a moment, not even to collect her basket and flowers, she lifted her skirts, running toward her horse, her hair coming loose and whipping every which way as a swift breeze wrapped itself around her. Angel pranced, unsteady on her feet as nerves took over. The mare was good and steady when Lorna needed her for her latest trick, but she was also skittish in the face of danger. A fact, Lorna had only realized on very few occasions. This being one of them.

Lord, she'd been stupid for coming up here. She should have listened to her aunt. Ugh, she should have listened to her older brothers. They hated her leaving the castle walls without an escort. In fact, it had been one of Magnus' rules since he became laird some fifteen years before today.

With that realization came the awareness of Beltane soon to be upon them. The anniversary of their parents' death. Perhaps this being the fifteenth year, those invisible enemies would once more crash their swords down upon them. And their swords would come clashing on her first if she didn't get moving. Lorna reached her horse's side, gripped the saddle and leapt onto Angel's back. The skirts caught around her left leg, making it impossible for her to get her foot into the stirrup.

"Damn it," she cursed, beginning to panic.

She caught a glimpse of the approaching riders and all sense seemed to leave her. She stilled, seemingly frozen as the distance between them closed.

Two warriors flanked a single man. Or demon.

The man appeared to be just as tall and dark as his warhorse. His black hair whipped around his head as did the horse's mane. The lead rider flew up one crest and down another, like a devil racing for time. He was massive, broad of shoulder and just from looking at him, she felt all the air around her vibrate, like it was being sucked in by him, leaving her little left.

The hilt of a claymore rose above one shoulder. Metal glinted from his arms, as though they, too, were strapped with swords.

Lorna swallowed. All three of them were fierce. But the one in the center… He was a thing of girlish nightmares, and yet she felt enticed. Excited. She couldn't goad her horse into a run. Couldn't even seem to get the mare to turn around—which wasn't surprising, given that she wasn't making her. Nay, Lorna sat like a duck in the line of an arrow, waiting to see just where this man and his followers would strike her.

And right now he seemed to have struck her all over.

Gooseflesh rose on her skin, the hair on the back of her neck prickled and she could barely catch her breath. He was magnificent, dangerous and… handsome. A handsome devil.

Somewhere behind her, the guards called, shouting over the din of hoof beats. And still she didn't move.

When the strangers were within a few dozen yards, the fire burning in their leader's dark eyes seemed to finally spear her into movement. He was close. Too close. What in all of heaven was she thinking just waiting and staring? She didn't recognize the color of their plaids. For all she knew, they were the enemy that had struck them in the soul fifteen years earlier.

"Zounds!" she breathed out, yanking Angel's reins and spurring her into a gallop with her right foot, her left foot still out of the stirrup.

The already skittish mare needed no further prompting. She whirled and, head down, made for home at a speed Lorna had yet to see her excel toward.

Lorna leaned low over the horse's neck, too fearful of falling off her mount at such a speed to grab hold of the long dagger she kept tucked beneath the saddle. Besides, it was entirely possible that she might end up stabbing herself with it.

The guards had begun to lift the portcullis, the gate opened wide now. Within moments they would be barreling toward her and her attackers, swords drawn. Oh, dear God! She was going to die...

If she thought Magnus would throw a conniption over her being out on the hill without an escort, then he'd be doubly mad if she came back covered in blood.

Tightening her grip on the reins, she called out to Angel, "Faster, girl! Fly!"

Pounding thunder chased her. And she might have thought that dark clouds were distending with long human-like fingers reaching toward her, ready to snatch her up into oblivion, save for the fact, she'd seen just who chased her.

A warrior. A god. And she couldn't quite figure out if she wanted to run toward him or dash away to the castle in hopes he and his men would simply disappear.

Somehow, even in the back of her mind, Lorna knew that the sight of such a magnificent man would never escape her mind. The vision of him would be forever burned there, invading her dreams and thoughts.

Jamie could hardly believe his eyes. 'Twas as though he'd been thrust fifteen years in the past, although this time the angelic apparition chose a horse to run away from him on instead of bare feet. Her hair still glistened like spun golden silk in the sun. But now a lass, barely older than a toddling bairn, was replaced by a full grown woman with curves that made him ache and a beauty that had him nearly undone. Mesmerized him.

With a flick of his reins he had his warhorse, Charger, barreling toward her. Toby and Donald called out for him to slow, but Jamie couldn't. Curiosity bade him move faster.

Was it possible that it was the same lass? And what was she doing out here all alone?

From the castle beyond, warriors spilled out like ants from a hill— probably seeing them and believing their lady was in danger. The thought almost made him laugh aloud, for if it weren't for him, she might not even be there racing toward home.

A deep frown creased Jamie's face. Had Sutherland not learned his lesson all those years ago? These were not simple times in which they lived, but brutal. Man against man. Let the most superior win. The English crawled all over the country—not trapped simply to the Lowlands.

A little minx of a woman was no match for an outlaw, nor an English bastard. She was lucky he'd been the one to happen on her. On his journey to Sutherland from Glasgow, he and his two best mates had encountered many a suspicious character and hidden themselves from plenty of bands of outlaws—fought several off, too. If his sisters, Matilda and Ceana, had so much as dared to venture ten feet past the gate without at least a guard with them, he'd have seen their arses flayed.

"Ye there!" he called out.

The woman turned her head to look at him, but her golden hair swept all the way around her face making it hard for him to see her. Not that he was certain he'd recognize her anyway. If it was she, fifteen years made a world of difference, not to mention she'd been a child and now was a woman. A luscious woman, at that.

"Stop!" Jamie shouted again.

That only seemed to make her go faster. And her guards shouted their own calls in return. Jamie rolled his eyes. He held up his hand, bidding Toby and Donald to keep back. The lass's attempt to increase her speed did little good. Her mare's legs were no match for Charger's. His warhorse stretched his forelegs forward, practically flying across the grassy moors and then he was within feet of her, swearing he caught the feminine scent of her. Floral and sweet.

Jamie reached out to grab hold of her reins before she killed herself, but the wench slapped his hands away.

"Dinna touch me!" she cried out, eyes warily flitting over him and then to Toby and Donald who sat their horses a dozen yards back.

Her men shouted a valley away, their words not fully sounding on the wind. Jamie growled, and this time when he grappled with the reins, he succeeded, yanking both their mounts to a halt.

But what should have been simple, was not. The woman was mad.

She wrenched a blade from beneath her saddle and brandished it before her like a miniature sword, her green-blue eyes blazing with fear and anger.

"Get away from me!"

"Lass, calm yourself."

"Dinna tell me to calm myself." Exasperation dripped from her words, and she stabbed toward Jamie.

He held up his hands and sidled his horse just out of reach.

"I'm nay here to harm ye," he said calmly, as though speaking to a crazed animal. He clenched his jaw to keep from laughing. She did look like a crazed animal at the moment. Hair flying and sticking out every which way around her face, cheeks flushed red, eyes blazing, and that mouth…

Hunger stirred within him. There was nothing mad about that mouth. In fact, he found the way her lips turned down in a petulant frown to be rather enticing. Full, strawberry-red lips. Perfectly kissable.

"Why are ye staring at me like that?" she asked, indignant.

Jamie cleared his throat, realizing that probably every lustful thought that had just crashed over him had shown on his face.

"I stare at ye in no way other than at a mad woman whose tried to get herself killed in at least three ways since I first saw her today."

Her mouth fell open and a haughty wash of air pushed out. "How dare ye?"

"How dare I? I was but coming to your rescue."

She narrowed her eyes at him. "I am not in need of rescuing."

"That ye know of."

"That I'm certain of." The haughty lift of her chin made him want to grin, but he kept it hidden.

Jamie shrugged. "I suppose a lass may not know when she's in danger."

She waggled her dagger toward him again. "The only thing dangerous here, is ye. And your underlings."

"Underlings?" He winged a brow and stared over his shoulder at Toby and Donald who looked on as if they'd not heard her just insult them. "I humbly disagree."

Her mouth fell open in exasperation. "Ye canna."

"Aye, I can."

"How?" She swept several errant strands of hair away from her eyes. The wisps appeared to be just as stubborn as she, however, and fell right back in the line of her vision. She puffed a breath and they flopped.

Jamie couldn't help but chuckle, which only seemed to enrage her more.

"I asked ye a question, stranger."

"Well, for one thing, Toby and Donald are hardly underlings. Ye insult their skill and intelligence." He leaned closer, breathing in her floral scent. "Ye dinna think ye're in danger, and yet ye lay upon the hill without an escort when any sort of man or animal could happen upon ye."

She rolled her eyes, but what Jamie found most pleasing was that she must trust him as she'd not tried to run away again, but rather stayed to spar with him.

"And I see I was set upon by animals."

"Is that an attempt to insult me and my men?" he asked with a winged brow, thoroughly enjoying his baiting of her.

"Humph." She rolled her eyes again, flicking her gaze toward the castle, probably gauging the distance of her brother's men.

"And what other ways was I in danger then, stranger?"

"The way ye ride. 'Tis reckless."

"And ye're as much of a worry wart as an old bat," she sneered. "Now, let me pass afore my brother's men arrive and cleave ye in two. I've no wish to talk with ye further on all the faults ye find with me."

"Och, lass. I find nary a fault with ye." Jamie let his gaze roam over her, taking in the beauty of her arched brows, high cheekbones and straight nose, the slope of her neck and the way her bodice hugged perky breasts and a waist that flared into round hips. Her legs straddled the horse, long, and he could imagine they'd be lithe beneath her skirts, hugging the side of her mare just as he wished they hugged their way around his hips. Desire shot straight to his groin. Again, he cleared his throat, hoping to clear his mind. "Shall I escort ye to the castle, lass?"

She rolled her eyes. "I doubt the guards will take kindly to it. As I said, I'm in no need of saving."

"Aye, but I might be," he teased.

"What?"

Jamie ignored her question. Only a few moments longer and her men would surround them. "What is your name?"

"I'm not accustomed to sharing it with strangers."

"'Haps we've met before," he offered.

"I doubt it. I'd recall your face. I'm very good at remembering faces."

"I shall tell ye my name, then, as I've already shared the names of my men. I'm Jamie, Laird Montgomery."

The lass's brows crinkled as she studied him, cocking her head to the side. "I dinna know any Laird Montgomery."

"May I have your name?"

"Nay." And with that, having caught him off guard, she kicked her horse into a run, never taking her eyes off him. "Many happy returns to ye, Laird Montgomery," she called, her voice carrying on the wind and fairly knocking Jamie off of Charger.

He was most certain, it was she.

And he'd not been aware until that moment, but he'd thought of her nearly every day since that time fifteen years before. Wondered what had become of her. Wondered if she ever thought of him.

Obviously, since she'd not recognized him, he'd not left a memorable impression on her. Jamie grinned. Nay, matter. He had at least a couple of days to remind her of who he was, because damn it all, he wanted to be remembered.

CHAPTER FOUR

*L*orna approached the open gates of Dunrobin, surrounded by her brother's men, without slowing her mount.

The castle guards had met her upon the moor, none of them uttering a word after she told them there was nothing to worry about and to put their swords away before they poked their eyes out.

Calls sounded from within the courtyard as the guards atop the battlements issued orders. She dared not look up at the gatekeeper who glowered down at her. No doubt he, too, would go and find her brother to complain about her having escaped once again and that it had caused him a near apoplexy to get the gate opened fast enough to send the warriors out after her.

But she needn't worry about that, because as soon as she was through the gate a wall of warriors stood in place of the double wooden doors and portcullis as Laird Montgomery and his two men pulled their mounts to a quick stop. She'd not told the guards who they were, wanting simply to be home and away from the man who made her feel things she didn't understand.

Lorna glanced over her shoulder at Montgomery and gave him a triumphant smile. If she were not safe behind her brother's men, the man might still be attacking her mind. She'd not let him grab hold of her reins again.

Pointing her nose in the air, she turned away from him, but before she could dismount on her own, rough hands grabbed her around the middle and yanked her off.

"Magnus! Put me down!" she shouted as a drop of rain plopped onto her nose.

"Not bloody likely."

Lorna's face flamed with humiliation and anger sliced through her as her eldest brother tossed her over his shoulder and marched, none too softly, up the stairs of the keep, each jar taking the breath from her. No amount of pummeling his back could coerce him to put her down. Once inside, he transferred her to Ronan's shoulder before disappearing out the door, most likely to see to the new warrior. Who was Laird Montgomery? The name was familiar, but not familiar enough she could place him. He'd seemed awfully confident about escorting her home. Was it possible he knew Magnus?

Oh, good God, what if he was a man Magnus hoped to marry her off to?

A shiver stole over her, and to cover it up she hit her brother on the back. "Put me down! Ye both are nothing but a couple of heathens."

Ronan ignored her, taking the stairs two at a time. As soon as he put her down she was going to punch him in the gut so he knew what it felt like to be carried over a brute's shoulder.

"How could ye do it again, Lorna?" he said, berating her like a bairn as he carried her up to her chamber. "Especially with Aunt Sourpuss here?"

"Aunt Sourpuss?" Lorna laughed, but the movement of her constricted ribs just hurt.

"Ye know the arrangements. When the Puss is in residence, the mice stay hidden."

Lorna rolled her eyes. "So ye won't yell at me for having escaped our laird's supervision or his men, but ye'll yell at me for having done it while Frigid Fiona's under foot?"

"Frigid Fiona, huh? I dinna think ye know what ye're talking about."

Lorna shrugged, though he couldn't see the movement. "She's as tight as a tree trunk. One wrong move and her spine will snap."

"And ye're as disobedient as an imp."

"And apparently I'm a frigid sourpuss."

Lorna's mouth dropped open just as Ronan's footsteps faltered in the center of the circular stair.

"If ye're planning to say ought but contemptuous things about a person ye might do so when they canna hear ye." Their aunt's voice was crisp and shrill.

They were both in trouble now. Lorna bit her lip as Ronan muttered his apologies. When they were children, Aunt Fiona would have taken a paddle to both their behinds if she'd heard their conversation. And Lorna wasn't too certain she wouldn't do it now.

"In the chamber with her," Aunt Fiona demanded and Ronan reluctantly rounded the last of the stairway, coming into their aunt's view.

Ronan obediently trudged down the hall to Lorna's chamber, entering when Fiona opened the door and depositing her on her feet with a look that said he'd pray for her.

"Don't leave me," Lorna mouthed.

"Ye shouldna have run away again," Ronan whispered in her ear, before giving her hair a tousle.

She'd be getting no help from him. He smiled then left, yet another sorrowful gaze expressed toward her.

Lorna swallowed and lifted her chin, flicking her gaze toward the shuttered window. 'Twas bad enough she couldn't see what was happening in the courtyard, but she couldn't hear a peep either. The blood rushed like a waterfall from her head and she swayed slightly. Straightening her shoulders, she forced her gaze away from the window and toward her discerning aunt. She was a grown woman. Aunt Fiona couldn't scare her now. But she did. Not for fear of physical harm, but for fear of whatever machinations she'd come up with and convince Magnus to carry out. Like a trip to Fiona's castle or marriage. Even the thought of it made bile rise up Lorna's throat.

The bitter looking older woman waited for Ronan to depart before she shut the door and turned her pinched face in Lorna's direction.

Every ounce of confidence Lorna possessed wanted to run out that door on Ronan's heels, but she couldn't let it escape her.

"Apologies, Aunt, for having disrespected ye."

Aunt Fiona made a snippy sound in the back of her throat, crossed her hands behind her back and walked slowly forward. Her hair was still mostly dark, with streaks of white going through it, pulled back in a bun so tight the skin at the sides of her temples was stretched to its limits. Her watery blue eyes were squinted as she assessed Lorna.

She was certain her aunt would find her lacking in most things this morning. But that wouldn't be anything new, and most times, Heather did something maddening before Fiona could finish with Lorna. But not today. Today she would stand up to her aunt. Spare Heather the harsh treatment. Remind her aunt of her own age—nineteen was no longer a child. Hadn't they just been talking of marriage several days before?

"I—" Before she could get another word out, Aunt Fiona held up her hand, lips thinning to white strips.

"Dinna say it, lass. And afore ye move forward, Heather is already engaged so I'll nay be distracted from the present conversation."

Lorna ignored the warning. "How—"

"I had a sister as well as a brother." She winged a brow. "Do ye nay recall?"

Lorna nodded, pursing her lips. Fiona was sister to the Sutherland siblings' deceased father, and whenever her aunt brought up that fact, it only made Lorna sad. A low blow on her aunt's part to remind her of all she'd lost, but really, that was Fiona's way. Almost as if she wanted everyone else to endure the pain she felt. Lorna's shoulders sagged.

"I dinna need a reminder of how old ye are, or that we were just discussing marriage not too long ago. I am well aware. I'll nay berate ye, nor order your brother to take a lash to your rear as he should. But I will say this, and heed my words carefully. When ye act in a rash manner, then all manner of consequences must be paid."

Lorna watched as Fiona reached up to swipe away a hair that was not there, tucking the imaginary strand behind her ear. Was the woman reminded of a time when she'd not pulled her hair so tight? Or 'haps staring at Lorna's disastrous mane was causing her aunt to twitch. Hmm... The latter seemed much more realistic. Lorna couldn't imagine a time Fiona wouldn't have pulled her hair steel tight.

'Twas hard to concentrate on what her aunt was saying, feeling, or the point she was trying to make when all Lorna wanted to do was look out the window to see what Magnus had done about the stranger. She wracked her brain for a clue as to who he was. *Montgomery... Montgomery... Montgomery...*

How humiliating that he'd witnessed her brother carting her off like a lamb to slaughter.

"When ye choose to do something, ye must think of everyone that will be affected by your actions." Fiona's long fingers gently tugged at Lorna's sleeve.

She felt her feet move across the floor as she followed her aunt's guidance to the bench before her dressing table. When Fiona pushed on her shoulders, Lorna grudgingly sat, watching her aunt pick up her brush, taking the first painful stroke through the knotted mass of curls.

Oh, Lord, so this was to be her punishment? A hair brushing. Lorna cringed, feeling the first tingle of a tear in her eye.

"Think of all those who would suffer if something were to happen to ye? Ye're fortunate that so many care for ye, lass. There are people in the world who have no one. And there are even those who have many but would still not be affected if they were gone." A wistful note came into her tone. "In any event, ye're very much cared for here at Dunrobin by your brothers and sister, cousins, your clan and by me."

With every passing moment the brush gentled, until finally her hair crackled and not a single knot was left. But Aunt Fiona didn't stop there. She separated Lorna's hair into portions and began braiding. Her aunt meant well, that was one thing Lorna did know. For all her rigidity, she was a woman who cared fiercely for her family. And she'd loved Lorna's father dearly, as well as her mother, taking it hard when they were murdered. A murder that had yet to be solved.

"Are ye listening, lass?"

Lorna chewed her lip, recalling every word her aunt had spoken as though hearing them through a distant tunnel.

She wasn't sure how to respond. Her aunt was making her sound flighty, as though she'd no notion of love and respect and responsibility. As if she didn't know just how many people cared for her, and as if she, too, didn't care for them in return. She feared opening her mouth, and something rude escaping. And yet, she couldn't let her aunt believe that Lorna was that much of a simpleton.

Fiona was making her feel…selfish. As if craving a moment of peace, a few moments of solitude was selfish. It wasn't. It was necessary.

But how could she phrase it so her aunt wouldn't get offended? The woman had devoted her entire life to her own family and now also to her nieces and nephews.

"Aunt Fiona," Lorna began, chewing the inside of her cheek. "Is there not something that ye enjoy doing above all else?"

Lorna tucked her fingers into her skirts and crossed them over one another, praying that Fiona would understand what she was trying to say.

Fiona's fingers stilled in the braid, as though such a question took her aback. "I enjoy serving God and my family."

Lorna resisted the urge to roll her eyes. Painfully obvious was that her aunt would fight her on this to prove her own point.

"And at the end of the day, when ye've said your prayers, and done all ye could do for your family, is there not something else ye enjoy?"

"The solid certainty that there is never enough praying one can do and never enough help my family needs."

Lorna jerked around, the motion so quick, the hair still threaded in her aunt's fingers yanked with a painful sting. She cringed, then looked up into her aunt's eyes.

"I serve God and my family, too, Aunt Fiona, but that doesn't make me a sinner when I take a moment to stare up at the clouds and embrace a few breaths of peace."

Aunt Fiona frowned, then pressed her fingers to Lorna's head making her turn back around. Begrudgingly she followed her aunt's nudge.

"Aye, lass. A few moments of enjoying nature's beauty is indeed no sin."

Lorna took a deep breath, glad she could make her aunt see the right of it.

"But doing so at the cost of your brother's men, your family's safety and your very life, is a sin." Aunt Fiona plucked a pale green ribbon off the dressing table as though she hadn't just told Lorna she'd be going straight to hell.

"Ye may think me a sinner, Aunt Fiona, but between the two of us, I've definitely got more to live for." Lorna shoved to her feet and walked toward the door with her aunt sputtering behind her. The light green ribbon trickling to the floor. "Your lessons and advice may have been welcomed by my brother while I was growing up, but they are no longer welcomed by me." Hand on the iron doorknob, Lorna twisted. "I'd hoped we could be friends. I'm a grown woman now, and I dinna need an instructor."

Aunt Fiona straightened her shoulders, looking down her elegant nose at Lorna. "We shall see about that."

Lorna kept her lips firmly closed, refusing to fall into another sparring match with her aunt. Instead, she inclined her head with respect and waited for the bitter woman to leave the room.

Lifting her skirts, Fiona swept from the room in a cloud of citrus and cloves—the way she'd smelled since Lorna was a child—the same way Lorna imagined a greatly revered queen would.

As soon as her aunt was gone, Lorna took a deep breath, letting all the pent up anxiety flow out of her. She shut the door, thoughts of her aunt pushed to the background as a sound outside reminded her of their uninvited guest. She hurried toward the window. What had Magnus decided to do about Laird Montgomery?

Flinging open the shutters, she searched the courtyard for signs of the dark warrior, and when seeing none, she looked for her brother. It appeared the two of them had disappeared. A glance over the moors gave her no further information. 'Twas entirely possible that her brother had sent the man on his way, and that he'd made such haste as to have disappeared from view already. Then again, he could be in the great hall now, drinking ale and laughing with her brothers.

Laughing about her.

Lorna frowned and did one more cursory glance around the courtyard, coming up empty-sighted and irritated.

Why today, of all days, did that brawny, handsome, wicked looking warrior have to ride to Sutherland? Why did he have to make an appearance now?

Jamie Montgomery… The name was so familiar… But he was a laird, and her brother often associated with other clan chiefs. She'd likely heard his name in passing. If that were the case, then why couldn't she shake the feeling that she'd met him before?

"Jamie Montgomery," she murmured, fingers sliding over the ridges of the shutters.

No bell suddenly tolled her enlightenment. She was still in the dark. But if he happened to be downstairs instead of on his way back to wherever he came from, she would certainly get to the bottom of the mystery. For her own sake. And not because she found him to be altogether very enticing.

The kind of man she could imagine herself getting married to.

The kind of man she could imagine spending the rest of her life with.

The kind of man she imagined bending her backward over his arm as he kissed her.

Lorna shook her head. What the hell was she thinking? She'd just brandished her dagger in the man's face! He'd scared the wits out of her. The last thing she should be thinking of was falling for him.

His soul could be as dark as his hair for all she knew. Lorna waved away her mad thoughts. For certain, Magnus would have sent Laird Jamie Montgomery on his way, and every thought she'd had of him since their encounter would be moot.

CHAPTER FIVE

fter being welcomed by the Sutherland clan, Toby and Donald were pointed in the direction of the barracks while Jamie was given a small guest room to wash up in before meeting the laird in his library.

A guard standing outside of Jamie's door, nodded. "This way, my laird," he said.

The man was silent as he led him down a flight of stairs and through a darkened corridor. They stopped at a wooden door and the guard rapped twice with his knuckles. On the other side, a voice bade them to enter.

The guard gave a curt nod to Jamie and opened the door, indicating he should enter first. Jamie took the lead, entering into a spacious library that much resembled his own. Large, imposing, but utterly masculine. A wide oak desk, tall wooden back chairs, a long high table, a grand hearth, shuttered windows, fur rugs, and shelves upon shelves of books and rolled scrolls. As the windows did not give off enough light, several sconces were lit upon the walls.

"Laird Montgomery," Laird Sutherland said, coming around the desk to stand a foot away. Jamie reached forward, grasping the man's arm in greeting.

A strong grip, for a moment they both competed for strength, before Sutherland broke away with a short laugh.

"I trust ye found ye're accommodations suitable."

Jamie grinned. "More than agreeable, Laird Sutherland. I'd not expected as much."

"Call me Magnus. No need for formalities. I didna forget what ye and your da did for my family all those years ago. I've never been able to find a way to repay ye, and I do hope ye call on me whenever ye've need of me."

A good opening as to the reason Jamie was currently at Dunrobin. "Any man would have done the same."

Magnus shook his head, his face growing grim. "Sadly, I dinna believe that."

And he was right. Many were of the mind that every man had to fend for himself. "Did ye ever find out who did it?"

Magnus' frown deepened. "Nay."

"I'm sorry to hear it."

"Aye, me, too. But that is not what ye came all this way for. As I've heard it, ye have a seat on the Bruce's council, a place within Wallace's own army."

"Indeed, and 'tis part of the reason I've come."

"Sit." Magnus backed away, shadows crossing over his features that made Jamie wonder if he'd be receptive to joining the cause. "Whisky?"

Jamie pulled back one of the wooden chairs from the desk and sat. "None, thank ye."

"None?" Magnus jerked back and winged a brow.

Not accepting a drink was considered rude. Highland hospitality bade Magnus offer, but it also required Jamie to accept. He ground his teeth. "I've had a long journey, my laird, and if ye dinna find it too offensive, I shall pass on the dram until I've had more time to rest."

He'd not tell him the real reason. The fact that he'd never liked the stuff other than for medicinal purposes. Because 'twas no secret in Montgomery country that when Jamie's father picked up a mug his fist usually landed on their mother. He'd respected his father. But he'd hated him for that.

Jamie had no interest in becoming a monster, and so he stuck to watered ale and wine, and left the whisky to others.

Magnus grunted. "Then I shall also refrain." He walked around the table and sat down opposite Jamie. "Let us speak plainly about why ye've come. Has it to do with my sister?"

Jamie held back his splutter, heels digging into the wooden planks of the floor. "Nay."

The man sat back in his chair and crossed his arms over his chest, a skeptical look upon his face. "Nay?"

Trying to offset the man's obvious doubt, Jamie leaned forward his elbows on the table. "I assure ye, my journey here had naught to with your sister."

"Huh. I'd assumed it did."

"Why?" Jamie frowned. Aye, the lass was intriguing, and a spit-fire, but marriage? Nay. Not yet. And when he did marry, it was likely to be to a woman who would submit to him. Not one that wouldn't think twice about wielding a dagger in his face.

"Well, she's of marrying age, and ye did save her all those years ago. And, ye were the one that brought her back to the castle. Stubborn lass that she is." He shook his head. "A man will have a hard time taming her."

Jamie happened to like a woman with spirit—but not for a wife. A daredevil was what Lorna was. Taming wasn't so much what she needed as training. Aye, and if he'd come for her hand, he might have offered to be the one to do it. As it was, his venture was far from anything to do with marriage. "Ah, so it was she," he said awkwardly to fill the space.

"Ye didna know?"

"She didn't tell me her name."

Magnus grinned. "Sassiest lass. Well, besides the hellion."

"The hellion?"

"My youngest sister, Heather."

"Apologies for any misunderstanding. 'Tis not that I dinna find your sister—"

Magnus raised a hand, cutting him off. "Och, Lorna is not quite ready to wed. Besides, I had hoped to cut ye off before ye asked."

Jamie grinned, although inside he felt a twinge of irritation. And why should that be? He'd not come to beg for the lass's hand. Yet, the idea of asking her to spend the rest of her life with him, having her sit beside him at meals, mend his shirts and lie naked in his bed was extremely appealing. He raked a hand through his hair and blew out a breath, reminding himself she'd more likely argue with him than acquiesce.

"Well, I didna come to ask." The last of Magnus' words seemed to hit Jamie all at once. "What do ye mean ye'd hoped to cut me off?"

Magnus looked at him gravely. "Ye live in the Lowlands. Not a place I'd want my kin to live, ye see."

Jamie nodded slowly, refusing to get into a battle on that fact. "I came on the business of the council."

Magnus looked relieved that Jamie had chosen not to continue with questioning his ideals. "What has that to do with me?"

"I'm hoping quite a lot. The Sutherlands are a powerful clan. Well respected not only in the Highlands but the Lowlands, too." He added that last bit after hearing the distaste the man had for his fellow southern countrymen.

"Aye, and?"

Hell and damnation, the man was going to make him work for it. "My laird, we need ye. Scotland needs ye. This fight against the Sassenachs, this fight for our own country's freedom, is costing us greatly."

"And ye want coin?"

Jamie nodded. "Among other things."

"Which are?"

Jamie leaned forward, keeping his gaze steady. "We need men. We need forces, weapons, supplies. We need support from the Highland clans in order to save all of us from Longshanks' tyranny. He's taking brides on their wedding nights and stealing their virtue for himself, allows his lords to do the same. Every man who weds is at risk of their wives birthing an English bastard. Not to mention we have no law that is our own. If Longshanks had his way we'd all be murdered in our sleep, and hanged just for breathing. We need your allegiance, and we need your allies."

Laird Sutherland sat back in his chair, crossed his arms over his chest and gazed off somewhere behind Jamie. 'Twas a lot to take in. Jamie had only been able to deliver the news so easily because he'd been dealing with it for some time.

Magnus stood up and paced the length of the room. "I'm in need of a whisky, Montgomery. I hope ye dinna mind."

Jamie shook his head. "By all means."

The man had more than one whisky, his jaw clamped tight between knocking them back. After a few minutes, he returned to the table and pulled out his chair, taking a seat.

"Ye have my allegiance, and if war comes to the Highlands, I will protect the lands and the people with every ounce of power I possess."

Jamie nodded. "We need more than that."

"I am uncertain if I can give ye more than that. Already this year I've sent a chest of silver to the Bruce. Any more than that before next year and I risk the safety and health of my people."

Jamie knew it would be hard to convince a man to support a war he could not see. "And what if Longshanks marches his men across the mountains, burning your villages and cotters?"

"He will never make it that far," Magnus said with confidence.

"How can ye guarantee that?"

The laird's nostrils flared in irritation. "Are ye threatening me, Montgomery?"

Jamie held up his hands in a show of yielding. "Nay, man, I am simply asking ye an honest question."

"I have scouts not only all across my land, but the Highlands themselves. He'll never make it to the village."

"Have ye that many forces on hand? Longshanks marches thousands of knights across our fields, trampling crops and murdering cattle, sheep. He does it for the entertainment and cruelty of it, not for the supplies. Whole villages have starved to death if they were not burned."

"What are ye asking for exactly?"

"Men. Supplies. For ye to encourage your allies to join our forces."

"If I send my men to the Lowlands and the bloody English defeat ye, like they did with Wallace not a fortnight ago, then they will march into the mountains and I am left without the men I sent to ye. We are unprotected. 'Tis best my men remain behind to protect the north."

"I disagree. With your men in the south, we can defeat Longshanks before he crosses the Grampians."

Magnus shook his head. "Too much of a risk."

"And if your future Scottish king orders it?"

"The Bruce?" Magnus leaned back in his chair. "Has he?"

Jamie frowned. He'd probably have more luck in convincing a virgin to have raw, sweaty relations in front of an audience—not that he'd ever done such a thing, but damn Magnus was making this difficult. "It has been requested that ye offer support in your country's fight for freedom."

Magnus' lips thinned in a line and he stared hard at Jamie. The man was stubborn. Good thing he'd not come to offer for Lorna's hand. Sutherland would no doubt come up with every reason not to agree just to get a rise out of Jamie. It appeared there were more than a few stubborn arses in the Sutherland family.

"I will need a day or two to think over what I shall offer. Is that suitable? In the meantime would ye and your men care to stay on as our guests? We'll have a Beltane celebration on the morrow, and I shall give ye my answer after that."

Now it was Jamie's turn to frown. He leaned back in the chair and crossed his arms over his chest as he assessed the Sutherland laird. Remaining at Dunrobin for two additional days was not in his plan. However, if he could convince Sutherland to send out messengers to the neighboring clans encouraging support, then it just might be worth it, and save him time in the long run. He truly needed to get back to Glasgow. Malcolm knew how to run the keep, how to protect their family, lands and clan, but Jamie was chief, and not a messenger. Glasgow was where he belonged.

He blew out a deep sigh. "Aye. I'll remain. But I'll need your answer no later than two days. And I'll need your word that whatever means of support ye decide on, ye'll send out word to your fellow allies, encouraging them to do the same."

Magnus gave a curt nod. "Ye have my word. And my thanks for allowing me some time to think over my answer."

"Your gratitude is nay required. 'Tis a weighty thing your future king has requested of ye. But it does not come lightly, nor without much appreciation. Your assistance will go a long way in helping free us from Longshanks' tyranny. The Sutherland name will go down in history as being part of that."

Magnus chuckled. "I but wonder what that history will be. My men are fully capable of fighting one on five to the bloody Sassenachs, but that's with me as their commander. Under another man, if they obey and he has not fully prepared for the attack, there is no telling what could happen."

"Wallace is a great leader."

"Aye, but he is not me."

Jamie smiled. "Ye and I are much more alike than ye may believe, Sutherland. I, too, care a great deal for my men. For my country. I'd not let your men be led into folly."

"I appreciate that." Magnus pushed back from the table, standing, he reached his arm across.

Jamie, too, stood and gripped his arm. "And I appreciate ye giving my request serious consideration."

Magnus grunted. "I was about to begin training with my men. Care to join us?"

Jamie's grin widened. He loved a challenge. And this would be a good chance to prove to Magnus that he was fully capable of leading the man's warriors into battle. "With pleasure."

~

So Magnus had *not* sent the wild warrior and his men away.

Lorna paused on the steps of the keep, and watched as the warriors filed out of the gate and onto the field where they would train for the day. Magnus and the warrior sparred with words, jabbing each other with their dumb fists.

Couldn't her brother see that this man was dangerous? A fool?

The two of them carried on like they were the best of friends. Well, she could ignore them both. Hopefully the wretch would be gone by the evening meal.

Lorna lifted her nose in the air and sailed past the men toward the stables, her *arisaid* full of apples and carrots for Angel. After giving her such a fright this morning—well, actually, after the stranger gave her such a fright—she felt she owed her mare a tasty treat.

"Lorna!" Magnus' voice had her pausing mid-step in the center of the courtyard. Should she turn and recognize him or just continue on?

If she just kept going, there was every possibility that her brother would follow her. As stubborn as he was, she wouldn't doubt it. Best to simply get it over with and be on her way.

Lorna turned slowly around and gave a haughty lift of her brow. The stranger's broad grin made her cringe. What did he have to be so happy about?

"Aye, brother?" she asked.

The two men approached her. "I wanted to introduce ye to our guest."

"Guest? Introduce?" She couldn't help her surprise. He was staying? At Dunrobin?

"Well, I suppose we've already been introduced. Twice, now," the man said with a chuckle that did irritating things to her body.

The sound of it tickled along her spine and sent a shiver racing into her chest. What was that all about?

"Twice? How so?"

"Lorna, this is Jamie Montgomery. The one who saved ye all those years ago."

All those years ago…

Her mind tunneled back, remembering those horrid sights. Her parents, her brother Blane, blood, screams of pain. Lorna flinched, nodded quickly and gave a jerky curtsy. Now she knew why the name had been so familiar.

"I see we have met. And ye're not as much as a savage as I assumed ye were this afternoon. My thanks for your assistance." The words tumbled out, monotone. She owed this man her life, for had he not the foresight to break away from the fight, 'twas very likely she wouldn't have made it home that day.

Lorna glanced down at the ground, suddenly not as full of spite as she'd been before. "I need to see to my horse. Nice to be reacquainted with ye."

Before he could respond, she whirled and took quick steps to the barn, tears blurring her eyes at the memories.

That day she'd been so scared, but when he lifted her up and held her tight, he'd made her forget her fear. He was her very own hero. A warrior she could love. If only in her dreams.

But now here he was in the flesh, and her body was doing all sorts of odd things, and her mind was racing with excitement, fear, and trepidation. Why was he here? Had he dreamt of her, too? Had he chosen to return to scoop her back up in his arms like she'd imagined he would one day?

Good Lord, she just hoped he went away. She wasn't ready. Not in the slightest.

CHAPTER SIX

'Twas the eve of the Beltane celebration and Magnus had chosen to begin the festivities early since they'd a guest present. Laughter, music and dozens of voices could be heard from the top of the circular stone stairs. After dinner there would be music and dancing.

Lorna's heart had not stopped beating erratically since she'd come across Jamie in front of the courtyard earlier in the afternoon. Would he ask her to dance? Would she even stay that long, or beg permission to leave the festivities early?

Lorna had taken extra time in her chamber to prepare for the evening feast, though she refused to explore the reason behind it. However, rounding the corner and entering the room, that very reason stood not five feet from her. Tall as a tree and as imposing as a mountain. Her belly fluttered when she caught his dark gaze.

She smoothed her skirts and swiped at invisible strands of hair. Not a single one was out of place. Her hair looked lovely, plaited and piled on the top of her head, in a high knot threaded with wild flowers, and she dazzled in a gown Magnus had given to her on her birthday. This one reminded her of spring. Light, sky blue and soft as a spring breeze. The one she'd wear for the Beltane celebration was as purple as a thistle.

Jamie stopped speaking to the men around him, his attention suddenly focused solely on her.

Lorna's mouth went dry as she felt the weight of his gaze boring deeply into hers. His gaze unlocked from hers and traveled, slowly, the length of her body, making her hands tremble and a shiver of… something…trailed up her spine and then back down again, circling her middle and settling in the pit of her stomach.

She swallowed. And swallowed again.

As the man assessed her, Lorna took the opportunity to do the same. He'd had a bath or a swim in the sea recently as the ends of his dark hair were still damp and hung loosely about his shoulders. His skin was bronzed from the sun, and clean. A shadow of a beard shaded the line of his jaw and around his firm lips. He wore a crisp linen shirt and a plaid similar to the one he'd been wearing earlier that morning. Just below his knees, leather boots hugged his muscled calves, but she found her attention drawn back to his knees.

Never before had she been so keen on a particular body part. But she was now. His knees… they were strong, brushed with a sprinkle of dark hair and so…firm. Lorna bit her lip, now sure that she was not the only one staring at his knees, for everyone was certain to notice that her eyes were riveted to that particular naked spot on his body.

But she couldn't tear her eyes away. In fact, looking at the curve of his leg had her imagining the way he'd bend to lift her on a horse, or how he might kneel upon the ground. When she was able to peel her eyes away and look up at him, her face quickly flooded with heat. Jamie's lips had curled slightly in a devilish smile and the intensity of his stare deepened. And, aye, there were others staring at the two of them. His two friends that he'd brought with him elbowed him in the ribs and chuckled as though they found the whole thing amusing. It only made her face hotter.

Zounds! As if she didn't have enough to worry over with her aunt and the marriage talk. Now, she'd have to deal with the rumors that would surely spark from her staring very inappropriately at their guest.

Forget that she liked the way he looked at her, or that she anticipated that swirling feeling in her belly and the shivers of excitement that rippled over her whenever he was near. She barely knew the man, and he was most likely dangerous.

Any man with knees as enticing as his *had* to be trouble.

Lorna lifted her nose a fraction and whirled her gaze away from the handsome devil in search of… what? What could she look at? Anything but him.

She headed straight toward her aunt. Probably the safest person in the room. If she needed to be straightened out of her odd thinking, Aunt Fiona would be the one to help. Or at the very least, give her a sound talking to that made Lorna never want to look at another man again. Especially his knees.

When she reached her aunt, Fiona gave her a side glance, but there was no reprimand as Lorna had anticipated. No scathing remarks. If anything, the woman had a scheming look about her. Fiona smirked, almost pleased with herself. But how could that possibly be? She glanced at her aunt's hands, half expecting to see a jug of near empty wine. But there was nothing. It was entirely possible she'd been partaking of wine before coming down to the great hall, but that was very unlike her aunt. Nay, this was something much different. Fiona glanced over Lorna's shoulder in the direction of Jamie, again a secret smile curved her lips as she caught Lorna's gaze.

Lorna frowned for a moment, not quite understanding why her aunt might look so—

Oh nay! Nay, nay, nay, nay… Her aunt was scheming all right and Lorna had a sneaking suspicion that it had something to do with Jamie and herself. That would not do. Not at all.

While her aunt's attention turned back to the few clanswomen she was discussing a new embroidery pattern with, Lorna snuck a glance back over her shoulder toward Jamie. A gasp stuck in her throat to see that he, too, was watching her. Her throat went dry. Underarms grew slick. Saints, but every time she was around this man she felt sick. Her stomach flipped, heart pounded.

His dark gaze was intense, and she had the sudden overwhelming urge to find out what it was he was thinking. But would she want to confess her own thoughts?

Nay, nay she wouldn't. For then she'd have to run to confession and explain to Father Hurley that she'd most definitely been having sinful thoughts—because she couldn't help but wonder what it would feel like for that brawny Highlander to put his arms around her, to brush his lips over hers and to breathe in his scent which had to be just as male as he looked. And just as intoxicating.

Again her face heated. She'd not felt herself blush so much in one day the whole of her life. She jerked her gaze back toward her aunt to find not only Fiona but the several women she'd been speaking with staring at her. Her aunt held the same pleased expression, and the other women smiled knowingly. Ugh. Lorna wanted to run from the room and vomit. Why did her interest in a man have to be a clan affair?

"What?" she asked, acting nonchalant with a slight lift of her shoulder.

Aunt Fiona tried to hide her smile while the clanswomen did no such thing—they grinned full out now from ear to ear.

"Do ye have a beau, lass?" Margaret, wife of the clan tanner asked, her eyes flicking toward Jamie.

Lorna's hand flew to her neck and she pretended offense. "Nay! I barely know the man. I only found out earlier that he'd been the one to save me when…" She trailed off, hoping the women would get the hint, but none seemed to notice, and she supposed she shouldn't have used such a tragic event to change the subject anyway.

"I barely knew my Angus," piped in Rebecca, wife of one of Magnus' warriors, while the other ladies chirped in agreement.

"Aye, love comes in time," Margaret said.

The muscles of Lorna's eyes burned to roll, but she held them steady. "I'm nay marrying the man," she whispered harshly. "Dinna say another word on the subject."

She was certain to be thoroughly chastised by Aunt Fiona for the way she spoke, but once again her aunt shocked her by simply smiling and nodding slowly.

Lorna huffed a breath. "If ye will excuse me." She whirled in an attempt to find her sister Heather, and smacked face to chest into the man in question.

Her hands came up involuntarily to protect herself and landed against hard muscle. Good God, he was like a wall. A thick, muscled, completely gorgeous wall. He smelled just as heavenly as she would have imagined and Lorna caught herself breathing deep of his earthy, spicy scent.

"Pardon me," she said, her voice breathy and distant to her own ears.

As if she'd only just recalled where her hands rested, she jerked them away. Blood rushed through her head, making her feel light-headed. Oh, why of all things, did this have to happen now? The ladies were sure to be gossiping about an upcoming wedding after that display.

Lorna cringed, gritting her teeth.

"Apologies, my lady. I was hoping to escort ye to the table." He held out a large elbow, obviously wanting her to take his arm, and blatantly ignoring her discomfort.

Lorna stared at the appendage, unsure of how to act. If she did take it, he'd feel how her fingers trembled over the sinew of his arm. And if she didn't take it, that would be rude.

Being rude to guests was unacceptable. Even if said guest made her heart go pitter-pat and caused the clanswomen to waggle their tongues.

Her gaze rose from his arm to his face, studying him. He raised a sculpted brow and shifted his arm closer. The man was invading her space, and shame on her, Lorna liked it.

"May I?" he asked.

Lorna gave a curt nod, forcing her hands to still as she wrapped her fingers around his upper arm. Dear Lord, he was nothing but sinew. Thick and hard. Her breath caught. No touch had ever made her feel so... Oh, she couldn't even describe it. Only that her breath left her, her heart beat faster and her belly felt like it had given birth to a colony of butterflies.

"My thanks," she answered, hearing the sound of the women whispering behind her.

Shame on them! Had they no decency? They embarrassed her more than anyone else. She'd not be surprised if by morning a wedding gown had been prepared. Just the thought of marrying the towering warrior made her belly flip again. Having a wedding meant having a wedding night...

Flames must have touched her face, for suddenly she was as hot as Hades.

She fanned her face as Jamie escorted her to the head table, while those around her also found their seats. When they reached her seat, he tugged it out and waited for her to sit before tucking her back in. So chivalrous. Of course, he wasn't the first man to pull out her chair, but for some reason it meant all the more that he'd done it.

Maybe because it showed that beneath his brute exterior, he was a gentleman? Or was it because she liked his singular attention? She was, after all, the only woman he'd chosen to escort to the table.

Lorna turned around, flashing their guest a smile—one that she hoped didn't convey just how much she was starting to like him. "My thanks."

"Ye're verra welcome." His voice stroked along her nerves in a delicious way, and she suddenly wondered what it would sound like if he whispered in her ear.

Ugh. Too many fairy tales. Growing up, her nursemaid had told many, and Lorna had taken over the task of telling them to Heather. Living in a world of fantasy and romance must have addled her brain.

Everyone took their places, leaving only one empty chair for their guest—right beside her.

Magnus swept his arm out toward Jamie. "Sit. Be our guest."

Jamie nodded and grinned down at Lorna before turning back to her brother. "My thanks, Laird Sutherland."

"Magnus, remember?"

"Aye, my friend." Jamie pulled out his chair and sat down, his heat and presence overwhelming in its closeness.

How could sitting beside a man give her such... Heart palpitations. Sweaty palms. Wicked thoughts. She found herself leaning closer to him and taking in extra-long breaths.

Jamie picked up a jug of watered wine and held it out to her. "Shall I pour ye a cup, my lady?"

Lorna nodded. Might as well. She could use a bit of wine to settle her nerves, else she'd end up crawling into his lap as she shoved her nose against his throat to breathe him in up close.

Jamie poured her wine, then offered to pour for Aunt Fiona on his other side. The sneaky woman nodded and peeked a glance at Lorna, that scheming smile on her lips.

Lorna plastered an irritated smile on her face, returning it to her aunt, so the woman wouldn't continue with her machinations. But Fiona didn't seem to care, she only beamed all the more as she said her thanks to Jamie, then told him how marvelous it was that he'd decided to join them.

Picking up her goblet Lorna brought the wine to her lips, wishing she hadn't spent so much time bating her aunt. Now she'd have to pay the price of her aunt's interference and the embarrassment it was sure to cause her. Not to mention Jamie. The man hadn't come here with intentions of sweeping her off her feet. 'Twas not a social call, but one of business, and he no doubt didn't want to walk away from it with a wife.

The only thing she could do from now on was ignore him. He had to have pride. He wouldn't simply agree to her aunt's plans if Lorna continued to brush him off.

Throughout the first half of the meal, when he attempted to speak to her, Lorna responded only in grunts, nods and shakes of her head. But by the halfway mark, and possibly her second goblet of wine, she found herself actually responding. Meeting his gaze. And all the sensations she'd felt before rushed through her in tumultuous waves. The man had a smile that could melt the ice atop the Grampian Mountains.

But every now and then, she caught sight of Aunt Fiona watching them, and then she'd clam up and ignore him. Stab at the roasted venison on her plate or shove an overlarge bite of bread into her mouth. Manners be damned. If she couldn't keep herself to ignoring him, perhaps he'd be disappointed with her eating habits.

Men liked women with a dainty appetite, and despite her petite figure, Lorna had anything *but* a dainty hunger for food. Not that it mattered, Jamie didn't seem to notice in the least that she ate nearly as much as he did.

After what felt like excruciating hours, the servants cleared away the platters and trenchers and pipers and fiddlers started to play the lively tunes that the Sutherlands enjoyed.

Nearly a quarter of the clan was dancing in the center of the great hall after shoving one set of trestle tables on the left side up against the wall. Lorna's foot started tapping and if it weren't for the man sitting beside her, she'd have gotten up to dance already.

Jamie leaned close to her, his voice low as he said, "Ye like to dance?"

"Nay," Lorna said adamantly.

"Your foot suggests otherwise."

She immediately stopped tapping her foot and flashed him a glance, but quickly looked away when she felt she could drown in his gaze. "Ye're mistaken," she whispered.

Jamie chuckled, the sound making her also want to laugh, but she kept her lips firmly together.

"Ye've been tapping your foot atop my toes in time with the music."

Lorna gritted her teeth. "Fine. I like to dance."

"Would ye care to dance with me?"

Her heart skipped a beat. "Nay!" she said, probably too quickly.

"Nay?" There was a hint of humor in his voice.

She glanced beyond him to her aunt, then down at the empty space where her trencher had been. "Nay."

"Come now, I dinna bite."

Lorna gasped. "I would hope not."

"Then why do ye refuse? Ye like to dance and so do I."

"It would…" She trailed off, not wanting to tell him the true reason.

Again he leaned close, his voice so low it sent a stroke of pleasure over her. "I promise one dance is not going to have your aunt insisting we rush to the altar."

Lorna flicked her eyes toward his, shocked that he'd guessed her hesitancy. Jamie's eyes were merry and danced with pleasure. He held his hand over his heart.

"I'll nay let ye be compromised, my lady. I simply wish to dance with ye."

What could be the harm? Besides the entire clan planning a wedding that he obviously didn't want—hadn't he just said that? And she didn't want it either for that matter!

"One dance," she said.

"Just one." He winked.

Oh, what a devil he was, winking at her like that. What did that mean? That he was saying one dance, but meant more? Before she could think on it, Jamie pushed back his chair, then pulled hers out and offered her his hand.

Lorna ignored the many eyes on them, and took Jamie's hand, her fingers sinking into his larger, warm grasp. A smile curled his lips, matched by her own. She liked holding his hand. A little too much. Just one dance, and then she'd excuse herself for the evening, lest she do something she regretted, like tell the man how his palm against hers was sending hot frissons up her arm, or how her legs shook a little as they walked toward the other dancers.

Jamie twirled her around, his body clashing against hers before he twirled her another way, and then they were both tapping their feet, and whirling around the others. But every time they came back together, Lorna felt the heat of her body increase. Sparks of some foreign emotion. Her belly wasn't the only thing fluttering either. An intense, confusing heat had started to build between her thighs. She wasn't naïve enough not to understand it either. She was attracted to the warrior. Dangerously so.

At the end of the dance, he bowed toward her, and she curtsied in turn.

"My thanks," she murmured. "If ye would excuse me."

Lorna did not say goodnight to anyone. Nor did she care that she would miss out on the bonfires being lit across the moors, there'd be plenty more on the morrow. Escape was necessary, else she be convinced to dance again. She trembled so fiercely at the reaction her body had to Jamie's, and confusion warred so intensely within her, she needed to escape to her room, to breathe in the air that couldn't seem to make it past her throat. She didn't wait for Jamie's response, but ducked out of the great hall and hurried toward the stairs. Her foot hit the fourth stair when he called out behind her.

"My lady, wait."

Lorna paused on the stairs, her heart hammering against her ribs. Should she turn? Run the rest of the way up without looking back?

She turned, seeing him standing at the foot of the stair. So tall he was—his head reached to her shoulders, and here she was four steps up.

"What is it?" she asked, her voice doing that breathy thing again.

"I—" He glanced away, seeming at a loss for words.

Lorna waited patiently, unsure of how to respond, and quite frankly, she wasn't sure she'd be able to find the words anyway.

"I wanted to thank ye for the dance, lass. And…" He stepped closer, eye level now. His voice lowered as he spoke. "I hope ye didna feel the need to run away because of me."

Lorna swallowed. He *was* the reason she'd run.

She stared at his lips, all the feelings she'd had inside the great hall colliding. Jamie's gaze flicked to her mouth, too. He wanted to kiss her just as much as she wanted a kiss.

Lorna licked her lower lip nervously, watching his eyes widen at the innocent move.

"I am tired, 'tis all," she lied.

"Aye, me, too."

"Good night, then" she whispered, retreating backward up another step, to put some distance between them, before she completely fell into her desire to press her lips on his and see if they were warm or hot.

"Sweet dreams, my lady."

Lorna turned and ran the rest of the way up the stairs, completely certain her dreams would be anything but sweet.

CHAPTER SEVEN

"*R*ise and shine, my dear."

Shafts of blinding light stabbed at Lorna's barely opened eyes. Who would torture her this way?

She rubbed her eyes, swearing it must have only been an hour since she fell asleep, or it might as well have been. A candelabra filled with nearly a dozen candles blazed bright on the table beside her bed.

"That's it, lass. Open your eyes. Ye've a big day ahead of ye." Aunt Fiona stood near the foot of the bed, a much too large smile spread on her face. "And I suspect the barrel of wine ye had didna help much."

Lorna shook her head and rolled away from her aunt. "I didna drink a barrel."

"Let us settle on half then." Her aunt had the audacity to chuckle.

"Isn't Heather causing mischief somewhere? Should ye not be attending her instead of me?" Lorna shoved her head under the pillow. How much wine had she drunk? What had made her do such a thing?

Jamie's face flashed before her closed lids. Ugh. The dreadfully handsome guest of Dunrobin.

Aunt Fiona's sing-song voice broke in. "Och, your sister is always creating mischief; I'll likely not miss out on any of it. Now out of bed with ye."

"Nay."

"Since ye didna budge when I came in an hour ago, and I saw the many times ye refilled your cup, I had Cook brew ye a special tea. Should make your head feel better. Besides, Laird Montgomery is likely to leave today." Her aunt's footsteps sounded closer.

"Why should I care?"

"Because he's the man ye're to marry." Fiona's voice was calm, so deadly serious, Lorna couldn't help but flip over in bed and sit bolt upright.

Aunt Fiona stood right beside her, a triumphant smile on her face.

"Are ye mad?" Lorna asked, her mouth falling open, eyes begrudgingly settling on her annoying relation.

"Mad? Nay. Ye need to marry, lass, and Laird Montgomery is the most suitable match." Her aunt shrugged like she was talking about which flour to use in the day's bread.

Lorna stared agape as her aunt set down the cup of tea on the side table and then sailed over to the wardrobe and threw it open, digging through the gowns.

"Stop. I'm wearing the purple," Lorna muttered, tossing back the covers and shivering at the sudden waft of cool air. Oh, how she wanted to curl back up beneath the sheets.

"Ah, purple, aye, that will be best." Aunt Fiona nodded, and tapped her chin. If a good idea came about and it hadn't been hers, Aunt Fiona always managed to find a way to make it so.

"Mmhmm." Lorna rolled her eyes, stood and stretched. Not only did her head ache, but the rest of her body felt as though she'd danced more than one round. 'Haps all the twisting and turning she'd done in bed. Whatever it was, she needed to heal as quickly as possible—as in by the time she'd finished dressing and left the room. If she didn't have all her wits about her, Aunt Fiona was liable to have her married by the time noon rolled around.

"Come now, we must get ye ready. I fear the man will be leaving us shortly."

That got Lorna's attention and she whipped her head around—a sharp pain in her neck making her wince. "Why do ye say that?"

"Are ye interested in the answer?" Fiona asked, whirling around, brow raised and an excited curl to her lip.

"Nay." Lorna waved her hand in the air, forced herself to frown. "I dinna care when the man leaves."

"Well, as a maiden, ye need to be out on the moors with the other maidens at dawn. 'Tis customary on Beltane."

The first of May. Lorna gritted her teeth, trying to think of any excuse to not go out and roll in the dewy morning grass with every other maid in the keep and village, but she could think of none. Besides, she enjoyed the ritual. It was the one time per year she was permitted to do the very thing she enjoyed—be one with nature, and no one could tell her otherwise.

A smile started to curl her lip and she tugged at the ribbons of her nightrail. Already her aching muscles were beginning feel better, her headache nearly gone.

"I'm glad to see your enthusiasm renewed," Fiona said.

Lorna tugged her nightrail off, pulled a new chemise on and grabbed the purple gown from her aunt. "Dinna get confused, my excitement is for Beltane and not the fictional romance ye have budding in your mind."

"As ye say," Fiona fairly sung.

Lorna bit her tongue to keep from retorting. 'Twould appear that nothing she said would matter to Fiona. She had her mind set on Lorna marrying and she'd clamped onto the first man Lorna hadn't turned away from in disgust.

If she were to be honest, and Lorna was in the least interested in marrying—and she was most adamantly not—she might have tried to entice Jamie. But as it was… What? What was barring her from marrying?

Nothing, truly, other than she wasn't ready to leave her family behind. Fear was what it was. And it was potent.

"I'll go roll in the grass, but ye must leave off about Laird Montgomery. I…" She couldn't tell her aunt. The woman was not understanding in the least.

Aunt Fiona studied her for a moment, tapping her lip in concentration. "What is it ye fear, lass?"

"Fear?" Lorna scoffed. How had she picked up on that?

Fiona gripped her gently at the elbow and steered her toward the bed, pushing her to sit, and then descending beside her.

"'Tis all right if ye are scared, lass. I, too, was fearful when my mother and father chose for me to marry. And for ye, it must be doubly hard because ye've not had a mother and father all these years. With only your brothers, and none of them married, ye've not had the proper guidance of a female. I've tried, but I fear, I canna be here all the time. Marriage can be a happy union, ye need not fear that. I sense that Laird Montgomery is a noble man. I think he'd be a good husband."

Lorna stared at Aunt Fiona, a woman who'd balked on more than one occasion that she'd not been so happily married. Their father's sister had been married off to a man as old as her grandfather—as his third wife.

But despite all that, Lorna's mouth parted in shock. Was her aunt right? She had a feeling she was. Aye, she'd seen many married couples within the clan, but none that she'd lived with, and she didn't remember how her parents were together. To her, marriage represented a stifling of her dreams and freedoms. Unless it was for love, like the stories she told to Heather and those she'd heard as a child. But fairytales weren't real.

And the last thing she would ever believe was that Jamie Montgomery was her hero—even if he'd saved her life once.

~

FROM THE WINDOW OF HIS GUEST CHAMBER, JAMIE WATCHED THE MOORS where women flounced with the abandon of dawn. The sun rose pink and gold, touching their cheeks and glimmering on the dew soaked grass.

But there was one maiden who caught his eye in particular—Lady Lorna. Her dress was as purple as the thistles that dotted the fields, and her skin as golden pink as the sunrise. Her hair shone in the light, reminding him of spun gold, and he wanted badly to run his fingers through it, curl a tendril around his thumb.

Jamie frowned down at the one woman who'd made him forget his next moves on the council and the war against the English. Tonight he'd find out from her brother if the council could count on the Sutherlands as allies, and then he'd be on his way.

He had no business watching a lass romp around the fields. No business in taking pleasure in the way her dew soaked dress clung to her breasts and hips and thighs. Joy filled her face as she held out her arms, face upturned to the sky, eyes closed. A picture of ecstasy, and he wanted to see that look again and again—preferably with her beneath him. Or over him. Didn't matter. Anyway he could have her, he'd be happy.

Entirely unrealistic. The lass wasn't likely to lure him into a hayloft or abandoned croft. Jamie had no intention of risking the council's business by seducing her and having her brother try to murder him. The only way he'd ever sink between her thighs was if they were married. And Jamie had no mind to get married now. Not until the English had been dealt with. A task that could very well last a lifetime if he didn't succeed in his mission to gain allies. The sooner the better.

He couldn't get involved with Lorna, or any woman for that matter. To do so would mean risking everything.

So why was he leaving his chamber? Why was he walking down the stairs and joining the other men in going to dance with the lassies on the hill?

In the Lowlands, many clans had stopped practicing the ancient ritualistic holidays for fear of retaliation by the English. He'd not realized how much he missed it.

The morning was crisp and a light breeze blew, cooling the skin, which was quickly warmed by the rising sun until it was cooled again by another bit of wind. Toby and Donald each swung their own lasses around—'haps one and the same with whomever they'd found to warm their beds the night before.

Magnus and Ronan, too, were running out to the hill, grabbing lassies and twirling them around with the rest of the lads. Everyone was laughing and pipers joined in, playing lively tunes.

Older clanswomen came out, including the fearsome matronly aunt of the Sutherlands, with crowns woven of marigolds.

"Here," Fiona said, thrusting a woven circlet into his hands. She nodded toward Lorna.

Jamie thrust it back. "I canna."

Fiona laughed. "'Tis all good fun. Give it to her and dance. 'Twill be delightful."

But Jamie shook his head again. It wasn't simply good fun. Giving her the headpiece was a statement. A statement of interest. Romantic interest. Perhaps even a promise. Not a promise or statement he was in any way capable of making. And yet, his fingers curled around the flowers and his feet took steps toward the lass whose braid had started to unravel and golden tendrils curled against her cheeks.

"Good morning, lass," he murmured, placing the marigold wreath upon her head, the backs of his fingers brushing her warm cheek.

"Good morning," she said breathlessly.

Her eyes lit on his, cheeks flushed. Jamie felt her waist beneath his fingertips before he realized he'd even gripped her.

"Care to dance once more?" he asked.

Lorna chewed her lip. Smile faltering and worry coming into her eyes. Was it possible she had the same trepidations about marriage as he did?

Jamie gave her a friendly smile. "'Tis just a dance. Nothing more."

She gave a short nod, relief showing in her eyes. Ah, so he'd been right.

"A single dance as it was last night." He winked and held out a hand.

"Then, I accept." Lorna's fingers tentatively reached for his, the slightest tremble quickly gone. She smiled up at him, vibrant, fresh and beautiful.

Jamie twirled her around the grass, finding himself laughing, lifting her into the air to whirl her around. There was more to her petite body then he'd first realized. Beneath her gown, each time he lifted her, he felt her muscles working. She was lithe, taut, and yet still full of feminine appeal.

"Ye're so beautiful, my lady," he said.

Lorna opened her mouth, looking shocked for a moment before she schooled her features into one of demure complacency. "Thank ye, my laird." Complacency was soon overrun by a teasing lilt of her lips. Lord how he loved the play of expressions. "Do ye always ask ladies to dance more than once when ye're a guest in their home?"

"Only one." *Ballocks!* He hadn't meant for that confession to slip out, but it had.

Lorna chewed the corner of her lip, a look he'd come to recognize as one that she used when she was deep in thought, or conflicted. Did he make her feel conflicted?

Hell, she was doing a pretty damn good job of making him feel the same way. He moved closer, his hand circling the small of her back, feeling the warmth of her body, the slight indent at the base of her spine. She glanced up at him through lowered lashes, her lips pink, plush and...

Jamie wanted to kiss her. To sweep her up into his arms and taste all that she was. To run his fingers through her hair. The primal dancing in the dew was making him feel feral in other ways. He dipped his head, inches from her lips, staring at her mouth. Her lips parted and she sucked in a breath, but she didn't move away. Was it possible that Lorna wanted a kiss just as much as he did? He'd thought so last night, too. No matter what the both of them thought of marriage or commitment, there was definitely an intense attraction, a tug and pull that had him flaring his nostrils to take in her scent.

As much as Jamie wanted to lean the rest of the way in, he was acutely aware they were not alone. Surrounded by her brothers, her aunt, her clan. Now was not the time for kissing, even if he warred with the decision inside.

Lorna's gaze flicked away from him for a second, then her hand clamped over her mouth, laughter filling her eyes.

Jamie turned around, watching as many of the young men ran toward the sea, stripping out of their clothes. Their tanned backs and pale white arses a testament to how they trained and worked with only their plaids wrapped around their hips. The women laughed, hiding their eyes and peeking between their fingers. Magnus gripped onto Jamie's arm and tugged him toward the water. As soon as they saw Jamie, Toby and Donald, too, ran toward the water, eagerly shedding all they wore.

Jamie glanced over his shoulder at Lorna as he went, her eyes riveted on him. He smiled at her while he unpinned his plaid, tugged off his shirt, dropped his sporran and then moved to unhook his buckle. As his plaid unraveled, she whirled away, making Jamie laugh hard.

When Magnus gave him his answer tonight, Jamie was going to have a damn hard time leaving Dunrobin and Lorna behind.

~

AN HOUR LATER, LORNA'S FACE WAS STILL FLAMING RED. IT WAS ALL SHE could do to keep herself turned away from the sea filled with naked men—and one in particular who she shamefully wanted to see.

Even now, standing in the courtyard by the well as Magnus and his men brought in a line of sheep they'd sheer in celebration of the coming spring, the fertility of their animals, clan and good fortune, she had to press her hands to her flaming cheeks.

Magnus came up beside her, a beaming smile on his face. He always loved Beltane and Lorna couldn't help but wonder if it was because many lasses clambered over themselves for his attention. Her brother was a gentleman to a point, but if a lass was a widow, or willing and not a virgin, he nearly always ended the evening with a bed partner on a holiday, though he refrained most of the time during the rest of the year.

Lorna smiled. Though he lamented that love was for fools, she

73

knew deep down, her brother would one day find his match. "How many lasses are vying for a spot beside ye tonight?"

"Och, Lorna, ye shouldna speak like that. Maidens dinna use such vulgar speech."

Lorna snorted. "Brother, ye know me not."

"I know ye well enough to see ye eyeing our guest like he is a sugar crusted almond."

She frowned. Was everyone going to be on her about Jamie? "I did no such thing."

Magnus laughed. "Aye, ye did. But ye know he will not be here for long."

"I know it."

"He'll be leaving most likely on the morrow, with my blessing, but without my men."

Lorna tried to hide her surprise, though she could feel her face paling. Jamie would leave already? And what blessing was he talking about? Oh, no! Not marriage… Her voice was barely above a whisper when she spoke, "What?"

Magnus glanced at her. "I suppose ye're no longer too young to know what goes on in the world."

Lorna swallowed, unsure if she was ready to hear everything he had to say. "And, that is?"

"War with the English."

"How naïve do ye think I am, Magnus? I've known of the war since as far back as I can remember. What is it that our guest has requested? He wants ye to fight?"

Magnus nodded. "Aye."

A shiver of fear stole over her, imagining foul English knights surrounding their castle walls. Every Scottish lass grew up fearing the knights. They had no morals, and wouldn't cease their goals of massacring all of Scotland. They raped women, children, beheaded them. Even took brides on their wedding nights before their husbands had a chance to touch them first. It was enough to make any girl cringe at the word—English.

"I dinna want ye to leave," she whispered. The heat left her cheeks, and she felt the blood drain from her head down to her toes.

When she thought of Jamie Montgomery now, she didn't see the wicked glint in his eye, but the fear of war and death. The man in question approached.

"Have a care, Lorna," Magnus warned just before their guest stepped within hearing distance.

Lorna dipped her head, keeping her gaze on the ground.

"My laird, ye know well how to celebrate our spring."

Despite her fear at why he'd come to Sutherland, Lorna couldn't help being drawn to his voice.

She glanced up at him through her lashes, remembering the last time she'd done so and how close they'd come to kissing. And how much she still wanted to kiss him—despite him bringing the war to her family.

"My thanks, Montgomery. I'm pleased ye were here to enjoy it with us." He clapped the warrior on the back. "Let us feast!"

The servants had pulled all the long tables out of the great hall, decorating the courtyard with them, filling the tops with flowers and candles. A dozen warriors started a blazing bonfire. Dogs romped around barking, and sheep bleated as they ran, newly sheered toward the gate to escape the chaos.

Heather ran up to Magnus grabbing onto his hands and begging for a chance to drink a bit of the spicy wine Cook had made. Her siblings walked off, arguing over the potency of the drink, leaving Jamie and Lorna to themselves.

"Ye will leave tomorrow," Lorna said, unsure of why she chose that certain line, but feeling as though they needed to discuss…whatever it was that was sparked between them. Or maybe it was distance they needed.

"Aye. But I'd come back again. If I had a reason."

Lorna lifted her brow, ignoring how her heart sped up at that line. "What sort of reason?"

Jamie reached out, stroked her chin, his lips curling into a devilish smile. "There is one reason I can think of in particular."

Lorna reached up, her fingers curling over his as she pulled them away from her face, but he didn't let them go. In fact, he moved a little closer, crowding her personal space and making her breath hitch.

"What reason is that?" Lorna whispered.

"Sutherlands have the best ale." His eyes twinkled with merriment, as he teased her.

Lorna yanked her hand away and swatted at him. "Verra funny, my laird."

"I jest not, 'tis delicious." He gripped onto her hand once more and looking around the courtyard, tugged her around the side of the castle out of view. "But there is one other thing I've yearned to taste."

Lorna's heart skipped a beat. "Taste?" Her voice was low, raspy.

Jamie leaned up against the stone wall and pulled her closer, keeping their fingers interlocked and wrapped his other hand around her hip, singeing her with his touch. Lorna pressed her hands to his chest, feeling the muscles ripple beneath her fingers. Their thighs brushed, and every part of her shivered.

"I want to kiss ye, lass." Jamie dipped low, his nose brushing over hers.

Lorna sucked in a breath, her eyes closing. Jamie's breath tickled her cheek and she leaned even closer into him. It seemed an eternity before his lips brushed over hers, soft, warm and infinitely spine-tingling.

Her fingers curled into his shirt, holding tight and she pressed her lips more firmly to his. Unfamiliar, but enticing, sensations skated along her limbs, knotting in her belly. She squeezed her thighs tight, humming at the spark of pleasure the move made, and the way her lips tingled against Jamie's.

She'd been kissed before. But it was nothing like this. Jamie's kiss was intense without being gratuitous, and she had the hardest time not begging him to deepen their kiss.

"Lorna!"

The two of them jumped apart at Heather's voice.

CHAPTER EIGHT

"*I* canna spare any of my men at this time, Laird Montgomery, but I will give the Bruce what he requires from me in supplies and coin. He has my support, and should the fight reach the Highlands, he has my word, my men will be prepared and ready to fight."

Jamie flicked his gaze back to Magnus who sat behind his desk in the library. While the revelers continued to be merry outside, Magnus had taken the time to pull Jamie inside to give him his answer. But Jamie was having trouble staying focused on the conversation. Instead, he'd studied the flames of the candles, speculating whether or not they were as hot as the flames burning his blood.

Nay, after kissing Lorna, he'd barely been able to think about anything other than the sweet honey-taste of her lips and the scent of her hair. Intoxicating. Stronger than any brew he'd tasted, or shied away from. His attraction to her was potent. Addictive.

Her youngest sister had promised Lorna not to say a word, but the secret was plain on his face he was sure. At any moment, Magnus would shove away from his desk and throw a punch toward Jamie's face. Shout at him for having touched his sister.

Truth be told, he should prepare to leave Dunrobin this very night, for no woman had ever struck him as Lorna had. No kiss had ever affected him as much. 'Twas a scary thing. He'd rather take on Magnus' anger any day than face the turmoil raging inside him.

Magnus, who must have noticed how oddly Jamie was behaving, had started to stare at him overlong.

Jamie cleared his throat, putting his focus back on the Sutherland chief. "I see. I will relay your message to the Bruce. And what of your support with your allies?"

"Ye have my word. I'll send out messengers first thing in the morning encouraging they also give support to the Bruce in any manner they can afford."

Jamie gave a curt nod. "On behalf of the council, we are most grateful," he muttered.

"A drink?"

Jamie had refused Magnus the last dram of whisky, and now he'd not the excuse of being tired from traveling. In fact, he wasn't sure he'd be able to sleep for a sennight given the racing of his thoughts. Though he'd not touched the stuff in years, again, Jamie nodded. "Aye."

Magnus poured them both a healthy portion of whisky, and grinned as he handed a cup to Jamie.

"To seeing the English beaten," Magnus said.

"To freedom." Jamie raised his cup to Magnus, and then they both drank heavily, perhaps each for their own reasons. The liquor burned a path down Jamie's throat, and he sucked in a ragged breath, forcing himself not to cough when his body was most adamant he do so.

"Strong stuff, eh?" Magnus asked, lifting the jug in an offer to refill.

Unsure of why he did so—well, in actuality he was certain why he did, to forget Lorna—Jamie lifted his cup. One more and he'd be through with it. This time when he took a sip, the burn was welcomed. But it did nothing to lesson his need for Lorna.

"I dinna suppose we'll be seeing ye again," Magnus said.

Jamie grunted. "Haps I will return on my way back south. I've several more clans to visit north, though ye've made my journey much easier with agreeing to send out messengers. My thanks."

"We'd be happy to have ye once more." Magnus wiggled his brows. "Many a lass was glad to have ye hopping in the North Sea with the rest of the lads."

Jamie laughed, though he could care less about any of those lasses. The one he had eyes for had turned her back. And, he admitted, he liked that all the more. Said something about her character. As much as she was willing to flirt, to taunt him for his arrogance, she wasn't so easy to win over. Jamie liked that about Lorna. He liked the challenge of chasing her, and damn but the reward had been sweet.

Again his mind shifted to that kiss, the heat of her body molding to his, the press of her lips. He'd not even kissed her as deeply as he wanted to, had kept it as innocent as he possibly could. For both their sakes.

Jamie tossed the rest of the whisky down his throat, then clunked the cup onto Magnus' desk. The hour had to be nearing midnight. The two of them had left the dancing and bonfires beneath the moonlight in order to speak, and now that they had, Jamie was considering retiring for the night, though at first he'd had every intention of returning.

"I should get some rest so that I may be off at first light."

Magnus finished his whisky. "Are ye certain? There is still yet a flame upon the wood."

Tempting. Because he could watch the way the firelight reflected and glowed on Lorna's hair and skin. But then again, everyone would see him staring, for he was certain his gaze could not be pulled anywhere but toward her. It wouldn't do for her brother to see him lusting after her when they'd just come to an agreement on a very important matter.

"'Tis probably best that I retire," Jamie said, unconvinced.

"Nonsense. Another hour at least." Magnus clapped him on the back.

"All right. Another hour."

He shouldn't have let himself be convinced, but if he were honest, it wasn't truly Magnus that swayed him to return to the festivities. It was the chance to see Lorna's face one more time. When morning came, she'd likely still be slumbering in her bed. Damn, but it would be nice if she were lying in his, their limbs entwined. When he felt his cock stir at the thought, he cleared his throat and held out his hand offering Magnus to lead the way.

They returned in time for the last maiden dance. Dozens of lasses danced around the fire in pure delight and abandon—and perhaps too much wine.

"Thank goodness not all the men are sotted," Magnus murmured. "Else we'd have many weddings come the morning."

Jamie chuckled, glad he'd not drunk enough to seduce Lorna. As a matter of fact, he was certain he didn't want to think on that at all. Jamie had oft followed the edicts of the other lairds and kept Beltane quiet. But with Malcolm at the helm of the Beltane festival at Glasgow, there was no telling what sort of deeds were going on. He'd often balked at the lack of celebration. Thank goodness his own sisters were already married off.

All thought left him as Lorna swung into view, her hair completely fallen out of its plait, curling in golden firelight, waves around her shoulders and down her back. She still wore the marigold crown upon her head, and her lips were curled in a smile of pure delight. Her eyes danced with merriment. She'd lifted her skirts just a few inches, revealing her ankles and bare feet. Enough skin showing to make Jamie's gut tighten, blood flow uncontrollably to his groin.

Magnus grunted. "'Tis about time Lorna was married." He said it so low, that it could have been to himself.

Jamie took it as encouragement, though he didn't say anything in return. Was Magnus hinting that he wanted a proposal? He flicked his gaze away, trying to look upon the other women to sway Magnus' opinion. It appeared to work for the man clapped him on the back and then took off after a dark-haired lass he'd seen him dally with earlier in the day.

And good thing, because Jamie could only keep his eyes off of Lorna for so long. He wanted to run into the circle, to pull her into his arms and finish the kiss they'd begun hours before. But dancing beside Lorna were her aunt and sister, as though they were both keeping her safe from him. Had Heather told their aunt she'd caught them kissing?

And why should he care? He was a laird, a ruler of his own clan. A member of the Bruce's council. He was powerful. It had only been a kiss. Maidens kissed warriors all the time.

Jamie crossed his arms over his chest and frowned. And at that moment, Lorna turned to gaze up at him, the rapture on her face momentarily stilted as she caught his stare.

He quickly regretted his irritation, and flashed her a genuine smile. How could he not? Every time he looked at her, she brought about feelings inside him of both joy and irritation. A war he didn't understand, and was reluctant to explore.

Lorna broke away from the maidens. From behind her, he was surprised to see that Heather grabbed their aunt from the line of matrons and tugged her into the circle. Neither Heather nor Fiona paid Lorna any attention. Instead, they continued to dance as though Lorna had never left their side.

He raised a curious brow, eyes never leaving Lorna as she sauntered toward him. The glow of the fire surrounded her. Cheeks flushed with excitement. It was a look he could have seen every day for the rest of his life and been happy.

"My lady," he said softly as she approached.

"I'd thought ye'd gone to bed, my laird."

"Not as yet." He couldn't tell her he'd come back outside to catch another glimpse of her. His gaze raked over her and he ground his teeth to keep from grabbing her and tossing her over his shoulder. Her gown was not immodest, but that didn't matter, it hugged her curves in all the right places and tempted his imagination with what might swell and arch beneath. All sorts of primal and possessive emotions spilled through him.

"I'm glad," she said, gifting him with one of her sensual smiles.

He was tempted to ask how much wine she'd had to drink. Jamie wasn't one to take advantage of a lass, even if she'd let him kiss her before, and even if his need to taste her sweet lips again was nearly overpowering him. Could it be the whisky? The two cups had warmed his blood, but seeing Lorna, that had put a true fire into him.

"As am I," he managed to answer.

"When do ye leave?" she asked.

"At first light."

Disappointment clouded her features. "Will another fifteen years pass before I see ye again?"

A bold question and one he wished he could answer, but in truth… "One can hope 'twill be sooner. Much sooner." He'd not meant to say that. Where the hell did that come from?

"One?" she asked, searching his gaze.

Och, why did lasses always want a man to expand on the things a man said? Didn't they understand men had only so many words of emotion they could utter?

"Aye, lass, I would hope to see ye before fifteen years passes us by."

"As would I." She frowned, chewing her lip. "My brother told me why ye'd come here."

"Did he?"

She nodded, but didn't expound on her statement. Instead, she fiddled with her fingers and what looked like a woven grass ring. Jamie couldn't help but postulate about what her brother had said. But that was the last thing he wanted to think about, so he forced himself to concentrate on the movements of her fingers.

"Did ye make that, lass?" he asked.

Lorna glanced up at him and nodded. "Childish, I know."

"Nay, 'tis not." He reached out, palm up and she placed her fingers in the center of his outstretched hand. He brushed a thumb over the grass ring. "Most of our lives ye'll find that things go in circles, just like this ring. There are reasons for everything, and everyone has a purpose."

Pretty green-blue eyes, dancing with firelight shadows, squinted up at him, surmising the meaning behind his words.

"The English have invaded our world, lass. Do not be afraid of what's to come, for we all must fight to live in our own world. Wrangle our freedom from tyranny's grasp. Some more than others."

"Why are ye telling me this?" Her fingers danced a little on his palm, a nervous tremor perhaps.

He didn't want her to be nervous with him though. He tightened his hold, an instinctual protective move.

"Because, I want ye to be prepared for what comes." He made a gesture with his free hand to their surroundings. "Here in the Highlands, ye've not got a firsthand look at what the devil Sassenachs are doing to our country. How they ravage it."

"We've seen."

"Some, aye. Ye've had a glimpse, but where I live, I see it nearly daily. I've had to wipe the tears and blood from a lasses face after she's been attacked in the wood. I've had to comfort a widow when her husband died, and find a family for an orphaned child."

Lorna blanched, and Jamie realized he'd said too much. No lass wanted to hear about the cruelties and realities of life. Especially on a night when she was celebrating her youth and freedom.

"Apologies," he mumbled, letting go of her hand, and glancing around at those who still danced and drank with merriment. "I did not mean to put a damper on this festive occasion."

Lorna pulled his hand back into hers. "Thank ye."

Jamie nodded, raising his brow in question. "I am not looking for gratitude, lass. Go and enjoy yourself."

"Nay, ye dinna understand. I thank ye for being honest with me."

That caught his attention, and he glanced back at her face, seeing her sincerity there.

"Ye were fierce and grave even at fourteen," she said, a smile curling one side of her mouth. "And now, here ye are, just as grave, and all the wiser for it."

"I dinna know about that."

"Haps ye should look inside yourself." She glanced behind her at her oldest brother. "Ye know, Magnus is wise as well. He has refused to give ye men, but coin and supplies instead."

Jamie nodded, and she met his gaze once more.

"'Tis because he believes he will need them," she said.

"He will."

Lorna glanced down at the ground, and her hands trembled for a moment. "I'm scared. As remote as we are, news has reached us that the English have many. They may not fight as well as we do, but they've got more men. More coin for their cause."

"'Tis a lost cause," Jamie grumbled.

Lorna stroked a finger over his knuckles as if she'd wipe away his consternation. "It may verra well be a lost cause, Jamie, but since when does a desperate man lie down in defeat when his need is so great he'd risk everything for it?"

"Ye speak of Longshanks?"

She nodded. "He'll never stop. Not until the day he dies."

Jamie frowned. "Ye know a lot about bad men."

She shrugged. "Having your parents murdered can do that to a lass."

Jamie had the sudden need to take away her fear. Her pain. "Let us talk no more of death and greedy men. Should ye like to dance with me?"

She chewed her lip. "'Haps ye'd like to give me a goodbye kiss instead?"

Jamie's heart pounded forcefully, and he held his breath, trying to replay what she'd said, uncertain if he'd heard her correctly.

"A kiss?"

Lorna laughed softly, giving him a coy look. "Unless, ye truly wished to dance instead."

Jamie shook his head. Never would he give up a chance to kiss her. "Nay, lass. I much prefer kissing ye."

Lorna's lips parted, perhaps shocked that he would admit as much. But the look in her eyes, the way she'd so boldly expressed her wish made him want desperately to pull her into his arms and give her exactly what they both wanted.

The key was keeping it to a simple kiss, for it could not go beyond that. He'd never take a maiden to his bed, and he had no plans to marry.

But a kiss was… just a kiss.

And so he glanced around and noting that no one seemed to be paying much attention to them, he took her hand in his and said, "Lead the way, lass." He wanted it to be about her, he wanted her to be in charge, for if he was to steal a kiss from a willing lass, at least he wanted her to be the one who chose when and where.

"Follow me." She let go of his hand and took off at a fast walk toward the stables.

Jamie kept a respectable pace behind her, hoping not to draw anyone's attention. Her two brothers had found willing lasses to dance with and her sister and aunt were no longer in sight—perhaps having already gone to bed. None of the other clan members seemed to be the wiser, all otherwise occupied, and that suited Jamie just fine.

A kiss. One kiss and that was all.

One kiss to say goodnight, and goodbye.

One kiss to last him the month or so it would take before he could return for another—a last kiss that would be. For then he'd have to return to his clan and his duties.

Ahead, Lorna opened the stable door and slipped inside. Jamie didn't follow her in that way, instead he snuck around the back and entered through there, finding her facing the front doors.

She startled when he cleared his throat behind her. It'd been a hard feat not to sneak up behind her and slide his hands around her waist. Instead, he waited for her to come to him, willingly.

Standing in the light of a single torch, Lorna looked like a heavenly creature come to liaison with a mere mortal. Her golden hair fell in waves around her shoulders, bits of marigold fell from her crown and tucked themselves within her tresses, a shroud of beauty. Her eyes were curious as she examined him, and there was a faint smile on her pink lips. Lips he remembered kissing, and wanted to kiss again.

"I didn't realize ye'd be coming in from the back," she said quietly.

"Better that no one see us both going in the front." Jamie ran a hand through his hair.

Lorna chewed her lip and took a tentative step forward. Jamie kept his feet rooted firmly in place, though his eyes roved hungrily over her form. Her breasts looked soft and pert, belly flat, her hips round, he could only imagine what she'd look like if he were to ever slip the gown from her shoulders, slit the ties with his dirk, and savor her bare flesh.

"Ye're right." She glanced up at him, her eyes slightly wide, pupils enlarged in the dim light, and she took a step closer. "My brothers would lock me away if they knew I'd snuck in here with ye."

"They'd toss me off their land. 'Haps even withdraw their support from the council."

"We risk much." Her bare toes touched the tips of his boots.

Jamie held his breath, until his lungs burned, and then he drew in a deep pull, her scent filling him, intoxicating him with its heady potency.

"Aye, lass, we do. But"—he reached up and tucked a soft tendril of hair behind her ear—"I canna seem to keep myself away from ye." He brushed his thumb along her cheek, cradled the side of her face.

Lorna turned her face against his hand, lightly kissing his palm. A shiver stole over him, tucking itself firmly in the middle of his back. Such an intimate gesture, and though slight, it rocked him to the core.

That tiny kiss was all the invitation Jamie needed. He stroked along the other side of her face, both hands holding gently to her cheeks one pinkie finger resting on the pulse at her neck. Her heart beat just as fast as his. Gazing into her eyes, he read her interest, her curiosity and desire. Lorna wanted him to kiss her, that much was evident from the way her body was reacting to his nearness, but he still wanted to hear the words from her lips.

"Lorna," he murmured. "Tell me what ye want, what ye need."

She wrapped her arms around his middle, tiny hands splaying along the sides of his spine. "I want ye to kiss me, Jamie. I need ye to kiss me. To escape for a moment from this world."

"Och, lass, 'tis the same for me." And then he lowered his mouth to hers, brushing her lips with a gentle swipe of his. "Your taste intoxicates me."

And this time he meant to taste her, to explore her mouth with sensual intent. Jamie slid his tongue along the seam of her lips, toying with the corner of her mouth until she parted for him on a gasp.

Though he wished to plunge inside, to claim what she offered, he kept his exploration gentle, dipping in to tease the tip of her tongue with his own. Swirling, savoring. Lorna tentatively mimicked his movements, but when she moaned he couldn't help sliding a hand around her back and crushing her form to his length. Supple, curvy and taut all in one, her breasts pressed to his chest, her pelvis tucked to his, and Lord help him, her warmth cradled his engorged cock.

Both of them gasped at the sudden increased intensity. Jamie claimed her mouth then, a possessive, demanding kiss. One that let her know just how much he desired her. One that if someone were to see them, they'd know exactly where he was headed with that kiss.

And with that thought, he tore his mouth from hers, both of them panting from desire and exertion.

"Lass…" he murmured, catching his breath.

"I'm no lass, Jamie, but a woman full grown," she replied, lips rosy and plump from his kiss.

"Aye, 'tis why we must stop, else I take your full grown body and press ye into the straw and make love to ye all the night through."

Her already flushed cheeks intensified in color and her mouth fell open as though she would say something. Whatever she was going to say remained stuck to her tongue, though her body pressed closer to his, giving him a clue as to what she desired. As much as he wanted to push her to the ground, undress and savor every inch of her in slow, delicious swipes of his tongue, Jamie had to recall who and where they were.

He growled a curse and turned away from her, hands on his hips, head facing the ceiling as he dragged in a ragged breath.

"Oh my God," Lorna whispered behind him. "Apologies, my laird. I dinna know what…"

Her retreating steps echoed in his head, forcing Jamie to turn around to see her back, nearly to the door she was.

"Wait!" he called.

Lorna stayed her tracks, and Jamie rushed up behind her. He slid his hands over her shoulders and bent toward her ear.

"Ye dinna understand, sweeting," he whispered. "I didna push ye away because I dinna desire ye, but because I do. 'Tis wrong for me to take the gift ye offer. We are both drunk on wine, on desire. In the morning ye'd regret it, for what more could I offer ye?"

A sigh left her, shoulders sagging. "Ye're right," she said. "There could never be more than this between us. My brothers would never allow me to go south and I... I..." But she didn't finish.

Instead, she pushed his hands from her shoulders and ran out of the stables, leaving him feeling colder, more alone, than he had been when he arrived at Dunrobin two days past.

CHAPTER NINE

$\mathcal{T}$he morning brought with it for Lorna, not only another vicious headache and queasiness, but a sense of regret. She rolled from her side to stare up at the canopy covering her bed. An embroidered brocade that her mother had worked on as a girl much Lorna's own age, in the hopes of giving it to her eldest daughter.

She gazed at the swirling knots contemplating her regret.

'Twas not for having kissed Jamie, but for having run out on him after saying there could never be anything between them. His kiss had been everything. All-consuming and filled with incredible power. Her body had lit on fire and she'd never wanted it to end. If she'd been willing to lie down in the straw with him, to give him everything she was worth—for a lass had nothing if she didn't have her maidenhead —then obviously there already something between them. A strong pull, a draw she couldn't get away from.

Now it was too late. He said he was leaving at first light and judging by the golden rays of dawn streaming through her window, Lorna had no doubt that he'd already gone on his way. And she'd never see him again.

Though he'd said he would return on his way back to Glasgow, she doubted he would now. There was no reason for him to. And hadn't that been his stipulation? She'd knocked that into the ground and squashed it with her bare heel.

The man she'd dreamed about since she was a child. The one she'd been waiting for as she turned her nose up at every possible suitor. For no one could match the bravery, the handsomeness, of the one who'd saved her life when she was a wee lass, and now he had swept her off her feet with his powerfully sensual kiss.

"Oh, Jamie," she whispered, sitting up in bed and rubbing her temples.

Regret filled her, because she'd pushed him away. And now she would be doomed to a lifetime of sadness and misery. Just as every other fair maiden was in the tragic romances she'd heard of. 'Haps she could prevail on her brother's kindness in sending her to a convent where she could at least serve God and the people of Scotland rather than wallowing in self-pity for the rest of her days.

A soft tap sounded too loudly at the door. "Who is it?" she called out, a nasty bite to her tone. She quickly covered her ears for having spoken too loudly, and groaned as she flopped back onto her pillow.

"'Tis me, lass," her aunt called.

"Go away," Lorna whispered, unwilling to bring back that sharp sting.

"I've brought ye some of Cook's tea."

That was enough of an enticement for Lorna to pull herself from bed and unbar the door. She didn't normally lock herself in, but last night she'd been so upset she'd wanted to block out everyone and simply be by herself. Or maybe it was because she was afraid she'd leave in search of Jamie, to finish what they started, and hoped the bar would somehow sway her to stay put.

She cracked the door open to see Aunt Fiona looking way too cheerful.

"How do ye feel, love?"

"Horrid." Lorna frowned and worked hard to get the cobwebs from her eyes.

Aunt Fiona chuckled. "I gather ye've drunk enough wine that past few days to fill a cellar."

"I'll not be drinking more for a while."

"Probably best." She set a tray filled not only with Cook's special tea, but a pewter dish full of apple tarts. "Sweets always help a queasy belly. Come now and have your fill."

Lorna's stomach turned and she gripped it, certain she'd be filling something else and not her belly.

Aunt Fiona chuckled again, the sound starting to grate on Lorna's nerves. She bustled over to Lorna and gripped her elbow, practically dragging her to the table, where she pushed her into a chair before taking the one opposite her.

"Drink. Take a bite."

Lorna shook her head. "I dinna think I can."

Aunt Fiona studied her a moment, her eyes narrowing as she assessed her. "I think ye're more affected by a broken heart than a splash too much to drink."

Crossing her arms over her chest, Lorna huffed a breath. "I've not got a broken heart."

"Huh." Aunt Fiona raised a brow, then plucked an apple tart from the tray, tore off a tiny bite and popped it into her mouth.

Lorna glared at her, took a sip of the wicked tasting tea and swallowed, feeling her belly calm almost instantly. Now if only she could get the pain searing across her temples to disappear.

"Huh," Aunt Fiona said again.

Lorna rolled her eyes, rubbed her temples. Why had her aunt changed her tune? Days ago she was getting the riot act about her morals, and now her aunt was being…comforting. 'Twas odd and completely out of character for her. "What does that mean?"

"Simply that ye're not telling me something." She leaned forward, as though they shared a secret. "Is there something ye wish to tell me?"

"I've nothing to tell." Lorna had an idea what her aunt was looking for. The woman had obviously turned an eye when she'd snuck off to the barn with Jamie, for Aunt Fiona had eyes *everywhere*. And if Lorna was nay mistaken, her aunt seemed almost pleased about it.

"I think ye have."

Lorna stared her aunt straight in the eyes as she spoke. "Ye've got too much time on your hands. Where is Heather?"

Aunt Fiona waved her hand in the air and then popped another minuscule bite into her mouth. "Och, she's after Ronan to teach her to sword fight."

Lorna took another long sip of tea then sat back in her chair, closing her eyes and willing the pain in her skull to disappear.

"Laird Montgomery has departed."

"I gathered." Though Lorna had known it had to be true, hearing the news drove the dagger of regret further into her chest.

"Does it bother ye?"

Devil take it, aye, it bothered her! Immensely. Which only made Lorna's frown deepen. Angrily, she grabbed at one of the tarts and stuffed an overlarge bite into her mouth. "Why should it?"

Fiona shrugged, appeared to ponder something for a few moments and then sat forward. "'Tis only I saw the two of ye sneak off into the barn. Another minute and I would have demanded a wedding."

Lorna ground her teeth together, the bite of apple tart settling like a thick, uncomfortable lump in her belly. She'd been right. The woman was all-seeing. "Nothing happened." Nothing that she would tell her aunt about anyway. The woman was liable to think that a simple kiss was enough to force a wedding, and Lorna refused to ever marry a man who didn't wish to be hers forever. Even if she'd been the one to push him away.

Aunt Fiona's eyes narrowed, squinting at her as though she'd see inside her soul. She was thankful in that moment that she'd not grown up in the woman's household, certain every naughty deed she would have ever committed would be quickly nosed out by the formidable woman. "He did nay compromise ye?"

"Nay," Lorna said, perhaps a bit too vehemently. "He did nay compromise me."

"Did he...kiss ye?"

"Aunt Fiona!" Lorna tossed her unfinished tart onto the platter. "The man took no liberties with me, and I am still intact. We...talked. 'Tis all."

Fiona frowned and set down the tart she'd barely touched. "Well, I must admit to being disappointed."

"What? Why?" Lorna couldn't help the exasperation in her tone. Did her aunt truly just admit she'd wished that Lorna had let Jamie take away her innocence? She sat forward, wondering for a moment if her aunt's body had been inhabited by a demon or fae or some other such fanciful creature that would take away the woman's faculties, for certainly this was not Aunt Sourpuss or Frigid Fiona sitting before her. "Aunt Fiona?"

Her aunt waved her hand away and stood. "Laird Montgomery was quite a catch. I'd have loved if the two of ye could have formed a match. Would have made all the parties involved pleased, to be sure, and then Magnus would nay have to worry over ye anymore. Lord knows he's got his hands full with your sister."

Lorna crossed her arms over her chest refusing to let her own desires for that very same thing affect her. Marriage to Jamie Montgomery would have been pleasing to her, too—if she was willing to marry. "Well, 'tis not to be."

"For lack of wanting on your part?"

The way her aunt gazed at her felt like the woman could see straight into Lorna's heart. 'Twas unnerving and left her feeling exposed for the fraud that she was.

"Aye. I've no interest in marrying *any* man, Jamie included."

"Jamie is it?" Her aunt again pursed her lips into a smile that said she'd caught her.

Zounds! Why hadn't she thought before speaking—a lesson she would have done well to learn.

"Lass, ye will have to marry someday, even if ye decide today is not that day."

Lorna nodded, though she couldn't swipe the frown from her face.

"Because there is no choice in the inevitable end result of your marriage to someone, I thought to help ye at least make a match that would suit ye best. Was not Montgomery better than MacOwen?"

"Haps Laird Montgomery did not want to marry me. Did ye think

93

of that Aunt Fiona? Just because I may or may not fancy a man, does not mean he is madly in love with me."

Aunt Fiona nodded. "'Haps not madly, but there was a spark. Sparks often grow into flames."

"Not when doused with a bucket of water."

"And what bucket is that?"

"Reality. The differences between us."

"I did not see so verra much."

Fiona picked up her partially eaten tart and started to walk toward the door. Lorna watched, and was startled when her aunt quickly spun around. "So few of us have choices in who we wed, lass. Some of us are forced to wed men older than our fathers, meaner than snakes or just downright ugly as boars. Consider yourself lucky that your brothers love ye so much and are willing to let ye have a say. I canna say whether your parents would have allowed such leniency. And even if ye were my own daughter, I canna say whether I would have considered your thoughts. But if I were ye, I'd make the choice sooner rather than later. For when we wait too long, the best choices are often far beyond our grasp."

Aunt Fiona didn't wait for Lorna's response, but instead whisked out the door, closing it loudly behind her.

Lorna sat back in the chair, feeling heavy and confused.

There was no one else she'd rather marry. And yet, she wasn't ready to marry him either. What of Jamie—was he prepared? She imagined him with another woman and felt a burning rage bubble up in her chest.

That wouldn't do. Not at all. Did that mean she really did want him for herself?

She'd certainly enjoyed their kiss. Felt magical tingles every time his lips had touched hers. Missed him when he wasn't near. Found herself looking for him and sneaking glances at him. Felt that her heart had shriveled now that he was gone.

Aye, the man had rescued her when they were children, but she'd only known him as a man for a few days. That wasn't enough time to decide if she wanted to spend her life with him. She shook her head. Not nearly enough.

And yet, there didn't seem to be a possibility of her getting to know him ever again. Jamie had taken his leave with no intention of returning.

She didn't regret at all having left the barn. Allowing Jamie to take her upon the hay would not have been wise. As much as she desired his touch, or to explore what more pleasure could be found in his kisses, she also respected herself. Knew that allowing a man a couple of kisses in return for lifting her skirts was less than she deserved.

In truth, she shouldn't lift her skirts for anyone other than her husband. To do otherwise would mean she was a wicked wanton, and yet, Aunt Fiona had planted a seed. If he were to declare his love for her, and she truly loved him in return, would it be so bad if she let him touch her? Should she not experience lying with a man, who she loved dearly before she was married off?

Frowning, she swiped at her matted, sleep-mussed hair. Lorna didn't know what the right answer was. In her heart, it seemed that if a man loved her and she loved him, that he would marry her. But in reality, she knew that was not always the case.

The question was, was she willing to risk her heart?

Lorna shoved another bite of tart in her mouth, barely tasting the sticky apple sweetness. Instead, the bitterness of regret coated her tongue. Worst of all, she'd never know if what she'd given up was worth it, or if it was all a fantasy. A question that would likely haunt her the rest of her days.

DEPARTING DUNROBIN SHOULD HAVE BEEN EASY. IN FACT, IT TRULY WAS. Jamie's horse had been saddled, his reserves filled. His men were in high spirits for having attended Beltane, and though he'd not gained any new men for the Bruce in the Lowlands, he had them set in the north and supplies going south.

All in all, his mission was proving to be a success.

Except that he felt heavy, and a cold lump had settled in his chest.

At least three hours had passed since they'd left the castle, and he'd regretted every minute of it. He should have said good bye to Lorna. Should have told her he'd return on his way southward, if only to see her face.

Then again, perhaps leaving was a good thing. He'd never been so… enamored by a lass before. Every sweep of wind reminded him of her hair. Every village they passed, the scent of peat fire in the air, reminded him of their kiss. Even the snorts of the horses, for they'd been surrounded by the animals as he claimed her mouth in the barn.

There was nothing for it. The woman had somehow implanted herself in his brain. And now he'd have to suffer the consequences.

"Ye all right?" Toby asked. "Been awfully quiet, my laird."

"Aye. Just fine."

Toby grunted, and on his other side, Donald did the same. He was surrounded by men who would pique his ire.

"What?" Jamie asked, exaggerating the syllable.

"There was a lovely lass at the castle," Donald said. "Hair as golden as the sun."

"Mind your tongue," Jamie growled.

"Och, but did ye nay notice her?" Toby drawled out. "Lips as red as—"

Jamie lashed out, punching Toby in the shoulder. A gut reaction, for he was certain they taunted him. Had he been so obvious?

Toby clutched at his shoulder howling with both laughter and pain. "I take it ye noticed her, then?" he asked.

Jamie growled and lashed out again, only this time Toby was fast enough to scoot his horse to the side before Jamie could connect.

"Dinna speak about her that way," Jamie warned. "She's a lady."

"Aye, a lady she is," Donald said.

Jamie whirled toward the man. "What do ye mean by that?"

Donald shrugged.

"Well?"

Donald shook his head, eyes wide as he studied Jamie's clenched fist. "Dinna want a punch like the one ye gave Toby."

"Out with it," Jamie demanded.

Donald moved his horse to the edge of the road and out of reach. "Only that your lairdship would not take too kindly to a man kissing his sister in darkened corners. Would ye?"

Jamie growled. Both angry at his man for pointing out the obvious and at himself for having taken advantage of Lorna and her red, plump lips. He was a cad, through and through.

"Och, a little kiss is nay a problem," Toby chimed in. "Donald's kissed many lassies and never shamed himself for it."

Jamie frowned and turned his gaze from one to the other. What were they about?

Donald grinned. "Aye, I have, and loved every one of 'em too. But not a one was a lady, nor am I a laird."

"True," Toby replied, looking deep in thought. "I kissed a lady once, but she slapped me soundly for it."

Jamie rolled his eyes. "Shut it, ye two." He'd had enough of their babbling about kissing, especially since it only brought to mind the one thing he was trying to forget—Lady Lorna.

The distant sound of chinking metal carried on the wind and made Jamie stop his horse in the center of the road. He held up his hand for silence from his men, and they, too, stopped to listen. The source was not completely clear, and judging from the distance, could have been a half-mile away, but nevertheless, Jamie could still hear its steady clink.

The only other time he'd heard that distinct, *chink chink chink* was when the English marched their horses past him on the road while he stayed hidden.

English. Here, in the Highlands?

How had they made it past the council's scouts? Unless the scouts were on their way now to find Jamie to warn him.

Recognizing the sounds for what they were, Jamie's men stared at him with looks of strain.

Jamie nodded, affirming their thoughts, then pointed to the woods. "We hide off the road. See how many there are. If 'tis not too many, I say we take them out before they can get any farther north."

And closer to Dunrobin. No way in hell would he allow them to hurt his woman.

His woman?

Before he could reflect on that train of thought, Jamie led his men into the trees where they hid away from view. Toby pulled out his bow and arrows, making ready to shoot should Jamie give the command. Donald held his broadsword in one hand and his targe in the other, reins linked through his hand that held the targe, same as Jamie.

They waited for about a quarter hour, the clanging of metal growing louder. The damned Sassenachs had yet to learn that the noise of their armor alerted men for miles of their approach. Jamie shook his head. They truly were imbeciles.

A dozen knighted English walked two-by-two on horseback down the dirt-packed road. They stared straight ahead, hands on reins, backs properly upright. Motionless, expressionless. Like they were the undead riding horses dressed in metal. It was chilling, and had he not had experience with the blasted bastards he might have been a little afraid of them. As it was, he was confident that between the three of them, they could take on these twelve.

Jamie nodded to Toby, who nocked his bow, took aim and let his arrow fly, slicing into the small space between the knight's helmet and his collarbone. The sensitive spot they'd discovered in battle months beforehand. Before the other knights had figured out what was happening, Toby had taken down four more. Eight knights held steady to their horses, turning in circles, shouting to one another as they tried to decipher from which direction the arrows had flown.

By the time they figured out that Jamie and his men were to the left, Toby took down two more. Six knights charged their horses into the trees—a bad move.

Jamie motioned his men to stand together as the six approached. Two against one were damn good odds, though he had been looking forward to more of a challenge. He supposed he should be grateful for Toby's skill with a bow—one of the reasons he'd invited him along this mission to begin with, besides him being a good friend.

"Morning, lassies," Jamie taunted the English. "Out for a stroll, and so far away from your border?"

The men bared their teeth.

"Not much for talking this morning, then?" Donald said. "'Tis fine with us. We'd much rather fight."

At that, all three of them smiled like hungry bears in the Sassenach's direction.

"Aye. We love to fight," Toby added.

"We've got ye outnumbered," the English knight who'd taken the lead said.

"Outnumbered?" Jamie replied. "Nay, laddie, ye've got just the right amount."

The knights moved restlessly in their saddles.

"Shall we?" Jamie asked, surprised he had to invite these idiots to fight. "Let us get on with it, for I'll not let ye go any further down the road. If ye wish to pass, ye'll have to kill me first."

"With pleasure," their leader growled.

And that was the last thing he ever said. Jamie, Toby and Donald, lunged forward, not holding anything back as they each took down one and then the second of their opponents within a minute. All six knights lay upon the ground, their eyes staring lifelessly into the clouds.

"Well, that was disappointing," Toby murmured. "Thought I'd get a bit more exercise than that."

Jamie rolled his eyes. "Ye killed eight men afore the nooning. Is that not enough to sate your needs?"

Donald chuckled. "Toby likes at least a dozen to fall beneath his sword a day—whether it be killing or rutting, doesna matter."

"Och, I take offense to that. I'd much rather be sliding inside a wench than a knight." Toby grinned and wiped his blade upon the grass.

Jamie shook his head. "Ye're both a couple of hounds."

The men laughed at that. They cleaned up the bodies, giving them a proper burial even if they were the enemy, for no man deserved to rot, and burying them hid the evidence of what they'd done should any other Sassenachs follow. The three of them waited an hour off the road to be certain no other English followed.

"Should have asked what they were about, afore we killed them," Jamie mused.

"Aye, but likely they'd not have told ye, my laird," Donald said.

"Likely." As soon as they reached the MacLeod clan, he'd have a missive sent back to Dunrobin.

Och, hell, he'd just as soon take the message back himself after securing allegiance from the MacLeods. Sad as it was, the English were yet again an excuse for him to see Lorna.

Jamie spurred his mount forward. The faster they got to MacLeod land, the sooner it would be that he saw her again.

CHAPTER TEN

*N*ight had long since fallen over Ardvreck Castle, and yet Jamie still sat in the great hall with not only Laird MacLeod, but Laird Mackenzie and the Laird MacKinnon's eldest son who was standing in for his ill father.

"I'd have liked to see ye and your men take down a dozen of those cock-sucking vermin," Laird MacLeod boomed taking a long draw from his ale.

"Aye, as would I," MacKinnon said. "'Twas one of the English bastards who killed my sister this summer past after abusing her relentlessly." He swiped a hand over his face. "Felt good to put the sot underground, but I've still a hankering to fight more."

Jamie blew out a hard breath at that news. 'Twas always hard to hear of a man suffering, and the death of a loved one, especially so violently at the hands of the English.

Laird Mackenzie nodded vehemently and sat forward. "Just what Montgomery here is offering, MacKinnon. A chance to avenge your family."

"Aye, Father was never the same after sweet Annabelle was found."

Jamie shook his head, and fixed his gaze on MacKinnon. "Join us, so that no other woman, child or man should suffer at the English's hands. We fight for Wallace. We fight for the Bruce to be king. We fight for an end to English tyranny and a country of our own. For Scottish freedom."

The battle might not have yet met the Sutherlands, but it had most definitely reached the Highlands. Jamie was damn glad he'd decided to head to MacLeod's holding now instead of later. He might not have been so lucky to happen upon the three powerful men at one time.

"I will," MacKinnon boasted. "For my sister. For my father. Thank God mother was already with the Lord when it happened."

MacLeod leaned forward and patted the young MacKinnon on the back. "'Tis all right, lad. Your mother was able to hold Annabelle in her arms after the ordeal, up in the heavens."

Jamie took a long swig of his ale. He couldn't imagine if any of his sisters had been ravaged by the English. Problem was, there was still the chance it could happen. Aye, they'd been married off to Lowland lairds with armies and well-fortified castles, but that didn't mean that if they left those walls they couldn't be attacked.

Flashes of Lorna riding alone on the moors assaulted him. The lass had no idea her actions were begging for the English to come and hurt her. And they were here now, judging by the dozen knights he'd come across in the forest.

The mere thought of one of jackanapes getting within feet of her sent a burning rage rushing through his chest and limbs.

"What's got ye so fired up, Montgomery? Ye must have had many run-ins with the bastards being in the Lowlands." MacLeod held out the jug of ale offering to refill Jamie's cup but he shook his head. He needed no more ale to cloud his judgment.

"Aye. Many run-ins." He cleared his throat, hoping it would clear his mind of all the vile imaginings of Lorna being assaulted. "'Tis why the council chose me." Jamie looked at each man, studying their faces. He'd already told them of the knights in the forest, which had riled them up beyond belief. MacLeod was ready to order his men out the gates now to scour the land, but Jamie had convinced him to sit tight for a little while longer.

MacLeod was easily twice his age, hair as white as snow and a face marred with not only age but battle scars. His bushy brows were dark as night, in contrast to his white hair and beneath his brows were eyes that seemed to know all. A fierce warrior he had been and still was. Mackenzie was closer to Jamie's age, his wife was MacLeod's daughter. He was red of hair and red in the face, as wide and thick as an old oak. MacKinnon was a few years younger than Jamie with a Viking look about him. Broad, fierce of body and hair as golden as Lorna's, but eyes as blue as the sea.

"Have ye come across any man who might go against the council? Perhaps claim no loyalty to the Bruce?" Jamie inquired, trusting these men after being in their presence for several hours to tell him the truth.

MacLeod blustered. "I'd bring my sword across any man's neck if I found him."

"Aye, I'd have him fed to the dogs," Mackenzie added.

But MacKinnon squinted his eyes, assessing Jamie as much as he had done moments before. Perhaps judging for himself who he could trust.

"Why would ye ask?" MacKinnon took a sip of his ale, never taking his eyes off Jamie.

Jamie didn't waver. "There is much strife in Scotland. Both Lowlanders and Highlanders must unite in the cause of freedom. Our men are dying. Our women abused. Children starving. And yet, there are some Scots who, for a price, will side with the English. Murder their own people. I'm not only here to ask for your aid in the cause, but to find out if ye would know of anyone who might sabotage us."

MacKinnon grinned. "I like ye, Montgomery. Ye dinna beat around the bush, nor skirt the issue as many men of the council do."

Jamie agreed, but still questioned, "Ye've met men of the council?"

"There is one on your council who came to me when my father fell ill."

Jamie waited, as MacKinnon chose his words carefully. No one on the council had told him of their visit to the Highlands, and he found that fact to be very suspicious.

"He did not come right out and say that should I be swayed to the other side there would be much for me to gain from it, but enough of what he said led me to that conclusion." He rimmed his cup with a finger, staring into the depths of his ale. "Of course, I praised the Bruce mightily and lamented of a time when Scots could be Scots through and through. I dinna think the man was aware of what had happened to my sister, else he'd not have come rooting around in that respect."

"Who was it?" Jamie was seething inside, having suspicions of one of the council members himself. But he kept his emotions intact, his voice steady and calm, direct.

"The Earl of Ross," MacKinnon said very matter-of-factly and without hesitating.

Jamie supposed he'd passed the test and MacKinnon trusted him.

"Did he come right out and say anything that could indict him as a traitor?" Jamie asked.

MacLeod and Mackenzie sat silently watching them speak. Neither sipped from their ale, nor seemed to breathe. As if one wrong move would make MacKinnon clam up again. Jamie wondered if the silent men individually plotted Ross' death.

"Nay, nothing outright. More a matter of how he said things. Such as, he'd heard the English were giving away lands, titles and castles— pieces of England and Scotland—to any man willing to join forces with them. Coin to any man willing to spy. Knew of the amounts of coin to be paid and which holdings were available. How would he know such intimate details, was what kept going through my mind."

"Aye," Jamie mused. "How would he?"

Ross would have known that because all the men of the council knew it. Had just discussed the problem recently. But they'd also sworn themselves to secrecy. The fact that Ross had gone and told MacKinnon, and God knew who else, was traitorous a move enough.

MacKinnon continued, "We've all heard tale of Longshanks making promises, yet not specifics. And besides, when a man starts talking about Longshanks' promises, most of us go into a rage and never get to the details as it is."

"Why, then, did ye let Ross get to the details?" Jamie asked.

"'Tis simple. I didna trust him from the moment he walked across our threshold. With my father ill, we've had more than one odd guest, coming to try and force an alliance or buy up a parcel of land. More than all the others, Ross had a greedy look about him."

"Aye, that he does." Jamie sat back in his chair, taking in the information and wondering what he should do about it. He'd had suspicions of Ross before. He'd not shown up to certain meetings, and feigned ignorance of their happening. The man was boastful and oftentimes argumentative. Little things like that had made many on the council distrust him, but none had come up with any reason other than the man being an arse to thrust him aside.

"We'll keep an eye on Ross, and be certain to get any news to ye as soon as we hear it," MacLeod said with a stern nod. His son-by-marriage also nodded just as firmly.

Jamie glanced at MacKinnon, gauging the man's thoughts. "And ye? Will ye tell me if ye should hear from Ross again?"

"I'll be with ye, Montgomery, but I'll leave word with my clan to keep their eyes open for signs of treason and English arse licking."

"With me," Jamie stated, rather than asking.

"Aye, my laird. I'll be joining ye, along with at least five score of the MacKinnon men." The man held out his arm. "I want the chance to beat these bastards into the ground where they belong. I know my father will approve."

Jamie grabbed MacKinnon's arm and shook. "Aye, man, me, too."

"Dinna leave us out of it. I canna go along with ye," MacLeod said, "but I can offer ye five score of our men as well."

Jamie shook the older man's arm, taking note that Mackenzie didn't want to be left out either.

"Five score of the Mackenzies will join the fight as well. I, too, canna join ye, with my lady about near to giving birth to our first bairn, but ye can rest assured that any English who traipse over Mackenzie land will be dealt with. Ye have our support undeniably."

"My thanks. The Bruce and the council will be pleased to know they have your support. If we are to win our freedom, we must do so as one." Jamie stood and set his ale on the trestle table. "I'll leave at first light."

"Where will ye go next?"

Jamie frowned. "I've a few more clans to visit and then I'll be returning to Dunrobin afore heading back to Glasgow."

"Back to the Sutherlands? May I ask why?" MacLeod asked.

Golden curls teased the recesses of Jamie's mind. "Aye, the Sutherlands." He didn't expound on it.

"Do ye mean to ask more of him?" MacKinnon asked.

"Aye. I wish to purchase his wool." A partial truth. Indeed, Sutherland wool was superior to all else. But it was not the soft wool he wished to feel slide over his fingers, but the silky tresses of Lady Lorna.

Several of the men grunted their approval.

"Their wool is unsurpassed. I've been brokering a deal myself," MacKinnon said. "In fact, would ye mind giving a missive to Laird Sutherland when ye see him? If I'm going south, I'll not have a chance to speak with him, and I'd like him to know my terms."

Jamie agreed with a nod, but his mind was completely elsewhere— imagining precisely what it would be like when he crossed under the portcullis and held Lorna in his line of vision again.

The following morning, Jamie gave directions to MacLeod, Mackenzie and MacKinnon on where to meet, with his word that he'd be there within a month and a half to join them.

Nearly three hundred warriors were now pointed in the direction of Glasgow. Jamie couldn't have been happier with his call to the MacLeod castle. And what luck to find the Mackenzie and MacKinnon men there. All three clans promised to send out missives to their fellow allies in search of more support.

With Sutherland funds and supplies and so many warriors now headed into the fray, Jamie felt his mission was a success.

So much so in fact, that after he stopped by another two clan holdings, he had time to go a little north in order to pay another call to Dunrobin before returning to Glasgow.

Certainly, he'd make it a pretense of purchasing wool, for he could not very well admit to Magnus that he'd come only to ogle his sister once more, perhaps kiss her one last time. Lord knew her sweet lips would be the last he tasted for some time. He'd no intentions of finding a bride, not with a war surrounding them. Jamie was married to Scotland. Married to the cause, and his brother Malcolm was his heir.

Just as soon as he returned to Glasgow, he'd have to see that his brother was married, and starting a family of his own to carry on their line. Like William Wallace, Jamie felt his duty was to country and country alone. 'Haps that was why they'd sent him on this mission after all. He truly was the best man for it.

"How much wool do ye intend to purchase, my laird?" Toby asked with a twinkle in his eye.

Damn the man for seeing right through his plans.

"Enough to make it worthwhile to Sutherland for allowing us to stay a few days."

Donald grinned. "Will we be taking home more than a few wagon loads of wool?"

"Naught but memories." Jamie frowned at the realization. "And 'haps a sack to start."

Jamie didn't like the way he'd left things with Lorna, the way she'd stormed away saying there could never be anything between them. That kiss proved there could be something—was something. Maybe that was why he needed to return, to find out for certain what it was. Even if she were to turn him away, at least he'd know.

A man going into battle with the possibility of no return, always wanted to know these things. Not that finding out if he had a chance with her could change things. Or would it?

Och, ballocks! The lass was messing with his head again and he was several day's ride from her.

And what if she refused to see him? What if she really meant she never thought there could be anything between them?

Was it worth it to travel all the way back to Dunrobin, when he'd only be disappointed? Aye, 'twas worth it. Then again, he was already disappointed, but at least he'd previously broken himself away. Having to do so again was likely going to prove more difficult.

"Well, I'm hoping Miss Mary is willing to make some of those memories with me," Toby mused, making a hand gesture that had Donald rolling and Jamie punching him in the arm.

"If ye've had her already, likely she'll be slamming her door in your face," Jamie taunted.

"Let us hope your lady doesna do the same." Toby yanked his horse away from Jamie's, fearful of the next blow to come his way.

Jamie set a grueling pace for his men, and by gloaming their horses were frothy and in need of rest, just as they were. With no storm in sight, they chose to set up camp within the wood, just a few paces from a trickling burn.

"Might I join ye?"

The men turned to face a priest in worn, brown robes that looked a little worse for wear. His hair was styled like that of a Viking, and he had a fierceness about him that was not often seen in a man of the cloth.

"Aye, Father," Jamie said, tearing off a hunk of bread and handing it to him.

They could use a man to confess to.

The priest sat down, wiping a bit of blood from his fingers on his robes.

Jamie caught his eye, raised his brow. "Run into trouble?"

The priest smiled. "Ye could say that. I may be a man of God, but I dinna take kindly to the English attacking a lass."

"Aye, me either," Jamie said, his frown deepening and his fear for Lorna increasing.

'Twas enough for him to have considered forgetting his plans to visit several other clans before traveling through the night to reach her. But his men would have only taunted him all the more. Besides, he'd been sent on this mission for one reason—to garner allies, supplies and men. Not a woman.

Not a wife.

Och, a wife? Why was he thinking along those lines again? He was married to Scotland. A man for his country.

And yet, his heart tugged him in another direction—toward Lorna. He tried to tell himself it was only because he wanted to be certain she was safe.

As long as her brother kept her within the walls of Dunrobin, Lorna would safe. Thing was, the lass was a daredevil taking any opportunity she could to sneak away.

Jamie took a long pull of ale. 'Twould be a long night.

CHAPTER ELEVEN

The door to Magnus' library had never seemed so imposing as it did today. Wide planked with iron nails and hinges, it could have been a door leading to a dungeon for all Lorna's imagination was running wild.

She smoothed her skirts and tried to quell the trembling in her hands. Magnus had summoned her just after dawn, which rarely happened. In fact, she could count on one hand the number of times it had occured.

Typically, if he wanted to speak with her, he'd simply find her. But to be summoned… Usually, it meant she was in trouble. Or worse, there was bad news. What bad news could there be? And she couldn't think of anything she'd done to warrant punishment—unless he'd found out about her kissing Jamie.

Had Aunt Fiona told him she suspected more than a mere kiss had happened behind the closed barn doors? Her face flamed, and she touched her cheeks, certain they were as bright as Cook's cherry cobbler. She could talk about how the heady wine, warm bonfire and magic of the night had propelled her into his arms, but that would be a lie, for even if it had been a stormy winter night, she'd have willingly gone into that barn for a kiss.

Acting loosely was certainly something her brother would be upset about.

But she'd turned Jamie away in the end and that counted for something, didn't it? Jamie was gone, and her virtue intact. There was nothing she had to worry about. With that thought in mind, she straightened her shoulders. Best to get this done with now.

Lorna tapped anxiously at her brother's library door.

"Enter!" Magnus called from within.

Lorna took a deep breath and blew it out slowly as she opened the door. Plastering a smile on her face, she greeted her brother as though she were not terrified to see him.

"Good morning, Magnus."

Sitting behind his desk with his fingers steepled beneath his chin, Magnus looked more than a little disturbed as he eyed her. Several scrolls sat before him, and it looked as though he'd stopped writing mid-missive to think. There were dark circles beneath his eyes and his hair was mussed. Had he slept at all? The man had taken on much since their parents died. At fourteen to become laird and protector of not only his four siblings but an entire clan had taken its toll on him. She dearly hoped he chose to settle down with a wife someday soon. He deserved to be happy.

"Please, sit," he said, motioning to a chair before him and moving his papers aside.

Lorna pushed herself forward to keep from running out of the room. Though she knew she had nothing to be ashamed of, the way Magnus was behaving had her nerves on edge. When she sat, the chair felt unusually hard. She squirmed a moment, pretending to arrange her skirts. It seemed hopeless. She'd not get comfortable and the longer Magnus stared at her the more she realized bad news was about to come.

Could it be about Blane? He'd been gone for over a month now, and she feared for his return. Aye, he was normally gone for months at a time, but still... Her heart skipped a beat.

When silence stretched into torturous minutes, Lorna finally blurted out, "Well, what is it?"

Magnus grimaced, his hands falling to the sides of his chair as he pulled himself to standing and walked over to the window. *Zounds!* This was not good. Only bad news would weigh so heavily on her brother's shoulders.

Outside, the sun hid behind gray storm clouds and rain fell in droves, splashing against the stone outside. A rather dreary day. Fitting for whatever it was he was about to say.

Lorna's stomach tightened as she studied his stiff back.

Would it be completely inappropriate to beg her brother for a dram of whisky before he started speaking? She never drank the stuff, but still... Desperate times called for desperate measures.

"Ye recall talk of marriage recently, do ye not?"

Aye, the whisky was definitely needed.

She was at once grateful that his summons had nothing to do with Blane, and filled with dread at the direction their conversation was about to head in. "How could I forget?" she asked, her heart sinking, mouth suddenly dry. This was not going to end well.

"I promised ye, I'd not marry ye off to MacOwen, and I'm keeping that promise." He paused, longer than made her comfortable. Lorna longed to stand and go to the window, to breathe in the damp sea air. As it was, she was starting to get light-headed.

"Magnus..." she drawled out, prompting him to continue. Did he not realize how much he tortured her?

Her brother turned toward her, his blue-green eyes that matched hers filled with sorrow.

"What is it?" Lorna asked.

"'Tis simply that this day has come quicker than I imagined, and ye're more than just my sister, but my friend, and like a daughter to me, as well."

Lorna swallowed. "Tell me. Please."

"We've been approached by the MacKinnon laird's eldest son. His father is verra ill and he'll inherit his title soon. I've heard he's pleasing to the eye which should satisfy ye, but most importantly, he wishes to strengthen our alliance. He's offered for your hand, and he's also offered a strong contract for our wool."

"So I am to be traded for a sack of wool?" Lorna gripped her skirts tight, anger rushing through her. "I dinna even know this MacKinnon! And I dinna care how pleasing to the eye he is. It does nay satisfy me. Ye promised me I'd have a choice."

Magnus withdrew his gaze, turning back to the window. Suddenly, her aunt's voice sounded in her mind, telling her how lucky she was to be able to choose a husband and that she should choose quickly before her brother changed his mind. Aye, this was the way for so many, but Lorna had higher hopes for herself. Had hoped for something magical, enthralling.

Perhaps she had let herself be swept up into a fantasy of her own making. Jamie's handsome face floated before her eyes. The crooked smile he showed her often, the dip of his lids when he bent to kiss her. His intoxicating scent and how warm and tingly she felt when he pulled her into his arms.

It'd been weeks since he left.

Jamie had been so close, nearly within her grasp. And yet, he'd stolen a few kisses, but made no promises. There'd been no declaration of love. No wishes for the future. And now…

She'd told him there would be nothing between them. Ever. And he'd left.

Oh, but it couldn't be too late! She couldn't marry a stranger. No matter if her brother thought he might be considered handsome, or how much wool he was willing to buy.

"Aye, I did mention to ye that I'd let ye have the choice. And I'm hoping ye will choose the future of your clan. Ye'll be mistress of your own house. Mistress to a clan. Married to a powerful man. He's about my age, never married before and will treat ye well."

A groan escaped her lips and she grabbed at her throat to hold back a painful sob. "I will nay do it." Lorna stood quickly, the wood of her chair legs scraping loudly on the floor. She pinched her lips together and glared daggers at Magnus' back.

Magnus turned slowly, his face resigned. "In time, ye'll understand, dear sister. We all have to make sacrifices for the good of the clan. For our family."

How could he lay that guilt on her? She was well aware of the sacrifices he'd made, but to make her feel guilty and selfish for not wanting to marry a stranger? Angry tears stung the backs of her eyes.

"I love ye, Magnus. I love this family, and I know all that ye've done for us. All ye've sacrificed for the good of the clan. But how can ye force me to a marry a man I dinna even know?" She chewed her lip, feeling on the verge of tears. At any moment the torrent would burst. "How can I love a stranger?"

Magnus stared her with sadness in his eyes. "In time, lass. Love will come to ye."

"What do ye know of love? Ye dinna court anyone!" She whirled, and stomped toward the door.

"Lorna, stop." His voice was not raised, not cruel, but flat and tired. "The MacKinnon visited weeks ago, and I've wrestled with the idea for as long as that. I am only doing what is best for ye."

Lorna could not recall the man's visit at all and wondered why it had been so brief.

Tears burned her eyes as she whirled on him. "Ye knew about this when ye teased me about MacOwen? Was it a test to see how I'd react? Ye made me out to be a fool." Her voice sounded shrill, foreign.

Magnus stepped forward, reached out his hands as though he'd pull her in for a comforting hug. But she didn't want his hugs. She wanted to punch him in the face.

"I wanted to gauge your—"

But Lorna cut him off, unwilling to listen to his reasoning. "How could ye? I'll never forgive ye for it!" This time when she rushed to the door, she didn't stop when he bade her. She ran all the way to her room, slammed and barred the door. Then she sank in a heap on the floor and cried.

Jamie was lost to her.

❧

HOURS LATER, LORNA STILL LAY ON TOP OF HER COVERLET, EYES stinging from tears, her entire face feeling swollen. She mourned the loss of so much—Jamie, love, a choice, and most especially her freedom.

How could she bring herself to become resigned to marrying MacKinnon? She knew nothing of him and even if he was handsome, that didn't reveal anything of his temperament.

What if he was cruel? Magnus said the man would be good to her, but what did he know? Nothing!

Lorna was an unconventional bride, for certain. Raised to speak out her mind, to value her opinion and thoughts, she wouldn't do well with a man who sought to quell them. Jamie had been the only man she'd ever met who didn't mind her tongue, seemed to revel in her wit and non-conforming charm.

Lorna flopped onto her back, arm across her eyes. Judging from the determined set of Magnus' jaw there seemed little she could do to change his mind.

If she was lucky, like Magnus said, in time she'd grow to care for her husband. Rubbish!

She had to do something. She couldn't just sit back and let her brother resign her to a fate that would leave her empty inside. No matter whom the groom was. MacKinnon could have been the most sought after suitor in all of Scotland, but the thing was, Lorna had already chosen who she wanted to spend her life with. Even if she'd pushed him away. It seemed to have taken that move, and this sudden onslaught of bad news to realize that she really wanted Jamie in her life.

Now if only she could figure out how to persuade Magnus to contact Jamie and forget about MacKinnon.

The rain had started to slow and through the darkened clouds in the distance, the sun shone in reaching streams of yellow. The nooning had passed and Lorna had not let her maid, Aunt Fiona, nor Heather in to give her a tray. They'd begged and pleaded, but she'd turned them all away. Her appetite had disappeared. She didn't know what worried them more—her loss of hunger or her sobbing for hours.

No matter, it was time to wash away her tears and move forward. She'd not settle. Besides, her stomach had started to growl.

Lorna heaved herself from bed and walked over to the wash basin, splashing cool water on her face, and wiping away the remnants. Just that little action made her feel immeasurably better, as though she not only washed away her tears, but her uncertainty. If she had to steal her horse away in the night and ride to Glasgow, she'd make it there somehow.

She'd stand before Jamie Montgomery, no matter how shameful it would seem to some, and declare her—

What? Her intentions to marry him? Her…feelings for him?

Was it love? Or desperation?

Lorna dare not say it was love. Not at all. She wiped the rest of the water from her face, then opened her door to find that the tray of food had been left for her outside. Cold chicken, bread and an apple. She brought the tray inside and set it at her table, taking a bite of chicken, and chewing on it thoughtfully.

Nay, she couldn't be in love with Jamie, but she was most definitely attracted to him. Relished his kisses, his touch. And she liked him a great deal, even cared for him. He made her laugh, smile, feel safe. He was a man she could and wanted to spend the rest of her life with.

Right now, that was all that mattered to her, because MacKinnon was a stranger, and Jamie her best choice—even if he didn't know it yet.

The tranquil breeze and misty rain were interrupted by the pounding of horse hooves and a call beyond the wall.

Oh, God! Had Magnus arranged for MacKinnon to come to Dunrobin so soon? Had he kept the knowledge to himself until this morning only because he knew he couldn't hold back any longer? Zounds, but she'd not even asked her brother when he planned to marry her off.

The hunk of bread she'd just swallowed into became lodged in her throat. She took a hearty gulp of ale, forcing the solid mass of dough down her throat. With arms that felt as heavy as tree trunks, she pushed from the table and made her way to the window, dreading all the while what she'd see below.

Clan warriors gathered around a trio of newcomers. Tall and broad, their backs were to the castle as they conversed with the Sutherlands and dismounted.

But it mattered naught that their backs were to her, for the man in the middle with thick dark hair and wide shoulders that begged to be stroked, she'd recognize anywhere.

Jamie had returned.

Hope soared with her and she gasped, clutching her hands to her heart. Though it had only been a few weeks since last she'd seen him, it felt like a lifetime. Her heart sped up, spiraling tingles of anticipation and fear through her. Why had he returned? Was it possible he…

Lorna shook her head. She could hardly form a thought. And she couldn't possibly get her hopes up too much. Nothing ever came that easy. Except, in her dreams, in her heart of hearts, Jamie was always her savior. The same dark-haired warrior who saved her from death as a child, might also be the same man who saved her from a future of unhappiness.

Jamie turned then, his gaze flicking up the castle walls until resting on her. Her ribs would surely burst, her heart pounded so fast. Lorna managed a smile, even though her teeth had started to chatter. Good God, what was wrong with her?

A second chance. When did one ever get that when it came to making choices about their future? Not many women did that she knew, and she would be forever grateful for the gift of his return. She said a prayer of thanks up to the heavens, ecstatic that God had heard her pleas.

It didn't matter that Jamie might not have returned to seek her hand, all that mattered was that he was here and she had the opportunity to change her brother's mind. And as stubborn as Magnus was, Lorna was by ten.

Her teeth ceased their chattering. Hands steadied at her sides. No more tears and wallowing for her.

"Oh, Jamie," she whispered, and hurried from her room.

CHAPTER TWELVE

*M*agnus eyed Jamie with skepticism, his brow raised as he studied him. "Montgomery, ye've returned."

"Aye, my laird." Jamie reached out his hand, gripping the other laird's arm.

As soon as he'd arrived, Ronan Sutherland had led Jamie to Magnus' library. But he couldn't get the sight of Lorna from his mind. She'd looked a heavenly vision up in her window, and rather than go to meet with the laird of Dunrobin, he wished to traverse the stairs and find the object of his desire.

Sutherland looked rather agitated, as though Jamie had arrived on the wrong day. But Jamie tried to ignore that. The man held vast holdings and had probably come across some news that he found displeasing.

"Why've ye returned? What's happened?" Magnus was abrupt and to the point.

Jamie completely understood Magnus' concern, as he'd probably read Jamie's warning of the English troops he'd met along the road that he'd sent weeks ago.

"Ye received my missive?"

Magnus nodded. "Aye."

"When I met with MacLeod, Mackenzie and MacKinnon, they all joined our forces. They'd seen and dealt with the English already. They are getting closer." Jamie ran a hand through his hair, ceasing himself from saying he'd come to be sure that Lorna was safe and well cared for. The man wouldn't take too kindly to such an inquiry as it would suggest he did not know how to take care of his sister, and if anything, Magnus was a damn good provider for his family.

Magnus frowned. "Aye, I'd feared as much. We'll prepare for it. Double up the scouts on our borders. When I got your missive, we increased the guards on the wall, and warned the crofters to be keen on any strangers in the area."

Magnus offered him a dram of whisky. Jamie nodded. Seemed whenever he was at Dunrobin, he indulged in the peaty liquor, though he tried to abstain wherever else he was. But he felt the fortification of liquid courage was necessary, for what he was about to ask the formidable northern laird may not be received well.

"Ye said ye'd met with MacKinnon?"

Momentarily distracted, Jamie nodded. "Aye, I nearly forgot. He gave me a missive for ye." Reaching into his sporran, he pulled out the rolled scroll and handed it to Magnus.

Jamie expected Magnus to set the missive aside, and then he'd come right out and ask him for Lorna's hand, but the man did not. In fact, he slipped his nail under the wax seal, but before opening it glanced back at Jamie.

"If ye'd excuse me, I've been awaiting MacKinnon's reply. I'll see ye at supper and we can continue."

Jamie agreed, disappointed. Magnus looked rather disturbed however, so it was probably best not to broach the subject of marrying his sister while the man was not in his right mind. That would only gain him a negative answer when what he wanted most desperately was an *Aye*, and a clap on the back.

"My thanks," Jamie muttered.

Magnus glanced up at him, almost as though he were surprised to see him there. "Ye're always welcome to Sutherland hospitality, my friend," he seemed to add as an afterthought.

Jamie nodded and retreated from the room, closing the door behind him, and wondering if all was well at Dunrobin. He admitted to not knowing Magnus well, but the man did appear truly out of sorts.

"Jamie," the hushed whisper came from around the corner and out of sight, but it sounded like Lorna.

His heart sped up.

"Lady Lorna?" he answered.

She peeked her head out from an alcove cut into the corridor, a wide smile on her plush lips. "Aye."

Jamie couldn't help but smile in return. Just gazing on her made this entire trip worth it. "Were ye spying on me?" he teased.

"'Haps I was," she answered.

Jamie took long strides to the alcove, slipping inside. "'Tis dangerous for us to be in here together. If your brother leaves his library—"

"Shh…" She pressed two fingers to his lips. "He will nay hear us, for I dinna plan on speaking."

Jamie kept his mouth from falling open by grounding his teeth together. Every muscle tightened at the memory of her kiss. His blood stirred, firing through his veins. Could she…?

"Lass…"

"Och, dinna scold me yet, Jamie." She wrapped her hands around his middle. "Kiss me first."

Her fingers burned through the back of his *leine* shirt, and his groin leapt to life. *Calm down, man*, he scolded himself, but it did no good. Jamie wrapped his arms around Lorna and did just as she asked. He dipped his head, capturing her luscious lips with his own and savoring her sweet flavor as though he'd never be satisfied. And, in fact, he might not be. Her kiss was heaven, sweet sunshine on a rainy day, and only reinforced his reason for returning all the more. Lorna sighed against his lips and Jamie tucked her closer, groaning with his need to envelope her.

The door to Magnus' library opened and closed with a click, forcing Jamie to yank away from Lorna, his body stiffening.

"Is someone there?" Magnus called.

Ballocks!

Lorna looked up at him in horror. What had he been thinking? What had she been thinking?

Lorna shook her head, fear filling her features. Jamie gritted his teeth. This was not the way he wanted to ask for Lorna's hand.

"I can hear ye," Magnus growled.

"Dammit," Jamie whispered. He pushed Lorna into the corner of the alcove, deeper into the shadows. "Stay here."

He stepped into the hallway, facing Magnus and prepared to ask just what he'd come here for, though it wasn't ideal.

"What are ye doing in there?" Magnus asked, looking over Jamie's shoulder, and blessedly seeing nothing.

Think quick, man! He lost his nerve to ask for Lorna's hand, not like this. Proposing marriage now might get him kicked in the ballocks.

"I needed but a moment alone," Jamie said evenly.

"Alone?" Magnus winged a brow.

"Aye."

Magnus scowled. "Then why did ye not go to your chamber?"

Well, he couldn't very well answer 'twas because he'd had his tongue deep in the mouth of the man's little sister. "A sudden need to pray."

"I didna take ye for an overly religious man." Magnus folded his arms across his chest.

"Aye, well, I'm not normally, but I've seen much in the last two years, that every once in a while I am struck with the need to get down on my knees and thank God I'm still living and breathing. We've the very devil on our backs, my laird."

Magnus' scowl deepened. "Aye, I know it. I canna imagine what 'tis like to be in the Lowlands right now. And ye've much heaped on your back with your clan and the council. Protecting all from the English bastards."

Jamie nodded solemnly. 'Twas true, even if it wasn't the reason for him being in the alcove. Lorna was blessedly quiet. And he was riddled with guilt for lying.

"Take a walk with me." Magnus didn't ask, he demanded.

Jamie obliged, wanting his future brother-by-marriage to find him agreeable. He fell into step beside Magnus as he made his way down the stairs to the great hall, and away from Jamie's quarters.

"I've received word from MacKinnon that he is going to Glasgow at your behest," Magnus said.

"Aye. He's sending nearly a hundred men to Wallace's army, along with his own pledge to fight."

They entered the great hall, which teemed with servants cleaning and mending. Magnus swept his hand in the air dismissing the servants from the hall. He didn't hesitate a moment in walking straight up to the hearth and hoisting a sword from the wall above the fireplace. He tossed it to Jamie, then pulled one down for himself.

"MacKinnon will marry Lady Lorna by proxy," Magnus said. "Instead of at Dunrobin in a fortnight as was planned."

The full force of a gale wind knocked into Jamie and he found it hard to stay steady on his feet. He blinked a few times, trying to remain calm and keep his face from showing how deeply this news devastated him. Marry another?

Jamie swallowed hard. Did Lorna know about this?

"A match well made," Jamie said, nearly choking on the words.

"Do ye think?" Magnus said, twirling the sword in the air.

"Indeed." Hell, no! It was not a good match at all. Not bloody at all. She belonged with him! "I spent several days with the man. He is honorable, wealthy and powerful. He'll make any maid a good husband."

"My sister," Magnus drawled, his eyes studying Jamie carefully as he said it.

The man suspected Jamie had an interest in Lorna, that was evident. He was warning him away, and while Jamie got the message, he wasn't in the least happy about it.

"Indeed," Jamie managed.

Magnus swung his sword, catching Jamie off-guard, but he quickly recovered, arcing up to block the blow.

Magnus put his face close to Jamie's, whisky on his breath. "Who were ye kissing in the alcove?" he growled.

Hell and damnation… "A maid," Jamie managed to say as he blocked another blow.

"A maid?"

"Aye. She invited me in for a kiss and well… It's been some time since I was with a lass." He blocked another crushing blow. If he weren't fighting the man over what he suspected was the man's suspicions about his sister, he'd have told him how much Wallace could use his prowess. "I meant no disrespect."

Magnus didn't seem to care what Jamie said, he wielded his sword at him as though he'd cut him down. 'Haps bent on thinking he needed to protect his sister's honor.

Arch after slicing arch, and Jamie blocked every damned one of them. But never did he lunge forward. This was a defensive fight for him, and Magnus was on the offensive, obviously needing to let off some steam.

"See that it doesn't happen again." With that, Magnus tossed his sword to the ground and walked out of the great hall.

A moment later, Lorna stepped into view, her face red and blotchy from crying. "A maid?" Anger sliced her features.

Jamie swallowed, and lifted the swords he and Magnus had used, putting them back into place over the hearth.

"What would ye have me say, lass? I was protecting ye."

"From my own brother?" Her snarl was nearly as vicious as her brothers'.

Jamie shook his head and walked toward her, wanting to pull her into his arms. "Nay, my lady. From ruin. Ye're betrothed." Jamie felt the truth like a punch to the gut. "Ye're not mine to have been in that alcove with."

"I'm not MacKinnon's either," she bit out.

But before he could respond, the lass had run from the room, tears glistening in her beautiful eyes.

Och, what had he done? Dunrobin was not the same as he'd left it.

He'd returned to Sutherland with the intent of seeing Lorna once more. Having decided once and for all if he not only wanted to court her, but marry her as well. One look up at the castle and seeing her in her window as he'd stood in the courtyard had been enough for him to be certain his decision was sound. But damn Magnus! He'd had to ask for the blasted missive from MacKinnon. How was Jamie to know it detailed the arrangements of their betrothal?

And why did sweet Lorna have to lead him on? Why did she pretend as though her betrothal was nothing but a myth when he knew it to be a fact?

Jamie did not want to be the plaything of a liberal woman. Nor did he care to share. He wanted Lorna for himself and now that seemed an impossibility.

A few moments passed as he stared dejectedly at the arched doorway in which Lorna had run. Inside, a war battled between running after her and letting her go. In the end, he stayed rooted in place until he was certain he'd not find her if he chose to change his mind.

Lorna Sutherland was betrothed to another. A man that he himself had great respect for. A man who'd joined his ranks readily and offered a hundred warriors to the war for Scottish freedom. He could not betray that man.

Why then, did it feel as though he'd betrayed himself?

Jamie walked dejectedly from the great hall. In his mind he knew there would be other women if he wanted them. But up until the day he'd met Lorna—well, the second time he'd met her—he'd believed that marriage was a thing never to be considered for him. A companion, a lover, a friend, for life was not to be his. But looking upon her countenance, kissing her sweet lips, he knew he'd been wrong. Lorna was the one and only woman for him.

But she belonged to another.

Forget the wool; Jamie wanted no reminders of the Sutherland he'd lost.

THE CLANG OF SWORDS STILL ECHOED IN LORNA'S HEAD. THE TWO MEN she cared about most had nearly hacked each other's heads off, and all because of her.

She'd been impetuous, spying Jamie and luring him into the alcove, but whenever she saw him, emotion seemed to rule the moment. As he'd exited Magnus' library, mouth pursed, brows drawn, she'd wanted nothing more than to smooth out those worried lines. To kiss away whatever tormented his mind.

At first, she'd only planned to talk to him, to tell him that she'd missed him and gauge his reaction, but the moment he'd filled the tiny space with his scent, his thick muscled body, she'd been overwhelmed. All reason had left her. Her heart sped up, her lips tingled and her body swayed toward him of its own accord. Jamie was like wine, instantly warming her and dulling her inhibitions. Kissing had been the solitary thought she had, and her only goal to get his lips on hers.

Sweet heavens, it had been magical.

But it didn't matter now. He'd rejected her. Told her brother she was some loathsome maid he could cast aside. A whore.

How was that protecting her?

But what could she have expected? With a sword at his throat, perhaps he'd simply thought of the first thing that came to mind that wouldn't end his life. A maid. And he'd not exactly said she was loathsome, nor a whore, simply that he'd not meant any disrespect.

Lorna shoved open her chamber door and slammed it behind her. She could make as many excuses as she wanted to, the fact of the matter was, when Magnus had confronted him about being in the alcove, insinuating that it had been with her, Jamie had denied it. If he had intentions toward her, wouldn't he have confessed and begged for her hand? Even with her brother stating she was meant for the MacKinnon?

That was another blow. Jamie had not fought Magnus or herself for the right to have her hand, for the contract with MacKinnon to be forgotten. He'd given in too easily.

Or, he'd never had intentions of being with her to begin with.

Lorna stomped across the room, wishing she'd headed outside

instead. A long hard ride was what she needed. Exercise to exorcise the demons in her mind.

No matter, what did she care?

She grabbed her uneaten apple off the table, whipped around and stormed back out of her chamber toward the stables. She'd have her ride, even if she had to crash through the gates and portcullis.

Jamie Montgomery was obviously not the man for her. Whatever spark, whatever pleasure and passion she'd found in his kiss, whatever connection she'd found when they spoke, or locked eyes, had to be entirely one-sided. She charged past those in the courtyard and felt only slightly better at the sight of her mare poking her head over the gate of her stall.

"I'd not expected to find ye here." Jamie's voice broke through her rapid-firing thoughts.

"Montgomery!" she gasped, whirling around to find him feeding a carrot to his stallion inside the stall across from hers.

Lorna was certain she'd never get over looking at him. He was handsome personified, even down to his godforsaken knees. Her belly did a flip and she swallowed, trying to find her mind, wherever it had gone to. Jamie pushed open the horse stall gate and raked a hand through his hair as he stepped into the aisle. He blew out a breath that sounded just as pent up as the one burning her lungs.

"I'd thought us on much more informal terms," he said, voice lowered, "Lorna."

"I…" Her lips flopped open and closed like a fish out water.

"I behaved abominably inside." Another rake of his hand through his hair and he stepped two feet closer.

Lorna backed up a step, uncertain if she could handle him coming nearer. Seemed every time he was near, all she could do was think of kissing him, and right now… Well, she needed a clear head.

"Is that an apology?" she managed, head held high.

"Aye," he said without hesitation. "Why didn't ye tell me about MacKinnon?" Jamie's eyes flashed with something she'd not seen before. An emotion she'd felt quite keenly moments earlier—loss.

Perhaps all hope was not forsaken.

CHAPTER THIRTEEN

$\mathcal{L}$orna stood stock still in front of Jamie, the scents of hay, horseflesh and leather surrounding them. Her feet felt suddenly constricted in her shoes, but she was afraid if she wiggled her toes she'd fall over, so off balance was she from his presence. Even her clothes started to itch. She shifted uncomfortably.

Jamie's gaze bore into hers, so intense that she could not pull her eyes away.

She swallowed hard, trying to find the right words to explain why she'd not said anything to him about MacKinnon. He had every right to ask her why she'd kept such a secret.

Especially after she'd tugged him into the alcove. Practically begged him to kiss her. Nay, she *had* begged him. Had sunk into his arms like a woman with no cares in the world but to be kissed, when in fact, she'd been trying to escape from the reality that her brother had made for her. Tried to decipher if Jamie really was the one she wanted. One look at him and she'd known. Judging by his own reaction, she thought he did, too. But he was too filled with honor to give them what they both wanted.

She flicked her gaze from his, unable to look him in the eye without a great amount of shame souring her belly.

"Lorna, answer me. Please." Jamie's voice was soft. Not accusing, but neither was it desperate. He asked her the same way he might request her to pass the stewed green beans.

She swallowed around the lump in her throat, then slowly raised her gaze to his, feeling as though the wind had been knocked from her.

"I only found out about MacKinnon this morning."

One brow raised in question. "And ye expect me to believe that?"

Such a question made her angry and she found her chin jutting forward, spine straightening. "Aye, because I'm not a liar."

Jamie grunted, obviously disbelieving her. "But ye'd kiss me when ye knew ye were promised to another?"

Oh, how her heart ached as he dragged his gaze away from her, the corners of his lips turned into a painful frown as he shook his head.

Was that disgust? Sadness? She desperately wanted to grip him by the shoulders and shake him. Force him to tell her everything that was on his mind.

Lorna took a few quick steps forward, hands out, imploring. "Jamie, aye, 'tis true. I should have told ye. Should have maybe stayed away, but I could no more stay away from ye than breathe."

Zounds! What had she just said? Words she most definitely should not have. Confessions of her heart, her inner most self that should have stayed hidden. Should not have been said to a man who was forbidden to her. Feelings she'd not yet found the strength to crush.

"Dinna say things like that, lass. I've no right to your affections." He stroked his horse's muzzle and for the moment she wished it were her cheek he so lovingly caressed. She yearned to leap into his arms, the place she'd been so welcomed weeks before, and just that morning.

"Haps. But there is nothing signed yet. There's still a chance..." She wished he'd look at her but he kept his eyes on his warhorse, paining her all the more. Wished he'd give her more. Some sign that she wasn't mad for thinking their connection was real.

"I've met the man." His voice was strained, the muscle of his jaw ticking. "I'll not make a cuckold of him. He's promised me men, service, coin, supplies. He's a good man, Lorna."

Lorna braved his possible rejection and took a few more steps closer to him. "MacKinnon fights for his country, for freedom, not for me," Lorna said. "How can ye make a cuckold of a man who I've not yet been linked with? He and my brother talk, 'tis all. I am yet unwed."

Jamie did look at her then, pain etched in the crinkles at the corners of his eyes and mouth. "They did more than talk, and ye're a fool if ye dinna think so."

A knot suddenly lodged in her throat and she tempted fate by placing her hand over his that rested on the gate to the stall. He didn't pull away and she sucked in a wavering breath. "What do ye know that I dinna?" Lorna asked, overwhelmed with a sense of dread. From what Magnus had told her, he was in negotiations with MacKinnon, but nothing had yet to be set in stone.

Jamie's eyes squinted as if he assessed whether or not to trust her. He glanced down at her hand on his, and still he didn't pull away, giving Lorna hope that just maybe, there could be a chance for them.

"Tell me. Please," she implored, closing a few more feet between them.

"I brought with me a missive from MacKinnon. He was to arrive a fortnight from now to wed ye, but given he's headed to Glasgow, he's requested to marry ye by proxy to ensure the union."

"Proxy?" Lorna's heart sank. Lord, what had Magnus done? "Ye brought his missive?"

Jamie's jaw clenched, eyes hardened. Lorna could barely look at him. She jerked her hand away and her heart squeezed painfully. If he'd brought the missive, met with MacKinnon, then he must have known all along what was happening, and yet he'd still swept her up in his embrace, kissing her as though his next breath depended on it. Or was that just her imagination? As it looked now, he'd never had any intention of claiming her for his own. She was nothing more than willing lips with which to kiss and she'd made a fool of herself.

When he didn't speak, she turned from him, busying herself with her own mare. She grabbed hold of Angel's blanket, saddle and reins, and set them on the ledge as she opened the stall gate and stepped inside. Tears of frustration, disappointment and hurt threatened to pour out, but she blinked rapidly to keep them at bay, chewed her lip to keep it from quivering. *Dinna ye dare cry in front of the man.*

What a fool she'd been. Lorna stroked a hand over Angel's mane, who nuzzled her shoulder looking for a treat. She gave her the apple, then stroked down over her back before laying the blanket over her and then the saddle. All the while she worked, Jamie said nothing, but she felt his eyes on her. Felt the burning of his gaze and wondered if it was because he wanted to kiss her or because he loathed her for whatever he thought she'd lied about. Well, he wasn't the only one feeling the pang of betrayal. Dammit, but he'd brought the missive and he'd still slinked into the alcove with her, pulled her into his arms and kissing her with such passion her knees still shook. And even with knowing he'd used her, she still longed for him.

"Lorna," Jamie said, his voice strained.

She ignored him, and settled the bit in Angel's mouth. She pressed open the gate and pulled the horse through, momentarily blocking her view of Jamie's brawny physique.

"Where are ye going?" he asked.

Lorna took a few more steps forward, her horse's hooves clopping rhythmically on the ground. She paused. "For a ride." And he wasn't invited. "Alone," she added to be sure he was aware of that.

A ride would do her good. To feel the wind in her hair... The freedom. Two more weeks was all she had before her life was forever stifled by a man she didn't know. Married by proxy. She'd not even meet him before her life was merged unbreakably within his. Till death did they part.

A shudder passed through her as she opened the stable doors and led Angel outside. She pressed her foot into the stirrup and mounted. A few of the clansmen looked up at her as they went about their duties, but she ignored them, and they returned to their tasks, uninterested. Lorna on a horse was the norm. As standard as the sun rising and falling.

Clucking to her mare, she urged her toward the portcullis, but the guards stopped her.

"Canna let ye out, my lady," one said.

She'd been waiting for that, and was ready to give them hell. Shielding her eyes from the sun, Lorna glared up at him. "Why not?" She didn't try to hide the frown from her face.

"His lairdship has forbidden it, unless ye've an escort. Troubled times we have now."

Lorna gritted her teeth. "I'll just be on the moor right there, where I always am. Ye can see me from up there."

He shook his head, his expression showing apology. "Not today, my lady. The laird will have my head."

She opened her mouth, exasperated and about to say something she'd most likely regret, when Jamie rode up beside her.

"I'll provide escort." He didn't even look at her, but kept a steady gaze on the guard.

Anger sliced through Lorna. He was the last man she wanted to escort her. In fact, he was the major reason why she needed the space to be alone in the first place.

"Nay, surely ye've much to do in the way of business with my brother," she said, glancing up at the guard. "Is there not one of ye that cares to join me?"

The guard looked at her warily, as if assessing whether or not he should indeed answer. She did not have the best reputation when it came to having an escort. Most of the time she forced them to race her, and then it was a game of hers to see if she could lose them in the wood, or soak their clothes in the sea. A lass had to have fun sometimes didn't she?

"Nonsense, my lady. I've already relayed my message to your brother."

Lorna flashed him an angry glare but was only greeted with a charming smile. Why did he have to do that? She felt her icy resolve starting to melt away, and hurried to block it back up. This man had known she was meant for another. He'd not even tried to fight for her.

Unless the battle in the great hall counted. Which it didn't, since he'd denied her brother the truth about them. She sniffed at him, and turned away, contemplating whether or not a ride was truly necessary. There was always a walk through the orchard. She could pick a few apples and ask Cook to make her a tart.

Jamie leaned close to her so that no one else could hear what he said. "It will nay do to argue, lass."

Lorna scoffed, feigning offense. "If I've no choice in the matter, than fine, but stay sixty paces behind me."

"Only sixty?" he drawled out, lips in a teasing curl.

"Ugh," Lorna snorted and glanced back up at the guards, who appeared to be too well entertained by her and Jamie's exchange. "Well, are ye going to open the gates? I've an escort."

They hurried to issue orders and the portcullis was lifted, the doors opened wide and the lush green of the moors presented to her. Lorna didn't wait for Jamie, she flicked the reins and leaned over her horse's neck, urging her into a run.

Angel responded the way she always did, forelegs reaching forward as she leaped into a gallop through the gates. The wind whipped Lorna's hair in a cloud around her face and she felt that immediate, intense surge of joy. The ground was still wet from the rain and Angel's hooves sank deep then flicked mud on the upward move. Splatters of rain soaked earth flung upward, sticking to her gown, arms and cheeks. Behind her, Jamie gained, and she got a nice feeling of pleasure at the idea of her mud striking him as well.

Yards of earth passed beneath her in shades of green, purple, yellow and white as she charged over the grass and wildflower covered heath. She veered to the left, riding around the thick walls of the castle and toward the beach. Above her, streaks of yellow fingered through the clouds, spreading the puffs of white apart to reveal the clear blue of the sky.

The North Sea came into view, choppy white swirls capped the top of waves as they lapped at the sands leaving foam in their wake. Fresh, salty sea air filled her lungs, helping to clear her mind and for a moment she forgot about Jamie's presence behind her.

Angel's gait sunk into the sand and still she pushed her

forward, until they reached the shoreline, splashing in the early summer water. Not near as warm as it would be a month from now, but worlds better than the frigid winter. They rode through the water, down the beach, leaping over large boulders and drift wood.

Normally she'd stop, leap off of Angel's back, rid herself of shoes and hose and let her bare feet sink into the sand and water, but with Jamie insisting on accompanying her, she felt the need to run him ragged, even if it meant running herself ragged, too. He'd get no special treatment, but the same trouble she gave her other escorts—if not more so for his betrayal.

They rode a mile down the beach, then two, her thighs tingling with that familiar burn she loved. Behind her Jamie kept his distance to sixty paces. Lorna couldn't decide if she was happy about that or irritated. After three miles, she pulled Angel to a stop and turned to wait.

Jamie stopped as well—sixty paces away from her. She suppressed the urge to roll her eyes. Was he following her instructions to bait her or impress her? Either way it didn't matter.

"Ye can come closer," she called over the din of the waves crashing to shore.

A seagull screeched and took off from a few feet away. Neither horse moved, nor acknowledged the sudden shriek.

"Are ye certain that would be wise, lass?" he asked.

Lorna narrowed her gaze. "Why would it not be?"

"I dinna know. 'Haps ye might try to seduce me once more."

It was extremely difficult to keep her mouth from falling open. "I, seduce, ye?" Exasperation sounded in her voice.

"Aye, lass. Ye canna keep your hands off me." He shrugged as if it was common knowledge.

If blood could boil and steam could burst from nostrils, both would be happening to Lorna at that moment. The man had the ability to make her sigh with passion one moment and scream with anger the next. No one had been able to pull the range of emotions from her that he had. No one. Which was why she'd thought there was a chance that maybe they could have a future together. A thought process that was obviously flawed.

And now he was finding it great fun to goad her. To tempt her anger, like a dog baiting a bear. Well, a dog could get crushed by a bear, and she was ready to crush him.

"I can keep my hands off ye, ye lout. This I promise, I'll never touch ye again." Lorna flicked Angel's reins again, urging her forward.

But Jamie had placed himself in a very inconvenient area. He'd positioned himself directly between two boulders, one of which the water kept lapping over, which meant it was deep enough her gown would get wet. The second boulder, leaned against a dune, and it would be tricky taking Angel up over that incline, especially with the sand soaking up most of the morning rain. Angel's hooves could very easily suck into the moistened earth.

That meant, she'd either have to face getting wet, leap a boulder or kindly ask Jamie to step aside. Lorna brought her horse muzzle to muzzle with Jamie's, cocked her head to the side and issued him a honeyed smile.

"Will ye please let me pass?" she asked, using a syrupy sweet tone that worked oft on her brothers.

"Nay."

CHAPTER FOURTEEN

'Twas not every day that a man could take such enjoyment in the wrath of a woman he cared for. Lucky for Jamie, today was just such a special day.

Waves lapped at his horse's feet, standing in just the spot he knew would irritate Lorna the most. She liked to escape him. To run from her problems. Hell, she'd been running the first times they'd met as children and adults, and she hadn't stopped since.

Well, he wasn't going to let her run from him any longer.

Every muscle in Jamie's face worked to keep the smile from curving his lips. Damn but the look of extreme anger that flashed across Lorna's features when he said *Nay* was impressive. And somehow entirely endearing. He wanted to swipe it from her face with a thousand kisses, but that only brought to mind why they were out here in the first place.

She was angry at him, and he was in turn, perhaps not angry, but definitely disgruntled, with her. The situation they found themselves in wholly stung. Betrothed to another... It'd been a blow to the gut for certain. Entirely unexpected.

And to think he'd come to Dunrobin in the hopes of asking her brother for her hand. In the back of his mind, the idea that she was betrothed didn't altogether cancel out his desire to ask for her to be his anyway.

What bothered him most was that she'd known about it when she'd pulled him into the alcove. What was it she hoped to gain?

He was flattered that even knowing she was betrothed to another, she still sought him out, but she was playing with fire, and he knew her to be an honorable woman—except where he was concerned, which if she were to be his, he had no problem sneaking into any darkened corner to kiss the breath from her.

A million questions swirled in his mind and not one of them could he answer. The upside of things was that he was out on the beach with her now. Just him and her. No one else about to remind them of the truth of things.

Only they could do that.

And he probably should.

But he was having entirely too much fun goading her. Gave him a nice sense of satisfaction, too. She'd lied to him, and now he was going to toy with her in retaliation.

The only thing was, he was starting to think that his own line of thought might backfire on him. He couldn't seem to get it through his mind that Lorna was off limits. And truly, he provided her escort on her ride, but it was entirely inappropriate given his feelings for her, and certainly if Magnus had been in the courtyard he would have forbidden it.

That gave Jamie pause. The right thing to do was to step aside and let the beautiful, fuming, blonde before him pass by. He should lead her right back to the castle, then gather his men and leave Dunrobin behind forever. The wrong thing would be to tug her horse forward until he could lean over and capture her lips in his. Why, then, was the latter so damn tempting?

The images that thought conjured heated his blood, and he shifted in the saddle, finding his cock suddenly filled with potent need. He ground his teeth, forcing his body to tame itself, else everything be lost as he tumbled her to the sand and showed her just how much she tempted him.

Jamie cleared his throat. "A truce, my lady?" he heard himself saying. Seemed he was too preoccupied with the devil between his legs to realize his mind had moved on to another path, and that he'd even spoken.

Lorna narrowed her eyes, pursed her lips as she studied him. Och, why did she have to do that? The pink pout was even more enticing

"What are your terms?" she asked.

Jamie caught her gaze roving over him and wondered at what she hoped the terms were. Brazen lass she was. Damnation! His body stirred right back to life.

He cleared his throat, shifted again, glad for his sporran which mostly hid his thickening groin. "We ride, side by side."

"And?" She cocked her head. Coy little minx.

"I want to get to know ye better." So much better. Stripped bare and spread out beneath him, all around him.

"Whatever for?" she sniffed, trying to act as though she was not interested, but he'd seen the curiosity flare in her eyes.

He had a lot more than mere curiosity flaring on his side of the beach.

"Because. Ye're nay married yet."

Lorna's lips formed the perfect little O. He'd shocked not only her but himself as well. Was he actually considering stealing her away from MacKinnon? Perhaps what she'd said about the man fighting for his country was true. He wouldn't suddenly turn traitor because Jamie stepped between the two of them. But what of respect? If he stole the man's bride, he could hardly expect him to follow his lead in battle—the man was more liable to lop his head off than his enemy.

Ballocks! MacKinnon would take it as a personal affront. Jamie cursed under his breath. He should call off everything. Insist Lorna return to the castle.

But just then, Lorna shoved her hand forward, her long slim fingers reaching toward him. Jamie stared at her outstretched hand. At the way the sleeve of her gown touched her delicate wrist, and the skin on her knuckles creased, how her manicured nails were short but still extremely feminine. He recalled how her hands had felt on his chest, on his back, in his hair. A rush of fresh desire tormented him.

"Well, Montgomery? When one asks for a truce and that truce is accepted, do we not shake on it?"

"Huh," he grunted. "Aye." But he didn't grip her arm as he would a man, instead, he held tight to her hand, tugged her forward and bent to kiss the knuckle on her middle finger. He lingered, breathing in her scent, the warmth of her hand and the softness of her skin. When he was dangerously close to flicking his tongue over her flesh he let her hand drop. "Truce."

"For now," she murmured, color high in her cheeks. "Shall we?"

"Where do ye want to go?"

"Ye wanted to know more about me." A mischievous twinkle came into her eye. "I've something to show ye. Something that gives my aunt a fit of apoplexy and makes my brothers shout at me."

Jamie shook his head, glancing toward the water. Many a maiden liked to take a dip in the warm ocean waters with not a stitch on. He'd spent many hours watching as a lad. What other act could she mete out that would have her family rail on her? As much as he wanted to see the ocean water sluice over her taut curves... Well, he was certain it wouldn't end with her a maiden any longer. "Sounds like a bad idea. I'll likely have both your brothers ripping swords off the walls and challenging me to a duel to the death."

"Not if ye keep it between us." Again she gave a coy cock of her head.

Dear God what was she going to show him?

"Stay right here," she demanded.

Jamie narrowed his gaze, suddenly not trusting in the least whatever it was she was about to do. Would she run off and leave him there? Was that her game, to ditch her escort? He wouldn't put it past her. Lorna was more intelligent than most females he'd come across. And dammit, but he'd learned rather quickly that she liked to play games.

"I promised the guards I'd be your escort, that means I canna simply stay put while ye dash away, even if we did call a truce."

Lorna waved her hand at him like he was a silly child. "Pish, my laird, I'll not be far. I promise to remain within your sight the entire time."

That was the problem. "Keep your clothes on," he warned.

Lorna's cheeks reddened and a short feminine gasp escaped her. "Saints, Jamie, what have ye got rolling through your head? Naughty laird that ye are."

He swallowed hard, unwilling to share exactly that, though she might have guessed and now he couldn't get the image out of his head. "I dinna wish to..."

"What? Marry me? Well ye needn't worry as MacKinnon has already staked his claim on this prized sow." She turned away, anger tightening the line of her jaw.

Jamie reached out, his fingers trailing up her arm. "That is not what I was going to say, lass. I simply did not want to compromise ye. And..." He gritted his teeth. "If MacKinnon had not gotten to your brother first, I would have offered."

She whirled back to him, mouth partially agape. "Then 'tis unfortunate that he did."

"Aye, that it is." He stared at her mouth, wishing he could capture her lips with his. One last kiss before he saw himself southward. "Now, if the task ye had in mind does nay involve ye removing your gown," he spread his arm out, "then by all means, I am your most captive audience."

"'Tis a good thing we're not to marry, because after ye see this, ye'd have likely broken it off."

She didn't leave him room to reply, but surged down the beach, her horse's hooves shoveling sand up into the air.

Jamie turned his own mount to watch, wondering what she could ever do that would make him not want to be with her. He couldn't think of a single thing, only that she trusted him so much that she was willing to show him. How had he ever garnered that trust? He was honored that she'd bestowed it on him, and his chest puffed a little at the realization.

Lorna didn't stop, but kept on riding down the beach. Far enough

139

away that he itched to chase after her, but not so far that she was out of sight. Then she stopped and turned back toward him. Had she changed her mind about escaping him? What was it she wanted to show him?

As he sat, perplexed by what it was she hoped to accomplish, other than making him into a drooling fool, she rode back toward him.

She lifted her hands up into the air, like she would reach for the sky, and his stomach flipped. She'd let go of the reins. What was she doing? But the next seconds had him gasping, his heart completely tunneling out of his body, and fear taking hold. The daft woman stood up on the horse as her mount galloped at lightning speed. Her body long, hands out to the side as though she would fly. Legs straight, head held high and regal. The horse didn't falter in its steps, but kept on running with Lorna standing in the saddle like some sort of warrior goddess.

If this was what a fit of apoplexy felt like, Jamie was most certainly having it. And he was also going to shout at her as her brothers did. He couldn't sit still, but raced towards Lorna, both fascinated by her daring and fearful for her life. The distance between them closed and he observed that Lorna's eyes were closed.

"Holy hell," he muttered. He had to reach her before something awful happened.

But the movement of his own mount must have spooked hers. Lorna's horse veered just a foot toward the water. The slight movement caught Lorna off guard, and she teetered on the saddle, eyes popping open in surprise.

"Lorna!" he shouted, reaching, nearly toward her, but not close enough.

She bent forward grappled with the saddle, but her mount seemed even more jittery. Jamie realized, too late, that he was probably the reason for that, and yanked his mount to a dead stop. He leapt off the animal and ran toward her on foot. But not quick enough.

He watched in slow motion as Lorna tumbled from her horse and into the ocean waves.

"Lorna!" he shouted again, splashing into the water.

Relief struck him in the gut, as he caught sight of her in the shallow sea, laughing, and a completely soaked mess. Hair fell in her eyes, her gown clung to her. Waves lapped at her bent knees.

"Told ye it would scare the wits out of ye," she said between laughs.

"More than that," he muttered, dropping to his knees beside her. He clutched at his heart, certain it had burst.

She laughed all the more and patted him on the back.

"Ye look as though ye saw a ghost." She laughed even more.

"I might have," he answered.

Jamie reached out his hand to her and Lorna slipped her fingers into his. He stood and he tugged her up. Her gown clung to her curves like a second skin. Jamie gulped, tore his eyes away from the enticing sight and tried to keep his gaze riveted to the water that dripped down her nose, over her lips and formed droplets on her chin. That, too, was wholly enticing. He swiped them away with the pad of his thumb.

"Ye nearly gave me a heart attack. What were ye thinking?"

All the laughter faded from her eyes and she glanced away. "Ye're just the same as my family. None of them understand me either."

"Lass, 'tis not that. I was amazed by ye, stunned. Ye handled your horse well, and your balance…" He raked a wet hand through his hair. "Truth be told, ye reminded me of a warrior goddess. Beautiful, confident and skilled. I just wish ye'd give me fair warning. 'Twas a dangerous trick ye pulled and ye're lucky ye fell into the water. What if ye'd fallen on a rock and cracked your head open? Or broken your neck?"

Fuming, she turned on him. "'Tis your fault, ye cad. I've not fallen off Angel in years. We practice that move at least twice a week."

"Twice a week?" He thought he might keel over right then.

"Aye." She chewed her lip. "'Haps I should nay have shown ye. I didna realize ye'd have such a fit over it."

Lorna sounded so downtrodden, Jamie couldn't help but stroke his hand over her cheek, threading the tips of his fingers into her damp hair. With his other hand he tilted her chin up so that she looked at hm.

"I was scared," he admitted. "Ye dinna realize…" Lord he couldn't confess to her what she meant to him. "The thought of ye falling or being injured tore me apart inside. I could nay live with myself if something happened to ye when I could prevent it."

"I relish the freedom of riding, Jamie. I love the feel of the wind in my hair, the thrill and excitement of doing something daring." She chewed her lip. "Any man is going to frown upon it. To stifle me."

Jamie smiled, choosing to tease her. "Any woman, too."

She rolled her eyes. "Ye know what I mean."

"Aye, lass, I know what ye mean. Ye've such spirit, such fire, it should never be stifled. I'd never suppress ye. 'Tis one of the things I adore about ye."

Hope that neither of them should possess sparked in her eyes. "MacKinnon will stifle me."

"Let us not talk of MacKinnon," he grumbled.

"Why? I'm to marry him."

"Dinna remind me."

"Tell me, Jamie. Tell me why ye dinna want me to marry MacKinnon."

Jamie growled, slipped his hands over her hips and tugged her close to him, feeling the warmth of her body slide against his and not caring that his hardened body told her exactly how much he desired her. "Because, I'd have ye for myself."

And then he kissed her. His lips crashed over hers in a torrent fiercer than the swirling waters. A kiss that claimed her as his own, even when he knew she was so far from being within his grasp it made his heart ache.

CHAPTER FIFTEEN

$\mathcal{L}$orna allowed herself to be swept up into the passion and pleasure of Jamie's kiss. There was no sea lapping at her feet, no gulls screeching overhead, simply the two of them and their mouths pressed hotly together.

She wrapped her arms around his middle, fingers splaying over the muscles of his back. A strong, sturdy back. Her nipples hardened, tingling and tugging at something within her. What was the power that Jamie wielded over her? Whenever he was near, she could barely think straight, and as soon as his lips touched hers, she was done for.

With his mouth taking control of hers, his lips sliding in a sensual rhythm, tongue gently exploring, Lorna was fairly certain she never wanted to come up for air. She sighed, and that little sound seemed to knock something within Jamie. His hands went from her face, down over her neck, shoulders, arms, and then burned a path around her waist until they both cupped her buttocks.

Jamie growled against her lips as he lifted her up on her tiptoes, tucking her length against his own. A sharp gasp escaped her as the rigidness of his arousal pressed indecently, and oh-so-deliciously to the very heated part of herself that had seemed to come alive the moment they met. She couldn't help rubbing wantonly against him, enjoying decadent frissons of pleasure as they radiated through her.

One thing was certain, she'd never be able to look at the beach again without feeling his strong hands on her behind, nor the feel of his thick erection nestled at the juncture of her thighs.

Feeling bold, Lorna let her own hands trail lower from the small of his back to the taut muscles of his behind. Thick muscle, hard, and yet pliant. She gripped him tight, reveling in the differences of their bodies. Jamie groaned, kissed her harder. The sound he made, the primal passion of his kiss, it took her over the edge. She wasn't sure she could come back from where she was. It was a swirling, tumbling, chaotic mass of emotions and bliss-filled sensations.

Aye, she didn't want this to end. Not now. Not ever. If they never parted, she'd die content with her lips on his.

"Lorna," Jamie murmured, sliding his lips along her cheek.

She let out a little moan of displeasure, turned her face to follow his lips, but ended on a gasp when he trailed a hot path to the sensitive part beneath her ear. Oh, aye, that, too, was lovely.

Nibbling on the lobe of her ear before sliding his tongue over the shell of her ear, she couldn't help but wonder how much more pleasure there could be with a kiss, with touching. It seemed that the more he kissed her, caressed her, the more pleasure she received. Like being intoxicated, only better, because on the morrow she'd not wake with a headache that only Cook's special brew could heal.

Her mood was quickly soured when she realized what kind of ache she'd end up with—heartbreak. In the morning, she'd still be betrothed to MacKinnon, and Jamie would still be heading back south after he reached a deal on wool with her brother.

The torturous thoughts were enough to make her pull back from Jamie a little. She stared into his heavily lidded eyes, searching for what, she didn't know—answers. Promises.

His eyes held many promises. Promises of more delicious kisses. Promises of pleasure. Promises that if she stayed right there, he'd fill her body with the wondrous heat he'd already given her.

Jamie dipped his head, touched his nose to hers. "What's pulled ye away?" he whispered.

Lorna gave a sad smile, bringing her hands up to his waist and clinging to the dampened fabric of his *leine* shirt. "The real world."

Jamie softly chuckled. "Och, the real world is for fools."

"Said a fool himself," she teased back.

Large, warm hands found their way up to her shoulder blades, massaging the taut muscles along her spine that suddenly felt pinched. She closed her eyes for a moment, enjoying the release of tension, the closeness of his embrace.

"I'm only a fool, it would seem, when it comes to desiring a woman pledged to another."

Lorna glanced up at Jamie, taking in his chiseled from stone features. He was hard, proud, and devastatingly handsome. A shadow of facial hair had started to grow on his face. She reached up, tracing the line of his jaw and feeling the stubble tickle against her fingertips. "'Tis not yet set in stone." Her voice came out soft, nearly a whisper. She couldn't trust her own words, nor his reaction to them, for she wanted desperately for Jamie to agree. To storm back into Dunrobin and demand that her brother break whatever negotiations he'd begun with MacKinnon.

"'Tis not as easy as all that," he said. "MacKinnon has pledged—"

Lorna couldn't still her tongue. "He's pledged himself to Wallace and to the cause."

Jamie's hands dropped from her back. They may have been the wrong words to utter, but they were the right words to her. Words he needed to hear. Jamie was being a stubborn arse and if he couldn't see that, then she needed to point it out. He himself had just said that he wanted her for himself. That he couldn't stay away. The same was true for her. And their kiss was any indication, then they *should* be together, alliances, negotiations and contracts be damned.

"If MacKinnon is a man of honor, he would not cease his fealty to Scotland simply because another had fallen for the woman he plans to marry, but has not even had the temerity to come and visit. Has it occurred to ye that he does not even wish to marry me? But does so only for some other reason? Would not a man wish to meet the woman he was to wed? He visited Dunrobin weeks ago and not once did he ask to see me."

"What reason could there be? Ye are the very woman a man dreams of being his wife."

Lorna snorted a laugh, thinking of every fault she had. "Ye are mistaken, Jamie. Blinded by my kiss." The latter she added in jest, hoping to regain his attention. "Anything that MacKinnon would have heard of me would most likely be about my willful spirit and ability to escape my guards."

He just shook his head, the muscle in his jaw clenching, nostrils flared. 'Twas obvious he was struggling inside. Just as she was. Lorna had a hard time not pummeling him with her fists. Why would he not see reason in this? He desired her. Cared for her. All that was obvious. Wasn't the logical thing to do, to petition her brother to consider his own offer over MacKinnon?

"Jamie..." How could she convince him? And just as suddenly as the question popped into her mind, anger consumed her. She shouldn't have to convince him they were meant to be together. Either he wanted it or he didn't. And he couldn't kiss her anymore if he wasn't willing to move beyond this beach with a sense of reason. "I need to get back to the castle. I've been gone long enough."

She didn't wait for his response, but disentangled herself from his embrace and grabbed Angel's reins. Her horse nuzzled her arm, and Lorna whispered a sweet word of encouragement. She'd just put a foot in the stirrup when Jamie's fingers wrapped softly around her upper arm.

"Wait," he said.

Lorna stilled, unable to move for fear he wouldn't speak. She even kept her foot within the stirrup. Chewing on her lip she stared at the ancient Celtic swirls sewn into the leather of her saddle.

"Ye are right, Lorna. I am blinded when it comes to ye. Willing to give up everything. Willing to risk an alliance in order to have ye for myself. But ye see, that is the problem—I canna give up the alliances. I am first and foremost a man of my country. Wallace and the council entrusted me with this, not to destroy alliances with MacKinnon and Sutherland in one day. Ye have to understand that."

Lorna pulled her foot from the saddle and turned to face Jamie. His eyes pleaded with her, his lips firmed into a thin line. She could turn away now, go back to the castle, forever giving up on Jamie as anything more than an alliance to her family, to the man she was to wed. But Lorna wasn't willing to give up just yet. He meant too much to her to simply walk away. As much as she wished to slap some sense into him, perhaps Jamie needed a gentler hand to guide him toward the right path.

'Twas obvious Jamie was not yet ready to cross the threshold of simple kisses to something deeper, and if she were honest with herself, she wasn't ready yet either. Not that her brother had really given her a choice. But if there was something there... Well, she wasn't willing to give up on that either.

Magnus would be furious with her, and while she could deal with his irritation for simple things, his fury over a lifelong decision would be extremely difficult. Better to ease both these stubborn mules onto the proper path.

Lorna thrust her hand forward and jutted out her chin. "To friendship."

Jamie stared at her hand, his face flat, making her long to know what was in his mind.

At last he took her hand in his, sliding upward over her forearm. Shivers passed over her, but she thrust them aside. Now was not the time for a physical reaction. She had to be smart about this if she was going to get Jamie and Magnus to see reason.

He squeezed her arm. "To friendship." His voice was soft, defeated almost, something else she chose to ignore.

❧

A SOFT KNOCK SOUNDED AT LORNA'S DOOR JUST BEFORE DINNER. SHE opened it to find Heather standing outside in the corridor.

147

"What is it?" Lorna asked, feeling exhausted from the emotional turmoil she was putting herself through.

Heather screwed up her face into a frown, and pushed into the room. "No need for such sourness, sister. Aunt Sourpuss has enough bitter for the both of us."

Lorna rolled her eyes and shut the door. She headed back toward her wardrobe, staring at the gowns that hung there. She'd found it hard to pick out what to wear this evening. Normally, she wouldn't care so much, but for some reason, she felt that it mattered. If she chose something too beautiful, it would be misconstrued. If she chose something too plain—yet again, it would be taken out of context.

Maybe she should just have her meal brought to her room. But if she did that, then she'd not be able to move forward with her vow to make the men in her life see reason.

"Ye've been moping around all day," Heather said. "What's happened?"

Heather plopped onto Lorna's bed, fluffed the pillows and sat back on it, elbows bent and hands behind her head like she was in her own chamber. Lorna happened to love that her sister felt so comfortable with her. Despite the hellion that Heather was, it meant much to Lorna that they were so close.

"Magnus told me something dreadful," Lorna confessed.

Heather's face fell. "Does this have to do with MacOwen?"

Lorna smiled bitterly. "Sort of. Though 'tis not MacOwen."

"Who then? Is it Montgomery? He is handsome." Heather smiled and sighed.

Lorna blew out a breath and tugged the green wool gown with the Sutherland plaid sash from the wardrobe. Plain, but elegant.

"No, the blue," Heather said.

Lorna shook her head. "'Tis not Montgomery."

"Oh." Heather sounded uncertain. "But I thought..."

"Ye thought wrong."

"There's no need for ye to be so angry with me, sister, I've done nothing to ye."

Lorna put the green gown back into the wardrobe and turned around. "Ye're right. I'm sorry."

She walked over to the bed and sat on the side. "Magnus has arranged for me to wed MacKinnon—without even a meeting. We are to marry by proxy, and then I'm to be taken to him some other time. After he fulfills his duties to William Wallace maybe." She shrugged. "I dinna know. But it makes me feel like one of the sheep. Just a body to be traded."

Heather reached out and tugged Lorna in for a hug. "I'm sorry. Why would he do that?"

"I dinna know. MacKinnon has promised to buy a mountainous supply of wool."

"That is awful!" Heather leapt off the bed. "I'm going to go tell Magnus just that, right now."

Lorna grabbed onto Heather's arm. "Nay, dinna!"

"He canna treat ye like that! He promised to protect us when Ma and Da were taken. Marrying ye off to a man ye've never even met is just cruel."

"He must have a reason for it," Lorna said, hating the defeated sound in her own voice and vowing once more that she'd make him change his mind. But she dared not voice that to her sister. There was too much at stake to share her plans with anyone. And to give voice to something that may not happen would only break her heart all the more in the end if she were defeated.

"Then let me speak to him," Heather said. "Please."

Lorna shook her head.

"Is…there another ye prefer?" Heather asked softly.

Lorna gazed at her sister. Wondering if she could trust the feelings in her heart with her younger sister. Heather was impetuous, mouthy and often blurted things out that were inappropriate. But despite all that, she was her sister, and Lorna needed someone to confess her feelings to.

"Promise to keep it to yourself?" Lorna asked.

Heather's eyes widened, and she nodded emphatically. Her sister was a beautiful wild child and would give a man in time a run for his sanity—and she'd love him as fierce as a gale wind.

"There is another I prefer." Lorna chewed her lip, reconsidering her confession for a moment before she blurted out, "Ye were right about Jamie Montgomery."

A wide smile spread on Heather's lips and she sat back down, grabbing onto Lorna's hands. "Does he have feelings for ye?"

Lorna shrugged remembering the passion he exuded each time they'd kissed. The fire in his eyes when he looked at her. The fear in his countenance when she'd fallen from her horse, and the laughter they'd shared.

Certain feelings, aye, many of which she could barely grasp herself. Hot, dizzying feelings. But she was not about to tell her sister of only fifteen years of age about that. The lass would learn in her own time about falling in love...

Was that what was happening?

Lorna shook her head, thrusting her thoughts aside and focusing on her sister who stared at her intently. "I think he does, but he is not willing to proceed with the betrothal Magnus has arranged. MacKinnon is an ally of his and he doesn't want to destroy that connection."

Heather heaved a heavy sigh—one that Lorna imitated.

"That is not good news," Heather said.

Lorna nodded. "I am doomed to a life of unhappiness."

"Then there is no hope for me, either."

Lorna gripped onto her sister's hand. "Haps all will be well. I've heard MacKinnon is attractive."

"So is Montgomery—and Montgomery has your heart."

"Aye, that he does." But was she willing to risk her brother's wrath, the future he had planned for her, and Jamie's alliances, in order to please her heart?

CHAPTER SIXTEEN

*T*hat night during the evening meal, Jamie brooded, tearing bites of venison from his eating knife with vigor and chewing as though his life depended on it. His gaze flew around the room, staring but not seeing. He was plagued with thoughts of Lorna in MacKinnon's arms.

MacKinnon pressing his lips to hers.

MacKinnon stroking up her ribs to cup her breast.

MacKinnon eliciting the soft sighs she made when he stroked his tongue over her lip.

Every thought worse than the first, until he was fairly snarling like a madman. Magnus eyed him with suspicion throughout the meal, and Lorna avoided him altogether. Heather kept sneaking curious glances his way and Ronan did the same.

Magnus tapped the tip of his eating knife on the table before Jamie's trencher to get his attention. When Jamie looked up at him, the laird raised his brow, a challenging expression on his face.

"MacKinnon plans on buying three sacks of wool. 'Tis seventy-two stone," he said.

A small ransom is what it was. Sutherland wool wasn't cheap as it was, and three full sacks? 'Twas nearly the size of eight Lornas. Most clans sold only ten to fourteen sacks a year, as it was. To have a single buyer for one third or a quarter of sales was like finding a chest full of gold. And MacKinnon was willing to put up the coin for it.

Jamie had to stiffen his neck muscles to keep from shaking his head and his fists. If he heard MacKinnon's name one more time… He shoved another bite of meat into his mouth, sinking his molars into it.

When Magnus stared at him, obviously expecting some sort of response, Jamie managed to choke out, "Indeed?" before taking a large gulp of dark ale.

"Aye."

What was Magnus getting at? Jamie could barely concentrate, he just wanted to shove away from the table, lift Lorna up and claim to all who would listen that she was his once and for all. "'Tis a good contract," Jamie lied, forcing himself not to growl out his response.

"Aye. Do ye think Wallace will want to contract for some wool?"

Jamie bent his head from side to side, cracking his neck. "I will mention it to him. I've heard your wool is beyond compare."

"'Tis that." Magnus flicked his gaze around the table, settling on Lorna for several heartbeats before returning to Jamie. "Think ye can do better than MacKinnon?"

Ah, the heart of the matter. Was he willing to trade in the marriage contract with MacKinnon if Jamie were willing to purchase more wool? 'Twas worth it to him to make the deal, but he was also offended for Lorna. Indeed, she was being treated more like a bargaining chip. And, hell, aye, he could do better than MacKinnon at everything—especially when it came to caring for Lorna. Though they weren't talking about that, but wool. Or at least, that's what Jamie had thought they were discussing.

"Better than MacKinnon?" Jamie shrugged. "In truth, we've been doing business with the abbey near to Glasgow."

A few sharply inhaled gasps sounded around the table. Jamie ignored them, tearing off a hunk of bread and swiping it in the juices on his plate before shoving it in his mouth. His stomach was filled with acid and the bread didn't seem to help.

"Then why are ye here?" Magnus asked, an edge of warning in his voice.

Ballocks! A painful jab stabbed at his eyes as he forced himself not to look at Lorna.

"The abbey's wool is sub-par. Good for monks' robes and nuns' habits, but I find our plaids are a tad itchy when wet. Men who spend much time without the comforts of home may be uplifted by at least a soft plaid. I'd hoped to purchase half a sack as a trial."

"But ye have said yourself our wool is unsurpassed."

"Aye. But it is also not cheap, my laird. Much of our funds are going toward the war at present."

MacKinnon must be rolling in chests of coin. The Montgomery clan was well off, but not well off enough to purchase three sacks of wool outright. 'Twas also about need. They didn't require that much wool. And what was Magnus about getting into a pissing match over how much wool MacKinnon was willing to buy? Jamie narrowed his eyes, studying Magnus. What did the man mean by all of it?

"Och, Montgomery! I am but jesting with ye. MacKinnon's wool is part of Lorna's dowry. We'd be glad to sell ye a half sack." Magnus slammed his fist on the table. "I take that back. We'll give it to ye, and if ye like it, then ye'll agree to purchase our wool instead of the abbey's. And recommend us to Wallace and the Bruce of course."

Hell and damnation. Jamie gave a stunned nod. He was grateful for the man's generosity, but he also understood Magnus' baiting. He'd wanted to rub it in his face about MacKinnon. Jamie had not been forgiven over the alcove incident earlier, and given that he was laird, Magnus probably knew that Jamie had escorted Lorna on her ride that afternoon.

Speaking of her... He'd tried to keep his eyes off her all night, but now he found his gaze drifting toward her again and again. She'd chosen a lovely green gown that brought out the lush emerald in her eyes, pushing the blue to the center. Lord, she was beautiful.

Magnus cleared his throat and Jamie pulled his eyes off the woman he'd come to think about morning, noon and night.

"Ye showed me your skill with a sword earlier today. Care to show me how well ye fight hand to hand?"

Jamie flicked his gaze back to Magnus, belying the sudden constriction in his throat. Why was the man challenging him once more? If he beat Magnus in front of all his clan, then he'd be showing the man great disrespect. On the other hand, if he let Magnus win, then he'd be proven weaker. A label Jamie did not want to have. If he won, then he'd be showing Magnus he was worthy of Lorna. Either way it seemed a losing situation for Jamie.

Dammit. Why did Magnus have to challenge him?

Pride filled Jamie's test. There was nothing for it. If Magnus wanted a challenge, then he'd give him one, no matter the consequences. The laird had been goading him since earlier that day and Jamie could use an outlet to let out his frustration.

Jamie grinned slowly. "Ye wish to fight me, my laird?"

"Och, I didna say fight. A friendly challenge." Magnus waved his hand out to everyone in the great hall. Those in attendance sat quietly, awaiting Jamie's response. "A bit of entertainment for the masses."

Jamie tucked his eating knife into his belt loop and pushed away from the table. He stood, pressed his hands to the table top and leaned toward Magnus. "I accept."

Lorna glanced up at him, pleading with her eyes. But what could he do? This was what Magnus wanted, and Jamie was not about to turn the man down.

"Excellent." Magnus, too, pushed away from the table. "Clear the way." He spread his hands outward and men and women stood from their places, pushing the tables back enough to form a good amount of space in the center of the great hall.

"Remove all your weapons," Magnus stated.

Toby jumped from his place at a table and came forward, taking Jamie's *sgian dubh*, dirks, daggers, sword and various other blades, including his eating knife. When he was thoroughly stripped of weapons, he faced Magnus, legs spread wide and ready for a challenge.

The man was cocky. And he had every right to be. He'd proven his skill with a sword that morning, and having been leader of his clan since he was fourteen—and prospering—he was obviously intelligent, too. But Jamie was skilled at hand to hand, too. A man never knew when he was going to be without a weapon, and he still needed be able to protect himself, and win.

"Ready?" Magnus asked.

Jamie gave a curt nod and put up his fists. A rush of excitement tunneled through his veins. The same that happened whenever he took up a challenge. Aye, Magnus was the brother of the woman he was fond of, and so this challenge meant more than most, but it was also a great past time of his. He wrestled nearly nightly with the men of his clan after the evening meal. 'Twas a great way to relieve stress.

Magnus grinned as though he owned the battle already. Jamie kept his face plain, not wanting to give away that he was about the kick the arse of the laird.

"Are ye ready, lad?" Magnus said. Though Jamie and he were born the same year, the man belittled him hoping to stir his ire.

"As ever," Jamie murmured.

Magnus held up his hands, walking in a slow wide circle around Jamie. A move that should have made Jamie feel cornered in the center, but if anything it gave Jamie the advantage. He'd let Magnus believe whatever it was that he had in his mind, but from that moment on, Jamie tunneled out everything in the room but his focus on his opponent, the tiny movements he made with his fingers and the way his eyes flicked over Jamie, assessing his own movements.

Magnus circled him several times before leaping forward, his fist thrusting outward. Jamie let it happen, ducking at the last possible second, Magnus' fist skimming the side of his cheek rather than hitting full on. Jamie leapt backward out of reach, not bothering to take a shot so close. He liked his challenger to underestimate him.

"Ye're either quick, or just lucky," Magnus commented.

This time Jamie did grin, though he didn't respond, a bit of arrogance taking over. Luck was not the only thing on his side.

Another circling and Magnus lunged again, this time faking a punch with his right hand to Jamie's face, and then pulling back to punch him in the gut. As the air rushed out of his lungs and pain radiated in his middle, Jamie grinned—finally an opponent he may just be evenly matched with.

Jamie didn't hold back this time. He jabbed Magnus in the side, hitting him in the lower side of his back hard, three times in succession until Magnus jumped back, pain registering on his face.

"Not luck," Magnus murmured.

"Nay, my laird," Jamie answered.

Some in the crowd grumbled, but most of the men moved to stand in a circle around them, shouting words of encouragement to Magnus. Toby and Donald were trying to hide the fact that they were taking bets.

Magnus bounced back and forth, fists clenched, teeth bared. "Time for your lesson," he growled.

Jamie chuckled and beckoned him forward. Magnus rushed him, bending low so his shoulder crashed into Jamie's belly. Normally, a move like that would have taken a lesser man out, but Jamie was prepared for it, and so he wrapped his arm around Magnus's neck and hooked his left leg around Magnus' right taking him off balance. With Magnus bent over, Jamie leaned over top of him, pressing him down further. The Sutherland laird wasn't about to be dropped that way though and he wriggled free, red-faced and furious.

The murmurings on the side grew deafening. This time Jamie didn't wait, he took quick steps forward, thrusting out both fists in a cyclical pattern. Magnus put up his arms to deflect, and ended up getting a few punches in himself.

Their fight went on like that for nearly half an hour. Both covered in bloody cuts, bruises and swelling. They hobbled like injured, elderly men, until Lorna pushed into the middle.

"Will ye both quit it? Each of ye are superb fighters. The best. Obviously. Neither of ye can be beat, now give it a rest." She sounded like an exasperated mother yelling at her young.

Jamie opened his mouth but quickly clamped it closed, nearly certain there was nothing he could say that would make her think otherwise. Magnus seemed to feel the same way.

He stared at Jamie and Jamie gave a curt nod. Magnus stepped forward and held out his arm, which Jamie did not hesitate to grasp in a show of respect and gratitude.

"Good fight," Jamie said.

"Aye, Montgomery." Magnus grinned. "Though I let ye have a few of those punches."

"Och, my laird, I did much the same for ye."

"Ugh. Ye both sicken me." Lorna threw her hands up in the air and stormed out of the great hall.

Jamie stared after her, wanting to run in her wake, but knowing that a move like that would only make Magnus tackle him from behind. Instead, he gulped the cold ale thrust into his hands and laughed with the men.

"Ye're not half bad, Montgomery," Magnus said.

Jamie nodded his show of appreciation. "Much the same to ye."

The perfect opportunity to chase after Lorna occurred ten minutes later when Magnus excused himself to go clean up. Jamie did the same. He rushed to his chamber, wiping off his bloody lip with a splash of water and then snuck down the stairs to knock lightly at Lorna's door. There was no answer.

Damn. Where could she have gone? Maybe to her sister's chamber, and he wasn't about to go knocking there in case he was wrong. So much for that idea.

Suddenly, he felt overwhelmingly suffocated. Cool night air would do him good. He took the back stairs and slipped through the kitchen and out into the gardens. The moon shone through a few wispy clouds, a sprinkling of stars glittering on the large black mass.

"I dinna need an escort in the gardens, Jamie."

The sound of Lorna's voice made him whirl. She stood in front of a rose bush, eyes glittering in the moonlight.

Jamie strode forward until he stood within a foot of her. He plucked a rose off the bush, scraping off the thorns with his thumbnail.

"Och, ye look awful." She studied his face, her hand coming up briefly to touch his bruised cheek and the cut on his lip. "Does it hurt?"

"Nay, lass."

"What possessed ye to fight like that?"

Jamie chuckled. "I'd not be a man if I didna."

"But ye are a fool."

He shrugged. "'Haps, but at least I proved that I'd not back down from a fight."

"That ye did…" She trailed off, her hand dropped, but her eyes lingered. Then as if recalling some grand detail, she flicked her gaze and took a step back, dismissing him. "Well, goodnight then. As I said, I dinna need an escort, Jamie. I'll be just fine out here by myself."

"I didna come to escort ye," he said, his voice gruff with pent up sentiment. He took a step toward her, reclosing the gap between them. He wanted nothing more than to pull her into his arms.

Her eyebrows jutted upward, surprise, and maybe hope filling her moonlit sparkling eyes. "Then why have ye come?"

He pressed the flower forward, tickling the petals on the tip of her nose before tucking the stem behind her ear.

"A breath of fresh air." And he meant it, for that was what she was to him.

"I gather ye've had more than one," she said, a teasing lilt in her tone.

He grinned stroking a thumb over the line of her jaw, feeling just the slightest tremble. "Aye, but I find the one I need is right here."

"What are ye saying?" she whispered, eyes connecting with his.

He lowered his mouth to hers, brushing his swollen, aching lips along her silky ones. In that moment, it appeared that everything would be well. All he needed was Lorna by his side and the world could be a better place. He was happy. Whole.

"I dinna want to be friends with ye Lorna. I want ye all for myself."

CHAPTER SEVENTEEN

*L*ightning could have struck and Lorna wouldn't have noticed. She was far too struck by the words she'd just heard uttered from Jamie's mouth.

Words she'd longed to hear. He wanted her. *Her.*

It didn't matter that Magnus had given her away to someone else already. Or that the man she was betrothed to had pledged his allegiance to Jamie. There was nothing else in the world, at that moment, that could have made her feel anything other than the elation she did at knowing he wanted to keep her all to himself.

Her head buzzed like a thousand bees had taken up residence and blood rushed and crashed in her veins making her a little dizzy.

Emotion, deep and consuming, welled inside her, settling like a giant, heated bubble around her heart. A slow smile spread over her lips as she gazed up at Jamie in the moonlight. His features were shadowed by the lack of light giving him an even more wicked, sensual appeal.

But there was more to it than simple physical appeal. Aye, she could kiss him for endless hours for the rest of her life and never grow tired of it, but she could also stand here in this very spot in the garden and gaze up at his handsome face for just as long.

The sound of someone laughing filtered over the gate that led around the side of the castle toward the courtyard. Lorna chose that moment to be bold. She grabbed hold of Jamie's hand and tugged him deeper into the garden, past the roses and shrubbery and toward the small apple orchard Magnus had planted for her several years before. The sweet scent of the fruit filled their noses as they got lost between the trees, invisible to whoever it was that sought a stroll in the gardens.

A thick bench made of willow bark sat beneath a tree and Lorna tugged Jamie to sit. But when he did, he pulled her onto his lap, cradling one hand behind her back and the other tucked around her hip, her legs over the side of his.

His gaze penetrated hers, and even in the dim light of the moon she could see he was concentrating on something hard inside his mind.

"What are ye thinking?" Lorna asked.

She'd hardly had to work to convince him of anything. All it seemed to have taken was a bit of a challenge from her brother. A frown creased her lips a little. Was it possible that he was only seeking her out now because her brother had issued the challenge? But his next words took that very thought from her mind.

"About how beautiful ye are," he murmured. The way the words rolled off his tongue, so easy, so seductive, made her head swoon.

Jamie always knew the right things to say to make her insides melt.

She curled her fingers, brushing the backs over his stubbled cheek and tracing her thumb along his jaw. If only they could stay in the orchard forever. In that moment, she realized how much trouble she was in. How much she cared about him. How deep her emotions ran, and what that welling in her chest had meant. What she'd tried to deny before, she could no longer ignore.

She loved him. Unequivocally, rip her heart out, loved him. A short gasp escaped her at the notion.

"Is something wrong?" Jamie asked.

Lorna shook her head vehemently, pressed her forehead to his. "Everything is absolutely right." She longed to tell him what her feelings were. To confess that she loved him. But she wasn't sure that such an admission would change their fates. Seemed that it would only make their lives that much harder, to know she loved him, yet she couldn't marry him. Even if he was willing to let her know that he wanted her, that wouldn't make a difference in Magnus' eyes.

"I will speak to your brother tomorrow," Jamie said. His voice was stern and full of conviction.

Lorna couldn't help her shock. Her eyes widened on his and her heart skipped a beat. "About what?" Lord, could it be?

"I respect MacKinnon. He's a good man. But every time I imagine him kissing ye the way I have, or sleeping beside ye, or…" He paused. "Or making love to ye the way I want to, a rage burns through me like I've never known. I dinna want any other man to have ye. Ye're mine."

He claimed her lips then for a kiss that said just as much. Passion possessed them as their tongues tangled in a heady dance. Lorna sank deeper into his lap, her fingers playing with the ribbons of his shirt before dancing over the muscles of his shoulders. They rippled as Jamie tugged her closer. Lorna was tunneled back to every other kiss, frissons of need firing along every nerve and her conviction that this man was the one for her all the more potent.

"I dinna want to marry him," she murmured against his lips between kisses. "I want to marry ye."

Jamie's fingers threaded into her hair and he captured her lips once more for an intoxicating swipe of his tongue. "God, lass, I've longed to hear it."

Ready to escape the tip of her tongue were the words. *I love ye*. But she held back. Why, she couldn't quite put her finger on. If she was willing to tell him she wanted to marry him, why could she not tell him how much she loved him? 'Twas as if that deep inner part of her, she wanted to save for the moment she knew she could have him in truth. Jamie, too, had not confessed his feelings outright, only the intense jealousy he felt toward MacKinnon. His longing to hear her words. 'Haps they both feared the truth of their emotions and the reality of Magnus' power of their future together.

Sadness threatened to dampen the joyous feeling and sensations crashing through Lorna.

"Let me speak to him first," Lorna said, suddenly fearful of Magnus' reaction. If he didn't realize that Lorna preferred Jamie it was possible he would deny him the answer they sought. And where would they be then?

Nowhere but a place called misery.

"Lass, 'twould not be right for me to send ye in my stead. Your brother is a man of honor. He will not take kindly to me not showing him the proper respect he's due as your guardian."

Lorna shook her head, consumed once more with overpowering emotion. She pressed her lips hotly to his, then pulled away just as swiftly. "Nay, Jamie, ye misunderstand. I simply want to speak with him first concerning my feelings for ye. Ease the way for your discussion with him. If he knows how much it would mean to me, then when ye ask his permission, he'll be more receptive."

Jamie clamped his jaw and thought a moment. "I suppose ye know your brother best. But I will speak with him myself just afore the noon meal. He will soon start to wonder why I've not yet left when I have such pressing business to attend for the council."

Lorna chewed her lip, knowing that what Jamie said was correct. Her brother was expecting the Montgomery men to depart within the next day or so and she could not imagine her life without him in it. What would she do?

She'd not realized how much she loved, and had grown accustomed to, looking out her window and seeing him stroll in the courtyard, or watching from afar as he practiced in the fields, or seeing his smiling face during meals. She liked the way he teased her, the way he looked at her, his kindness to her family, even his arrogance. Everything about him pleased her. She couldn't get enough of him. But… he was right. Her brother was expecting him to leave—as were his men most likely.

Which prompted her to ask, "What do your men think?"

Jamie grinned. "Toby and Donald? They know my heart, lass, and they support me."

His heart… Did that mean he loved her? Oh, heavens, she hoped it did. For she certainly loved him. He was her breath, her every heartbeat.

Lorna took his hand in hers and pressed it over her heart. "Ye have my heart, Jamie Montgomery."

"Och, lass, ye've had mine all along. Even as a wee thing, ye stole me away."

Lorna smiled, staring into his adoring eyes. What would it be like to be married to this man? To have him all for her own? She knew exactly what it would be like. Joyous and magical. Aye, they'd have their ups and downs like every other relationship, but that would be so minuscule compared to their infinite happiness.

Jamie bent closer to her, pressing his lips softly to her mouth. Not a claiming, nor a frantic need, but one that Lorna felt was full of love, bursting with promise. He slid his lips over hers, touched his tongue gently to the seam between. She opened, allowing the warm velvet of his tongue to touch hers.

They kissed like that for some time, swept up inside each other. But when Lorna threaded one hand in his hair and used the other to stroke the muscles of his chest, gently scraping with her nails, their kiss took a different turn. Jamie stroked a path up her ribs, leaving shivers of anticipation in his path. His thumb caressed the side of her breast and she gasped, her nipples hardening into tingling knots. Oh, the things he did to her body.

Lorna arched her back, searching out the new heat of his hand, nipples aching with the need for…him to touch them. Stroke them. Love them. Goodness, but she was a wanton. Wicked in every sense of the word, but that didn't stop her. She wanted him to touch her. To experience the pleasure that the simple caress of his thumb on the side of her breast promised.

He didn't deny her.

A gasp of both pleasure and surprise pushed past her lips as his hand covered her breast. Warm with just a bit of pressure, he cupped her. Her nipple was hard as a pebble and pressed against his palm. The friction of the sensitive flesh rubbing against the fabric of her chemise

163

and gown and his palm was almost more than she could take. Such sensations she'd never felt before. It was new and wondrous and intoxicating.

"Good God, lass…" he murmured against her lips. "Your body is reacting to just the slightest touch. So much passion ye have."

More passion than she knew how to deal with. Lorna gripped tight to Jamie's shirt while his lips traveled a heated path over her neck. Her head fell back as his lips grazed her collarbone and then hovered torturously-hot over her nipple.

"I want to taste ye so bad I ache," Jamie said, his lips brushing—or was it just her overactive imagination—over the tip of her nipple as he spoke.

Taste her? Oh, aye! *Aye!*

She arched her back again, pushing her breast up toward his mouth. The heat of his tongue flicked out over the fabric covering her nipple, followed by the covering of his lips as he nibbled and teased her. Lorna's breath came in shallow pants and she squirmed in his lap, unsure of anything and everything, except for the pure joy of his mouth at her breast.

Something hard pressed against her hip, it hadn't been there before, and Lorna knew exactly what it was. Had felt it when he'd kissed her before on the beach. His arousal, thick and pulsing. She writhed in his arms, loving the feel of that thickness pressed to her hip. Jamie growled, gently nipped her breast. Lorna reacted immediately, her body bowing with need.

"Lass, if ye dinna stop moving like that, I'm likely to upend your skirts and make love to ye right here."

Oh, what a vision he'd given her. To make love for the first time with the man she loved, beneath the starlit sky in one of her favorite places? 'Twould be perfect.

"Aye, Jamie, I want ye to."

He pulled back, his expression registering shock. "Nay, lass. I'll not take that from ye. Not yet. Not until we're wed."

He spoke the truth. 'Twas smart for them to wait. Magnus was likely to give them much resistance, but his opposition wouldn't change the way they felt, and what they wanted. And since when did she take what was morally right over what *felt* right. "We'll be wed. Tomorrow morn, my brother will give us permission. We can be married by the nooning." She pressed both hands to the sides of his face, lips tingling and swollen from his kisses. "Dinna make me wait. Not when we're here in this magical place and ye make me feel so… So wonderful."

Jamie pressed his forehead to hers. "Och, lass when ye say it like that, how can I think 'tis wrong?" He nibbled at her lips. "Everything with you feels right."

"'Tis exactly how I feel." Lorna glanced around. They were completely hidden in the foliage of the orchard. Privy to no eyes but their own. The balmy evening air licked tantalizingly at her skin, only adding to the heady steam they were creating.

Lorna pushed off his lap, standing between his deliciously naked knees. Nervous as hell, her limbs quivering and legs threatening to buckle. Never having done more than kiss a man, she wasn't sure how to proceed. Knew she should let Jamie take the lead, but she couldn't. Not if she was going to be the one making this decision. It was her virtue to give away, and she wanted him to have it.

By God, her brother had better see them wed.

She reached out, fingers trembling, and swirled her forefinger on the crisp hair of his knee, her nail slightly scraping the center until he groaned. She remembered staring at those knees weeks ago. Recalled how floored she'd been by something she'd seen on any number of men thousands of times. She was still stunned.

"Ye have beautiful knees," she said.

Jamie gave her a crooked smile. "Och, the wine has gotten to your head."

She shook her head, tendrils that had come loose from her plait falling into her eyes. "Nay, Laird Montgomery. I adore your knees wholly sober."

Jamie reached for her, gripping her hips in his hands. He tugged her closer so her knees hit the bench. "Why did ye pull away from me,

Lorna? Was it to tell me about my knees? I want ye back on my lap so I can kiss ye some more."

She chewed her lip, knowing exactly why she'd pulled away, and it wasn't because she wanted to be further from him, nor deny him more kisses. Quite the opposite in fact. "Because I canna remove my gown while sitting on your lap."

Jamie sucked in a breath, shook his head, cursed beneath his breath, "*Mo creach.*" His gaze grew serious as his eyes hungrily roved over her. "I am the luckiest man in the Highlands."

Lorna reached behind her, tugging at the laces of her gown. When the fabric loosened she tugged one shoulder off, the warm air touching her skin like a kiss. Her chemise was thin, only held onto her shoulders by the tying of two ribbons, no sleeve. 'Twas the only way she could stand so many layers in summer.

Jamie's eyes widened as he watched her, filling her not only with anticipation, excitement, but nervousness, too. His desire for her was obvious, but she'd never been nude with a man before.

"Will ye make me the luckiest lass?" She slipped off the other shoulder and shimmied so the gown fell in a pool around her ankles. Though she stood in her chemise, she felt like she was naked. Exposed. Her nipples pressing like two ripe buds against the fabric.

While she was anxious for what would happen next, she wasn't afraid. This was Jamie. Her love.

Jamie stood up, closing the short distance between them, the heat of his body surrounding her as he tugged her into his arms. "Och, I'm going to make ye a verra, verra, lucky lass."

CHAPTER EIGHTEEN

*J*amie's arrogance and promise of pleasure only endeared him more to Lorna. She loved his confidence, and judging from his kisses, she was certain he would indeed have her feeling more than lucky. There was nothing better to her, than a man who was determined to see her pleased.

Already she felt blessed to have met him. Not only because he'd saved her life, or because he made her skin tingle with urgent need, but because he allowed her to be herself, encouraged her even. A gift she couldn't ask more for. When she used to think of marriage as suffocating, that she'd lose her freedom, she now realized that life with Jamie wouldn't be anything like that.

It would be a dream come true.

Her dream come true.

Jamie gazed on her with something akin to admiration. His lids were lowered, heavy with desire, and the only thing that would have made the setting more perfect was a torch by which she could better see his eyes.

He touched his fingers to her shoulder, skimming two beneath the strap of her chemise, but he didn't try to remove it, just placed his fingers there. Her skin burned where he touched, and she shuffled from foot to foot in an attempt to ease the urgent pulse between her thighs. Every inch of her skin was suddenly alive, over sensitized. Her mind hummed.

"Will ye let me kiss ye?" he whispered.

She'd let him do a whole lot more than that, but her voice had vanished, caught somewhere between her emotion thickened throat and nervous tongue. Lorna nodded and tilted her face up. Jamie met her halfway, curling a hand around the small of her back and lifting her slightly off her feet.

Their bodies slid easily together, her softer curves melding against his hard flesh in a tantalizing mix of raw, potent sensuality.

"I canna believe what your kiss does to me," Jamie murmured as he nibbled her lower lip. "I burn for ye."

Lorna's eyes closed in pleasure as he teased a path with his lips and tongue over her throat, stopping just over her heart which beat so frantically, she was sure it must have vibrated his mouth.

Jamie set her back down, unpinned his plaid and tugged off his *leine* shirt, laying it on the ground beside them. Lorna gasped at the sight of his nude torso. Aye, she'd seen it before near the sea when he'd joined the other men on Beltane, but it seemed to shock her once more because now... Now she could touch him.

With tentative fingers she reached out and traced her fingers over his collarbone, down the center of his chest and then over the thick muscles of his chest, her palm covering his nipple. Crisp hair tickled her as she explored and the sudden urge to kiss his skin, to breathe in his scent, took hold.

Lorna leaned forward and pressed a kiss over his heart, feeling rather than hearing the pulse beat there. Jamie sucked in a breath, his muscles rippling beneath her lips. He cupped her face and kissed her tenderly, before sweeping her into his arms and laying her down on his shirt.

"I've never made love in an orchard," he said, smiling at her as he came down over top of her. "Never made love to a woman like ye. Never felt this way about anyone."

So many firsts for him, Lorna was thrilled to know she wasn't the only one experiencing firsts, but she was also glad he knew what he was doing, for she was clueless.

Jamie rested with one thigh on the outside of hers and the other between her legs, pressing gently to her heated center. His elbows held up his weight as he leaned forward to kiss and tease her mouth. Fingers traced her breasts, her ribs, and with each passing moment, Lorna knew with conviction she was doing the right thing.

"Are ye nervous?" he whispered.

Lorna shook her head. "Nay. Not with ye."

"Good. I dinna want ye to be nervous." He tugged at the hem of her chemise, pulling it slowly up to her hip, his fingers splaying on her bare thigh, moving to stroke the inside of her thigh, edging closer and closer to the place that sparked like fire. His fingers feathered over the hair on her mons, slid between her folds, over a knot of flesh that had her gasping, hips involuntarily bucking.

"Aye, lass, let me know what ye like." He nibbled at her ear lobe, kissed her neck, all the while his fingers rubbing small, fiery circles over her slick flesh.

Lorna could hardly breathe. Could hardly control the movements of her body. She jerked, hips rose and fell, thighs opened. Pleasure radiated her being and she was certain she'd drunk from some forbidden pool to feel so decadent. Jamie moved lower, tugging a nipple into his mouth as he slid a finger inside her woman's sheath.

All sense left her. "Oh!" she cried out, her insides pulsing, quickening, reaching for something. She threaded her fingers into his hair, tugging, pushing, unsure if she wanted more pressure or less but absolutely certain she wanted more of these feelings.

Jamie didn't remove his finger, but pushed in another all the while the pad of his thumb continued to circle over the overly sensitive flesh near the top of her sex. She held her breath, stilled, not wanting to move in case the pleasure stopped.

"Let go, love," he murmured against her breast. "Breathe, feel."

She let out her breath, only to gasp as he quickened the pace of his fingers. One breath, two breaths and then she cried out as something inside her shattered, firing off potent waves of pleasure in every direction. Seconds passed where all she could do was feel, ride out the storm of ecstasy. Finally, the waves subsided, leaving her feeling warm, calm, and yet, eager for more.

"Did ye enjoy that?" Jamie asked, gazing down at her.

Lorna nodded, certain her voice wouldn't work.

"That was your pleasure, your release," he said.

"I…" She cleared her throat. "I didna know it was possible."

"Want to feel it again?"

She nodded eagerly.

Jamie winked at her, a grin splitting his face. "Wanton woman ye are," he teased. "Perfect for me." Jamie moved to kneel. He held out his hand to her and pulled her into a sitting position. "We must remove this." He tugged at the laces of her chemise, then pulled the fabric over her head. "Good God, ye're beautiful."

He stared intently at her, reached forward and cupped her breasts, then leaned down to kiss each in turn, swirling his tongue over one nipple and then the other. Lorna moaned, that aching pulse between her thighs building anew.

Abruptly, Jamie pulled away. "I want ye so bad, lass."

"Aye, I want ye, too."

Lorna reached for the belt of his plaid, and kept her eyes locked on his as she undid the hooks. The fabric fell around his knees revealing his hips, muscled thighs and the thick length of his arousal.

She drew in a deep breath as she stared at him, never having imagined a man's sex would look so enticing. With three brothers, she'd seen it before, but never like this. Not aroused, and fairly begging entrance to her body and her wanting to part her thighs for him. Deliberately, she glanced up at his face, to see that Jamie stared at her with intent question.

"Are ye all right?" he asked.

"Aye, Jamie. More than all right."

"Thank God. I dinna think I could walk away without sinking inside ye."

Lorna lay back on his shirt and reached for him. "Me either."

Jamie positioned his knees between her thighs, then sank on top of her, Lorna's arms wrapping around his waist.

"Lift your legs, love," he whispered against her ear as he teased the sensitive flesh there.

Lorna did as he asked, lifting them up around his hips, feeling the night air kiss her wet sex just before he covered her with his body. The thickness of his erection pressed hotly to her, making her wonder just how this would work. But she didn't have to wonder for long.

Jamie reached between their bodies and began to stoke her fire once more with his fingers, his mouth finding hers and kissing her with such fierce passion, she felt the stirrings of her release once more. And then he was pushing against her, the thick tip of his shaft pressing at her opening.

"This may hurt a little," he murmured against her lips. But he didn't give her a chance to question him.

He pushed against her slickness, and she felt her body stretching to accommodate, then as he surged forward, a painful pinch made her cry out and stiffen, fingers digging into the skin of his back.

Jamie stilled, pulled his face back and stared down at her. Concern etched his features.

"Does it pain ye much?"

Lorna didn't want to be seen as weak, but it had been painful—like stubbing a toe in the dark, or slicing your finger when chopping carrots. But the pain had lessened. She wiggled beneath him, noting that not only had the pain almost disappeared, but that she *liked* the feel of him inside her.

"The pain is gone," she said, smiling up at him and wiggling again.

Jamie groaned. "Dinna do that."

"Why?" She did it again, sucking in a breath when his pelvis rubbed against her firing nub.

Jamie lowered his forehead to hers, their noses touching. "Because I'm already close to losing control."

"Is that a bad thing?" Lorna trailed her fingers up his back at the same time she lifted her legs a little higher. The move had Jamie sinking deeper inside her and Lorna moaned. "It feels so good."

"Aye, love, so good." Jamie slid out slowly, every inch he moved sending ripples of pleasure through her.

When he pushed back inside, his pelvis tucking into hers, she raised her hips, crying out at the sudden, shocking sensation.

"I like this," she murmured.

"I love your passion." Jamie took her mouth in a heated kiss as he continued to move slowly out of her, then drive back inside.

The friction made her dizzy with need, desire. Every movement pushing her closer and closer to that pinnacle point she'd reached before. Now she understood what real desire was, what the bards and minstrels sang about, the deeper meaning beneath their words was revealed to her in Jamie's arms. Pleasure was intoxicating, delicious, and what made it more so was that she shared it with a man who she loved beyond reason and made her feel the same way.

Jamie buried his face in the crook of her shoulder, kissing, licking, nibbling on her skin. His pace increased, and Lorna found it even harder to breathe. Blood rushed through her ears and spark after radiating spark fired inside her.

"Jamie!" she cried.

Her back arched of its own accord and she locked her ankles around him, writhing as a climax even more powerful than the one before tore through her. The primal cry of pleasure that tore form her throat sounded surreal and distant compared to the pounding sensations whipping through her.

"Oh, Lorna, aye, love, let it come," Jamie growled, thrusting faster and faster.

Clinging to him, she knew she'd never be able to let go, completely unable to resist the potency of his lovemaking. Wave after wave washed over her, drowning her, until finally she was able to catch her breath. But Jamie didn't cease his torment, in fact, moments later, he clutched at her hips as he pounded harder, shuddering and crying out. He collapsed over her, for a moment, resting his weight on his elbows, until both their breaths had begun to quiet.

"That was breathtaking," Lorna murmured.

"Unearthly," Jamie replied. He kissed her gently on the lips and stroked her face. "Ye're a passionate lover, Lorna."

"As are ye." She smiled up at him, feeling proud of herself for having been able to please him as he'd pleased her.

"Saints, lass, but ye've had me undone." Jamie kissed her on her lips, then moved to rest his face on her belly, tracing his finger over her hip bone before kissing the spot. "I look forward to us being man and wife when I can make ye call out my name again and again, night after night."

Lorna's belly rumbled loudly, causing her cheeks to flame hot. From his place on her stomach, Jamie chuckled. "Your body is in need of sustenance."

Jamie sat back on his heels, reached up and plucked an apple from the tree. He took a big bite, juice dribbling over his chin and then pressed the apple to Lorna's lips.

"Mmm," she said around a crisp bite. "I've never had an apple that tasted so good."

"'Tis a special apple," Jamie said, taking another bite.

"How so?"

"Because it has witnessed something beautiful."

"A starlit night?"

Jamie grinned and winked at her. "Our love making."

Lorna blushed. "'Twas beautiful."

"Nothing is more beautiful than ye, love."

LORNA ROSE BEFORE THE SUN, WELL, IF A NIGHT OF RESTLESS BLISS AND endless magical dreams counted as sleep. She tugged on her clothes and rushed from her room, certain she was the only one awake. She had to speak with her brother before he went down to break his fast.

There was absolutely no way that she'd be able to sit through an entire meal of porridge without bursting.

Indeed, she couldn't wait another minute.

She knocked on Magnus' door, hoping he wouldn't be too angry at her for waking him, but really how could he be when she had such wonderful news to share with him? She was in love!

No answer came. She knocked a little louder, and still there was no reply. Not wanting to wake anyone by pounding on his door, she turned the handle and stepped inside. The room was darkened still, and his bed rumpled but empty.

Magnus usually rose early, so there was no surprise that he wasn't in bed. She could only pray he was in his library—else she'd have to search the moors and sea for him and it didn't seem likely that she'd have luck when the sun had yet to rise. Besides, the guards wouldn't raise the portcullis for her, and she'd have to somehow steal away through the postern gate without the guards there seeing her. Unlikely.

Lorna hurried down to Magnus' study and tapped at the door.

"Aye?" Magnus' voice sounded heavy with suspicion.

Lorna sighed heavily with relief. "'Tis Lorna," she called.

"Enter."

Lorna thrust the door open. There was no going back now. She beamed a smile at her brother who sat behind his desk studying several scrolls.

"Good morning, brother."

Magnus frowned. "'Tis not even light yet. What's got ye out of bed?" He set down the letter he was working on and stared hard at her.

Lorna shut the door and hurried forward. "I've something to tell ye." Her stomach suddenly plummeted. What if Magnus brushed her feelings aside?

Saints! After last night, she knew there was no going back. Even now she felt the glow of a woman well-loved on her skin.

"Out with it. I'm trying to finish these letters afore the whole of the castle rises."

Lorna swallowed hard, finding it difficult to put forth the words she needed. She took a deep breath, folded her hands in front of her and spoke. "I've fallen in love, brother."

Magnus sat back heavily in his chair, his eyes wide with surprise, mouth turned down in a frown. "Love?"

Suddenly her throat felt constricted. Her fingertips cold. "Aye," she said softly. "I wish ye to break my contract with MacKinnon."

Magnus shook his head vehemently. "Not going to happen. Who is the cur?"

Anger burned like fire around her heart. "He's not a cur! Dinna ye want me to be happy?"

"Lorna—" Magnus cut himself off as he stood and came around his desk. He put his hands on her shoulders and stared into her eyes. "I canna break the contract. 'Twould ruin our reputation for our word, our honor."

Tears came swiftly, stinging her eyes. Lorna shook her head. "Did ye hear me, Magnus? I love another! Please dinna make me marry MacKinnon. 'Twill ruin my life. I wish to wed the man I love!"

"Who is it?"

"Promise me!" She wouldn't give him Jamie's name, not if he intended to exact revenge simply because she loved him.

"Nay, lass. I canna." His voice was stern. More so than she was used to and it shook her to the core. His tone belied his gaze which held regret and sadness.

What did he have to regret? To be sad about? He'd just sentenced her to life with a man she didn't love. He'd sentenced her to heartbreak.

Lorna beat at Magnus' chest with her fists. "I hate ye! Ye've ruined my life!"

As she ran from the room, her brother's voice trailed after her, "Dinna do anything ye'll regret, Lorna. I canna undo what has been done."

How true and deep his words cut to the truth—more so than he realized.

CHAPTER NINETEEN

*L*orna did not come to breakfast.

Nor the nooning.

Throughout both meals, Magnus stared Jamie down as though he'd a nest of maggots on his nose. Pure disgust. He could only surmise Lorna had told her brother everything. Yet, the laird said nothing to him. Only watched him with unwavering revulsion. Which made Jamie wonder if she had not confessed his identity, and the man simply was suspicious.

Either way, he needed to find Lorna and speak with her, *before* he sought out a private meeting with the Sutherland chief. As soon as men started to rise, Jamie set down his spoon, even though he'd only eaten about half of his soup. He'd spent so much time worrying over where Lorna was and why, that he'd not eaten, and though his stomach growled, he didn't have time to finish his meal. He had to find her. Now. The tension was eating him alive.

He'd woken in a dream state, elated. Visions of the night before dancing behind his eyes. She'd been beautiful, passionate and his feelings for her soared. Full of vigor and energy, he'd leapt from bed, eager to speak with Magnus about marrying Lorna. But with every passing hour his urgency to meet with the laird depleted.

His left his meal unfinished and shoved past a few lingering warriors in his haste to leave the room, but Magnus' voice stopped him in his tracks.

"When are ye taking your leave of Dunrobin?" Magnus asked just as Jamie's foot touched the first of two stairs leading out of the great hall.

He turned around and walked back toward the laird's table, hands behind his back. 'Twas a question he'd been expecting. Dammit!

Now was not the time to answer such a question, for what he really should be doing was asking Magnus for a private audience. Hell, the man's sister's scent still lingered on his skin. Jamie glanced around the great hall, praying that by some miracle, Lorna would have shown up and he could have some sort of clue as to whether she'd spoken to her brother. He'd promised her he wouldn't speak with Magnus until she had. And now the man was asking for his departure date.

Jamie drew in a long lingering breath. He'd have to lie. "Day after tomorrow if that is acceptable to ye, my laird. I had thought to wait to hear back from a few more clan chiefs who knew I was headed this way. I'm expecting several missives." Not entirely a lie.

Magnus nodded. "Aye. I believe ye had one come this morning. 'Tis in my library. I'll have Ronan fetch it for ye."

Ronan Sutherland stood from his place beside his brother and left the great hall. It seemed at that moment everyone else chose to depart as well, leaving Jamie and Magnus alone.

Magnus set down his spoon and turned to face Jamie. "Have ye been leaving my sister alone like I bid ye?"

Jamie kept his face cool as he stared at Magnus. The man was forever testing him. How was he to respond to that? That he'd not only *not* left his sister alone, but he'd been well and truly inside and outside of her the night before? That he'd stolen her innocence and she'd cried out her pleasure beneath him?

Nay, that would likely get him a bloody lip again, at the least and murdered at worst.

"I have done nothing but treat Lorna with honor, my laird." Honor due a wife…

Magnus grunted. "Ye've sisters, aye?"

"Aye."

"Are they married?"

Jamie nodded.

Magnus shoved his soup away. "When she was born, my parents signed a betrothal contract between her and the MacKinnon lad— soon to be laird as his father is gravely ill. My parents are gone. His mother passed awhile back and his father's mind was never the same after, and yet we still honor this contract. 'Tis a mess since she fancies herself in love with another. I dinna know how to break it without destroying our alliance. With times the way they are, 'tis best not to make enemies."

Jamie reeled from Magnus' confession. Lorna was in love? A near two decades old contract? For the love of all that was holy… Lorna had not confessed to Magnus that it was Jamie, only that she loved another. Loved *him*.

He couldn't speak, stood stock still ready to spill his guts to her brother, but knowing that doing so would likely get him well and truly gutted.

Magnus wasn't going to break the contract with MacKinnon… Which meant that Jamie wasn't going to marry Lorna. He felt as though his heart was being ripped savagely from his chest. To find out this way was horrid—he could not react to the devastating news, which made it doubly hard. He kept his features cool while inside he boiled.

He loved her. Oh, God, how he loved her! He'd not realized it until now. Not until Magnus told him he'd never have her. Hell, he knew he cared for her deeply. That he thought it was a feeling that could grow into love. He adored her, wasn't lying when he told her she held his heart.

"Here 'tis." Ronan's return startled Jamie from his profound thoughts.

He cleared his throat, trying to regain some semblance of control. Neither of the Sutherlands realized how close he was to losing it.

"My thanks," he managed, taking the missive from Ronan. "If ye would excuse me."

"We'll be practicing in the field later, if ye care to join us. My men seem to have taken a liking to the way ye fight," Magnus called after him.

"Aye, I'll be there." And he would, if only to have the chance to beat the piss out of Magnus.

～

Lorna had never felt so miserable in her life. Well, perhaps she had the day her parents were murdered, but what she remembered most about that time was Jamie, and here he was haunting her again.

She sat in her room, the shutters drawn closed and her candles left unlit. It wasn't completely dark, but dark enough for her tastes. After her horrible conversation with Magnus she took to her chamber, barring the door, refusing anyone entrance—even Heather who'd arrived with a tray full of Cook's hot honeyed buns and a bowl full of freshly picked berries. Not even her favorite treats could entice her to come free of her despair.

Lady MacKinnon would be her new name, and not Lady Montgomery as she'd come to dream of. Jamie had her heart, she'd given him her virtue.

She pressed her hand to her belly. Even now life could be sparking within her womb. Her breath caught. MacKinnon would know she wasn't a virgin on their wedding night, and if she quickened with a child, he would always wonder if it was his. Knowing her tongue, she'd probably tell him the truth anyway.

Their marriage was doomed before it even began. *Oh, Jamie!* Had Magnus already sought him out, having guessed who it was she'd fallen in love with? Her brother would have to be blind not to realize who it was.

A deep sigh blew out slowly from between her parched lips.

Maybe if she stayed in her room forever, refusing food and drink Magnus would see the right of it. Och, who was she kidding? He was as stubborn as an arse! What was the reason behind his refusing to break the contract anyway? He'd not given it to her. Unshakable mule that he was.

A soft tapping sounded on the other side of her door.

She looked away from it, hoping that by ignoring the knock the person would go away without her having to tell them so.

The knock came again, a little louder now.

Lorna stood from her place in the chair by her closed up window and trudged over to her bed where she burrowed her body beneath her blankets and her head underneath her pillows. After a few minutes, she popped her head up and listened. Nothing.

Good. Whoever it was, had given up.

Lorna yawned, too tired and drained emotionally to deal with the day. Just as she was starting to doze, the knocking came again, incessant and irritating.

She leapt from her bed, yanked off the bar and ripped open the door, prepared to give hell to whoever it was that insisted on disturbing her.

Jamie stared back at her with shock.

"Jamie," she gasped.

"What is wrong?" he asked, his face filled with concern.

"I'm in mourning," she said sardonically, turning away from him and going back to her bed, not caring at all that he'd followed her into her room and shut the door behind him.

Totally improper. But so was what they'd done in the orchard when she was betrothed to another man. What would Aunt Fiona say? Something about her being an immoral sinner.

'Twas enough to make her chuckle just before her head slipped beneath her pillows.

A blast of air hit her as Jamie plucked the pillows away. "What are ye mourning, lass?"

She rolled over, looking up at him and instantly remembering how he'd looked above her in the orchard the night before. Her body tingled, coming alive, and she felt her skin flush.

"Dinna look at me like that," Jamie said.

She raised a brow. "Like what?"

"As though ye wish me to make love to ye."

"But I do."

Jamie shook his head. "Ye spoke with your brother?"

Lorna looked away. "Aye."

"I take it, the conversation didna go well."

"Not at all."

He didn't look surprised.

"Did ye talk to Magnus, too?" Lorna asked.

Jamie turned from her and grabbed the chair she'd vacated earlier and tugged it over to the side of the bed. She propped onto her side to see him better.

"Aye."

"When will ye leave?" she asked, her eyes stinging with tears.

"Not without ye."

"How?"

"I dinna know yet, love, but I will figure it out. I canna live without ye."

"And I canna live without ye either."

Jamie sat forward, his elbows on his knees and he swiped his hands through his hair and then over his face. "Did he tell ye about your contract with MacKinnon?"

"Only that I have no choice but to follow it. Oh, Jamie! How can I ever go through with it? Especially after last night. I'll run away before I marry him." She swiped angrily at her tears. "I know he's not a bad man, nor has bad intentions, but I just canna. We are not meant to be together, MacKinnon and I."

"Ye dinna have to explain it to me, love." He reached forward and wiped at a tear, then planted a kiss on her forehead. "Your brother wishes he could break the contract. 'Twas signed by your parents and MacKinnon's, and now they are all gone—well, except his father

181

who's not in his right mind now anyway. Magnus and MacKinnon were simply following the edicts of those who ruled in the past."

"Then why doesn't he just break it?" she asked, exasperated.

"He's afraid that breaking it will ruin the decades old alliance that was formed." Jamie shook his head. "I've got to come up with an idea to help Magnus out of it. I swear it, if it takes me until the end of my days, I will."

"Oh, Jamie, would ye?" Lorna sat up now, launching herself into his arms.

"I will do my best. I'll be relentless. Ye have my word." He put his arms around her, burying his face in her hair.

Lorna closed her eyes, sinking into his embrace, wishing he could carry her away from Dunrobin today.

"One way or another we'll be together," Jamie said.

"Did ye tell him that ye wished to marry me?" she asked.

Jamie shook his head. "Magnus was in a foul mood, love, and practically tackled me with questions about whether or not I was staying away from ye as he'd warned me to. When I couldn't find ye all morning, I assumed your talk hadn't gone well, and I thought it best to speak with ye first before broaching it with Magnus."

Lorna nodded. "That was best, I think. 'Haps we can figure out a solution ourselves."

"I think we have one already," Jamie said, his fingers sliding over her hip and back to cup her behind. "I will confess to your brother that I've already claimed your virtue. He'll have no choice but to wed us."

Lorna pushed away, shaking her head. "Nay, not that way. I dinna want Magnus to be angry with me."

"Then we'll figure it out another way. One thing is for certain," Jamie said as he laid her down on the bed and pressed his body on top of hers. "Ye will be my wife. I love ye, and I'll never let another man have ye."

Saints! He'd said he loved her!

Lorna felt herself melt into the mattress, a puddle of emotion.

"I love ye so much."

"How did I ever get so lucky?" Jamie murmured against her lips.

Lorna had no chance to respond as he claimed her mouth in a torrid kiss, bringing about all the passion she'd felt the night before in the orchard. Her body remembered just as vividly as her mind how much pleasure he could bring her, and she in turn could give him.

Their kisses became frantic, their hands just as wild as they stroked each other, yanked at clothes. Lorna wrapped her hand around his thick arousal, feeling it pulse against her palm.

"Oh, saints, lass, I've never..." He didn't seem able to finish, for Lorna had started to stroke her hand up and down his length.

The feel of his silky steel in her hand was mesmerizing, filling her with a power she didn't know she could possess. With her touch she had rendered him immobile.

Well, not entirely. For not a moment later, she found herself completely flipped as Jamie rolled over and pulled her to straddle his hips. He settled the apex of her thighs over his turgid length and grinned up at her.

"Can we..." She raised a brow, feeling wicked and sensuous and totally desirable.

"Oh, aye, lass, we can. Let me show ye." Jamie's voice was thick with desire.

He slid his hands under her gown and up both of her thighs leaving goose flesh in his wake and making her shiver with anticipation. Her nipples strained the confines of her clothing, and she leaned forward, gripping the ties of his *leine* shirt. She tugged open his shirt and spread her hands over the warmth of his chest.

Jamie's hands touched her bare hips and he shifted beneath her, making her cry out at the movement of his erection against her hyper-sensitive center.

With his fingers dancing magic between her folds, Jamie leaned up on an elbow and captured her lips. Lorna rocked her hips back and forth in time with his fingers, amazed at how her body responded to him. She wanted him to feel just as wonderful. She slipped her hand between her thighs to find his shaft, but the fabric blocking her hand from feeling the silky smoothness started to irritate her.

She shoved his plaid up around his waist and sighed when her hand met the nakedness of his sex. Then she explored the length of him, the indentation at the tip, the ridges around the top. Ran her finger over a pulsing vein to the base, and then discovered something else. A soft sac. Jamie gasped when she cupped the sac, massaging the two orbs within. Touching him only heightened her own pleasure.

"I've got to have ye," Jamie growled against her lips, skimming lower to tease her nipple through her gown.

He pushed her hand from his shaft, replacing it with his own as he guided it to her entrance.

"Please," Lorna begged when he hesitated.

Jamie growled and thrust upward, filling her with intense pleasure. She arched her back, gripped tight to his shoulders, her head momentarily falling back.

"This feels good, too," she commented, completely mesmerized with this new way to make love.

"Damn good," Jamie agreed.

He tugged at her gown and chemise until one of her breasts popped free, then captured the stiffened nipple with his lips, sucking hard, as he drove up inside her again and again.

Lorna rocked back and forth, finding it awkward at first to match his rhythm, but within a few moments she'd found it—and it felt… wicked, and so incredibly amazing.

"Ye look like an angelic vixen when ye ride me," Jamie murmured.

Lorna opened her eyes and gazed down. Staring up at her was a vision that would keep her up at night, wishing she was tangled with him. His eyes were heavily lidded with desire, lips damp and curled in a mischievous grin, and cheeks slightly flushed. Looking at him made her shiver, had her nipples tightening all the more.

"Ye look like a wicked warrior bent on ravishing maidens." She grinned. "And I'm happy to be that maiden."

Jamie chuckled softly, then cupped the side of her face and leaned up to kiss her. Their tongues swirled and slid against each other, every breath taken ratcheting up their need another notch until they kissed with frenzied passion and their bodies rocked hard back and forth.

When the first twinings of release caught hold of Lorna, she grabbed onto his shoulders, her fingers wrenching his shirt into her curled fists and she moaned into his mouth, letting the pleasure take hold of her and push her off the abyss.

Jamie reacted to her climax with a fever of his own, fingers gripping tight to her right hip, and the other around the back of her neck, holding her mouth to his. Faster, harder he thrust. And then he was growling as his body trembled and quaked beneath her.

He collapsed backward, tugging her with him so they lay chest to chest, her head tucked against his shoulder, completely sated and ready for a nap.

And then her stomach growled again.

Jamie's chest rumbled against her cheek when he laughed. "I see in the future, I should have a feast prepared for each time we make love."

Lorna playfully slapped his shoulder. "Not a feast, a simple platter would do just fine."

"Let us sneak into the kitchens to see if we can find ye something to eat."

"Together?"

"Aye. Why not? Everyone will know soon enough that we mean to wed. I love ye, Lorna, and I've already made ye mine."

"I love ye, too." She kissed him quickly, then jumped from the bed to right her clothes.

Jamie did the same, and moments later they were sneaking toward the servants' stairs that led toward the kitchen.

'Twas only when they rounded the corner that Lorna caught sight of her aunt lurking in the hall. She opened her mouth to speak, but Aunt Fiona held her finger to her lips in gesture for her to remain quiet, and then turned from them.

Lorna's mouth fell open in shock. Her aunt's plan was all falling into place. And Lorna wasn't the least bit irritated with her for it. In fact, she was pretty darn smitten.

CHAPTER TWENTY

*W*hen Magnus asked Jamie to remain at Dunrobin an additional week to train his men in the ways of fighting with the English, Jamie couldn't resist the opportunity to stay on. Toby and Donald had been instrumental in that move, befriending many of the warriors and alluding to the fact that the English fought differently—which they did. Magnus' own men had approached him about the three of them staying just a bit longer.

Surprise was an understatement.

Jamie could tell the laird asked him to stay begrudgingly, but that didn't matter. Any extra time he could get with Lorna, Jamie would gladly take. He'd not been able to come up with a valid reason yet to push for their union and breaking with MacKinnon, and he was hoping inspiration would strike.

Over the past two days he'd trained the Sutherlands from morning until night, stealing moments between exercises to secretly court Lorna.

While the men took a break to clean and sharpen their weapons, Jamie had handed his off to Toby and then snuck away to the barn where the wool was stored. Lorna had told him to meet her there for a private picnic—and he hoped a tumble within the soft fur. He could not resist her.

The barn was situated well away from the men, and there was no need for any of the other clan members to enter, which was why they'd chosen the spot for the day. Up until then, they'd snuck into the orchards or one of their chambers, but with two near collisions with others which would have revealed their affair, neither of them was willing to risk losing a good thing, especially since Magnus had yet to find out and they were not ready to tell him. Over the past few days with the training, the Sutherland chief had grown to respect Jamie a great deal. It was only a matter of time before Jamie felt confidant Magnus would want to break the contract in favor of Jamie.

MacKinnon he would deal with when the time came.

Jamie circled around to the back of the barn and opened a single door that stood slightly ajar. Inside, the barn was dimly lit by shafts of golden light that came through the thatched roof and a few high, slim windows. Wool was stacked in sacks along the walls, and a large pile of yet to be sorted wool pooled in the middle—topped with what was enough to take a man's breath away.

Lorna lay gloriously naked upon a pile of freshly shorn wool. Her hair was spread out around her like a golden blanket, her creamy skin quickly flushed when their eyes locked. Two beautiful breasts topped with rose-colored nipples, already hard and taunting him. A flat, muscled belly led to the golden curls between her thighs. Thighs that he thoroughly enjoyed nibbling on. Thighs he wanted wrapped around him that very second.

"Ye're a vision lying there like that," he said, his voice coming out gruff.

Lorna grinned liked a wicked minx and crooked her finger at him. "Get undressed Montgomery, and come show your future wife exactly how much ye love her."

How could a man refuse a demand such as that?

Jamie quickly divested himself of his clothing and stalked toward her like a hunter on his prey. And he was more than ready to devour her. He knelt on the ground, parting her legs so that the pink petals of her sex were exposed to him. Already they glistened, making his cock stand on end, pulsing with the need to thrust inside her deliciously tight sheath.

Lorna reached out for him, but Jamie shook his head. There was something he'd been wanting to do to her since she took off her gown in the orchard.

"Nay. I'm going to make love to ye with my mouth."

"What?" She gasped and pushed up on her elbows, but Jamie ignored her.

He parted her legs further and dipped his face toward the sweet essence of her womanhood. As soon as his tongue flicked over the pearly bundle of nerves, Lorna fell back into the wool, a short gasp on her lips.

"Oh, my," she murmured, then moaned when he swirled his tongue around.

Jamie stroked his hands over her body, massaging her breasts, hips, thighs, all the while laving at her sensitive flesh. He flicked his tongue over the bud, fluttered in circles, thrust it inside her snug opening. He couldn't get enough of her, loved her scent, her taste and the way she was moaning with pleasure and raw abandon. Watching her face, eyes closed, lips parted, cheeks pink, he was enamored all the more with her. His cock was rigid as steel, and just from this act, he was close to spilling his seed.

Suddenly, Lorna arched her back, her hips bucking upward. Her sex fluttered around his tongue as she cried out. He continued to suck and nuzzle at her until the waves of her pleasure subsided. And then he could wait no longer. He crawled up the length of her body, gripped his cock and pressed the tip at her entrance. They locked eyes as he thrust inside her, both crying out at the sudden joining.

"What in bloody hell are ye doing to my sister!"

A bellow that Jamie would hear for a lifetime. He quickly pulled away from Lorna, and pushed her behind him, hiding her nakedness but not caring at all for his own.

Magnus stood at the back entrance of the barn, fury in every bunched muscle and his contorted features.

"Magnus, get out!" Lorna screeched.

"Like bloody hell I will." He stormed forward and Jamie leapt to his feet, continuing to block Lorna from her brother's view.

"Stay back, Magnus. Let your sister dress."

Magnus growled, but did still his steps and gave them his back. Behind him, Jamie heard Lorna gathering her clothing.

"Be quick about it, lass, else ye witness a murder," Magnus growled.

Jamie was certain the man meant every bit of his words, and he was prepared to fight. Though, he was naked and unarmed, Jamie would not back down from this.

Lorna thrust Jamie's plaid into his hand, and then stepped in front of him. But Jamie couldn't dress, not when she was trying to protect him. Besides, Magnus may have given his sister time to dress, but he would definitely not give Jamie the same courtesy.

"Wait, love," he murmured, trying to pull her back behind him.

But Lorna resisted, shaking her head stubbornly. Thrusting her chin up in the air, she stood off at her brother like a man facing down his enemy at war.

"Ye canna hurt him. He is the man I love, and we intend to wed."

Jamie gripped her arm, hoping to pull her away from her brother so that he could face him, explain that, aye, they'd not been smart about their love, but they were indeed true.

Magnus eyed Jamie's hand on Lorna's arm, and bared his teeth.

"Get. Out." Magnus spoke through clenched teeth to his sister, but his gaze never wavered on Jamie.

Jamie intended to protect Lorna and her virtue, no matter how naked he was. Before she could move, he stepped in front of her, prepared to face Magnus down.

"'Tis true, my laird, we plan to wed. My intentions are nothing but honorable where your sister is concerned."

Jamie wasn't certain how it was possible, but Magnus' face filled all the more with rage.

"Ye've defiled her. Ye've defiled my home. My family." His arms moved violently as he pointed to Lorna and toward the direction of the castle. "Ye will die here today." The man was so enraged spittle flew from his lips.

"Nay! Magnus, nay!" Lorna screeched.

But Magnus took Lorna by the arms, tossed her over his shoulder and marched toward the door. "Stay out." He set her down through the opened door and then shut it in her crying face, and that was the last straw for Jamie.

He rushed toward Magnus, intent on punishing the man for his cruel treatment of his woman, sister or nay. But Magnus heard him coming and whipped around punching him square in the gut. Jamie doubled over, glad the man hadn't aimed a few inches lower, else he'd be on the ground crying for certain.

"How dare ye come here and take my sister's honor!" Magnus raged.

He pummeled Jamie, coming at him like a man with murder as his only goal. He shouted insults, threats, and vicious names. Jamie blocked many of the hits, but in the end, he knew he deserved to have his arse handed to him by Lorna's brother. He should never have taken her innocence without being certain her contract with MacKinnon was broken and his own contract with her approved. Hell, with a punch to the jaw that he was sure left it dislocated, he conceded that he never should have looked at her at all. But the fact remained that he did, and he loved her fiercely.

Jamie did manage to get in a few good hits, but he just didn't feel right about it.

In the end, Magnus left him bloodied on the barn floor. With a final kick in his arse, the laird spat, "Put your bloody plaid back on and get your arse off my land."

"Not without Lorna," Jamie croaked, refusing to give in.

Magnus swung back and kicked him again. "Whether ye choose to or nay, ye'll be off my land within the quarter hour and *without* my sister."

Outside the barn, Jamie could hear Lorna's hysterical cries and they tugged at his heart. His own eyes filled with stinging angry, sad tears.

"Get dressed." Magnus didn't bother with any other parting words before he left the barn, kicking an apple—part of their picnic—toward Jamie.

Seeing that piece of fruit only broke his heart all the more. A few brisk words were said to Lorna by Magnus outside and her sobs ceased.

Jamie rushed to dress, wiping the blood from the cuts on his brow and lips. Already one eye was swollen shut. His ribs ached. His arse ached. Everything felt like it had been pummeled by a giant wielding a boulder. He shook his head, disappointed mostly with himself. There was no one else to blame, he'd brought this upon himself and Lorna.

When he exited the barn, Ronan stood—murder in his eyes— beside Toby and Donald.

"Best get moving afore I decide to take up where Magnus left off."

Jamie opened his mouth to protest, but Donald quickly stepped forward. "We'll be seeing him off ourselves."

Jamie searched the courtyard for Lorna with his one good eye as both of his men held onto his arms and tugged him toward the stables where his horse was already saddled. There was no sight of her. Not even a hint of her golden hair. He struggled with mounting his warhorse, but refused the help of his men, preferring the pain over appearing so weak in his already defeated position.

The courtyard was eerily empty when they reemerged from the stables, save for Magnus by the open gate.

"Tell Wallace I will still back his army, but I will never allow ye to lead my men." Sweet parting words.

"I will send for your sister," Jamie wheezed.

Magnus growled, but before he could pummel him some more, Toby grabbed hold of Jamie's reins and tugged him through the gate.

"Pardon my bluntness friend, but the lass is better off with ye alive than dead," Toby said out of earshot of Laird Sutherland. "Get back to Glasgow, complete this mission and then send for her. Donald and I will talk to MacKinnon, force him to give his blessing if we have to."

But Jamie didn't want them to force MacKinnon to do anything such as that. He wanted Lorna, but not in such a cowardly way. As soon as they reached Glasgow, he'd write a missive to Magnus apologizing for compromising his sister, but offering for her hand, postulating at his love for her. There need be no dowry if that made Magnus understand how deep Jamie's love went for Lorna. He'd take her with nothing, because he wanted to provide her with everything. He couldn't live without her.

Pain radiated deep in his chest, and it wasn't just the bruises he was sure already covered him, but his broken heart. Where had things gone so wrong? How could they have let their affair get so carried away? How could they have been so careless?

The only answer he had to that was that he'd been blinded by love. Blinded by his need for her. There'd never been any question over his intentions toward her. The moment he'd seen her riding her horse across the moors he'd decided she would be his. Hell, the moment he'd caught her fifteen years ago, he'd decided.

There was no world for Jamie without Lorna. No life worth living.

Whatever it took, he would have her as his wife. Even if he had to beg for her hand year after year until they both were grayed and shriveled. He'd never stop.

Lorna Sutherland would be his wife.

CHAPTER TWENTY-ONE

*L*orna was inconsolable.

All the clan had seen her rushed from the wool barn in a state of disheveled dress by her brother, tears streaming down her face. They'd all surely seen Jamie tossed from the land—which she hadn't. She'd not even been able to say good bye to the man she loved.

Magnus had taken that from her. Beat him to a bloody pulp. She'd not been able to watch, but she'd heard the beating all the same. When Ronan had rushed to her he'd tried to force her away, but she'd refused. In the end he'd had to hold her back, kept her within his comforting embrace the duration until Magnus came out and ordered her to her chamber.

She was to be confined to her bedchamber. Though he'd not said it yet, she knew how her brother worked. He'd inform the MacKinnon that a match was not to be made and then he'd ship her off to convent, shaming her and never speaking to her again.

What she'd done would be inexcusable in his eyes. He didn't understand love. Didn't understand the melding of two hearts or the uncontrollable need to be in a lover's arms. Magnus was cold inside, and while she wished her brother would find love, she was starting to think he was incapable of it. Not after the news of him sending her off as a trade for wool and then the way he'd treated Jamie.

If it had been any other man and she was just having a torrid liaison, that was one thing, but that was the furthest thing from their minds. What she and Jamie had was beautiful. What they did together was beautiful.

Jamie had told Magnus he wanted to marry her. Had made every attempt to secure her honor, but Magnus had tossed her out of the barn like she was a whore rutting with every warrior that came in her path.

Lorna threw herself onto her bed, heard the click of the lock on the outside of the door and knew that Ronan had been ordered to do so by Magnus. Probably to keep her from running away after Jamie.

"I'm sorry, Lorna," Ronan called through the door.

"Dinna bother," she screeched back, anger and pain taking hold of her anew. She picked up the closest object to her—her wash basin—and chucked it at the door.

The clay piece shattered on the spot, falling to the floor. She'd liked that bowl, too!

Lorna thrust her face into her pillow and sobbed, feeling nauseous and full of righteous pain.

How dare Magnus!

The happiest moments of her life had been in the last month of being acquainted with Jamie. And he'd taken all that away from her.

A soft scratching sounded at the door. Probably Heather or her maid. Maybe even Aunt Fiona as the woman had seemed to come around lately. She ignored them. But the scratching persisted.

"Go away! I'm locked in here like a prisoner anyway so it's not as though I can open the door."

"Are ye all right?" It was Heather. She sounded scared.

And if anyone had judged what had happened just by the looks of things, they might have thought Jamie took her violently, but that was anything but the case, and she didn't want her little sister to worry over such a detail.

So, instead of ignoring her questions, Lorna wailed, "Magnus sent my love away!"

There was silence on the other side of the door for a while and Lorna thought that her sister might have left. Then her voice sounded through the door again. "Want me to steal the key and arrange for a horse?"

Lorna couldn't help but give a bitter laugh. "Oh, but I wish ye would."

"I would, Lorna. I will. Tell me aye and I'll leave now to find Ronan. He gives me everything I want. I'll convince him I need to give ye some tea."

'Twas a good idea, but Lorna knew without a doubt, she'd never make it through the gate without getting caught. "I thank ye, dear sister, but I do not think it will work."

"I'm so sorry."

Lorna wished she could open the door just to give her sister a hug. There was always the two of them, and even though Heather was a complete hellion, she loved her all the same.

"Ye have nothing to be sorry for. 'Tis my fault." And while she blamed Magnus for his reaction, she knew deep down that it was her fault.

When she'd gone to Magnus and begged him not to make her marry MacKinnon and that she was in love with another, she should have told him it was Jamie when he asked. For he had asked, and she'd refused to answer. This entire mess could have been avoided if she'd simply told him the truth and proclaimed that she'd not marry anyone but Jamie. If Magnus was simply looking for an alliance to strengthen the clan, then Jamie was the best choice, for he had a seat on the Bruce's council and the ear of the future king.

Oh, what shame! Her face burned with it, but even knowing that all the clan had to be talking about her loss of virtue, what hurt the most was the loss of Jamie. How was she going to get to him, or he to her?

She'd not give up. She'd not let her brother ship her off to a convent never to be seen again. Nay. The nearest window would be where she'd toss herself if all else failed, for she could never live without Jamie in her life.

"Could ye get Aunt Fiona for me?" The woman had been on her side before. Had wanted her to marry Jamie.

Maybe she could convince Magnus that though they'd made the wrong choices in bedding each other, that they were in love and a good match.

"Aye, I bet she can talk some sense into Magnus," Heather said.

And for once, Lorna was actually looking forward to her aunt convincing Magnus of something where she was concerned. A circumstance she would have laughed at months ago.

Lorna sat up and wiped away her tears. Enough crying. This would work out. It had to. And she had to be strong if she was going to make certain that it did.

A WEEK LATER, WITH BRUISES THAT WERE NOW MOSTLY YELLOW, JAMIE nudged his horse under the wide gates of Glasgow Castle.

Not only was his brother there to greet him, but a few members of the council—thankfully not Ross—and William Wallace himself.

"Damn, brother, looks as though your mission beat the piss out of ye."

Jamie grunted. "Ye could say 'twas something like that."

"What happened?"

Jamie dismounted, handing the reins off to his groomsmen and glanced over at Toby and Donald. "I'd probably be dead if it weren't for those two."

"A woman," Wallace said right away as though he could see right into Jamie's mind.

He gritted his teeth.

When Toby and Donald didn't say anything, Malcolm's eyes widened.

"Ye got your arse kicked over a woman?"

Jamie nodded. "Dinna ask."

"Och, ye canna come home covered in cuts and bruises and not expect to tell us the story," Wallace said.

Just then MacKinnon came from the stables. "Thought I heard voices," he called as he headed toward them. "Welcome back, my laird."

"Uh, well if ye dinna mind, my laird, I think Toby and I ought to be seeing to our families," Donald said, suddenly looking extremely uncomfortable.

Jamie turned around to ask what he meant, given the two of them were not married, nor did their parents live, and out of eight combined siblings, none resided at Glasgow. But the two were off at the first sight of MacKinnon. Bastards, Jamie thought with a chuckle.

Malcolm, too, noticed the odd timing and looking from Jamie to MacKinnon, but Wallace was none the wiser.

"Laird Montgomery, 'tis good to see ye." MacKinnon held out his hand.

Jamie stared at it, unsure of what he should do. He'd cuckolded the man. Been caught with his arse up in the air and his cock inside the man's betrothed. Word had not yet reached Glasgow, but it would any day now.

But a head of red curls caught his attention. "What is Ceana doing here?" Jamie asked.

Sadness fell over Malcolm's countenance. "Her husband was killed in a fight."

"A battle?" What all had happened while he was gone?

Malcolm shook his head. "Nay. A fight. Seems the man was a right ornery bastard. With no issue, she was allowed to return home."

Ceana retreated into the gardens, not having noticed him. He'd have to talk with her later.

"I say, Montgomery, ye look like hell. Was it the English?" MacKinnon broke in.

Jamie swallowed back the knot of irritation in his throat and stared at the man who had no idea why Jamie would be so cross with him.

"'Twas over a woman," Wallace boasted. "I bet I know who, too.

One of the reasons I sent ye on the mission was my hope the two of ye would rekindle. I'd heard of her spirit and knew ye'd be the right man to tame her. Guess ye tamed her too well."

Jamie raised a brow. What the hell was Wallace talking about?

The warrior elbowed Malcolm. "I gave up on love a long time ago after…well, ye know. But I could nay allow your brother to forsake love. He's become such an arsehole. Needs the touch of a woman."

"Who's the lucky lady?" MacKinnon asked. "And ye must tell us about the arse whooping ye got for it."

Jamie ignored them all, changing the subject. "I must speak with ye about a member of the council. In fact, I'm glad MacKinnon is here, 'tis he who shared the details with me," Jamie said to Wallace.

"Och, we've already had that conversation," MacKinnon said.

"Dinna hold out on us brother," Malcolm said.

Jamie couldn't take it. He had to get away from them. He'd not tell them who it was, not in front of MacKinnon and not until he'd had a chance to write a series of letters to Sutherland begging for Lorna's hand.

Damn, but staring the man in the eye whose bride he'd stolen made him feel like warmed over shite.

"The suspense is killing me," Wallace said. "Come now. Did ye see Lorna Sutherland?"

Jamie stilled, his blood going cold, teeth clenching. How had Wallace guessed? Lord, but he'd been harboring the hope in his mind Wallace meant someone else entirely.

Behind him he heard MacKinnon say, "Lorna?"

There was an indrawn breath, he wasn't certain whose, but when he turned around, MacKinnon looked ready to kill him.

"What's he talking about?" The northern laird glared glacial spears at Jamie.

"I rescued Lorna Sutherland fifteen years ago."

"During the attack on her parents and brother Blane?" MacKinnon asked.

"Aye," Jamie said curtly.

"So, ye've a history with the Sutherlands?"

"Aye."

"I think it best ye tell us what happened to your face." MacKinnon's tone was deadly serious, and it didn't seem that Jamie would be walking away as easily as he pleased.

That being the case, Jamie still didn't think it best at all to discuss it. Malcolm moved to stand beside his brother, perhaps certain there would be a fight at any moment.

"'Tis a matter I'd rather not discuss." Ever.

"Considering Lorna Sutherland is the woman I am betrothed to, *I* think it *best*." MacKinnon was fairly seething as he spoke through gritted teeth.

Jamie looked for any reason to stall this conversation. "I'll meet with ye all in my library after I've had a chance to clean myself of travel dust."

MacKinnon looked as though he wished to argue, but in the end conceded.

Jamie gave curt nods to all the men and then headed into the castle, as he did so, he spotted Ceana again, and she was looking past him to the trio of men he'd just left. MacKinnon was staring back.

Was it possible…?

Jamie shook his head. Nay. Ceana had just been widowed and MacKinnon seemed quite angry about hearing the possibility that Jamie had dallied with Lorna. But, damn if his eyes weren't seeing things. For it looked as though Ceana and MacKinnon gazed at each other with the same intensity he felt for Lorna.

CHAPTER TWENTY-TWO

*T*wo months passed and Magnus would not relent. No matter what Lorna said, nor Heather, nor Aunt Fiona—and even Ronan had started to beg on her behalf.

Word soon came that MacKinnon had heard of the relationship between the two of them and was breaking the betrothal. Magnus flew into a rage. Not because of the broken betrothal, but because MacKinnon was actually pushing for Jamie and Lorna to be together *and* he'd agreed to purchase the three sacks of wool that were to be part of her dowry.

Magnus didn't let her read the letter, nor did he give her the details, but it was enough to enrage him all the more that everyone was on Jamie and Lorna's side.

Lorna no longer participated in clan activities. She barely ate. Barely slept.

She kept to herself most all the day, unless Aunt Fiona or Heather forced themselves within the room. Ronan came by and tried to entice her out for a ride on Angel, but not even a ride on the heath could make her leave her room and her perpetual state of mourning.

Heather wrote letters to Jamie, begging him not to forsake her, declaring her love, and praying he'd be patient until Magnus accepted them. She paid the messengers double their usual fee to sneak the letters out without Magnus any wiser to the fact.

Jamie's replies were just as gut-wrenching to Lorna, filled with love and finally an explanation as to MacKinnon's easy release of the contract—he, too, had fallen for another. In fact, he was courting Jamie's sister Ceana. A marriage was planned close to Samhain, when Jamie felt it wouldn't be looked upon oddly for her to marry so quickly after the loss of her husband.

The alliance between the MacKinnon clan and the Sutherlands was still strong. Unbroken.

Why, then, was her brother being so damn stubborn?

Was he so deeply against love that he would make Lorna suffer for believing in it?

Or was he completely filled with rage at how she'd gone behind his back and claimed Jamie for her own when he'd made other plans?

On the other hand, she was certain part of his anger came from having the visions of her and Jamie making love stuck in his mind. She certainly wouldn't want to see any of her brothers making love. It was an image that may give him night terrors.

That thought always made her laugh. Her brother was acting a fool, however, and she had to find a way to make him see reason.

That reasoning came rather quickly—in the form of several bouts of nausea which resulted in a trip to the chamber pot morning after morning. Finally, on the third day, her maid wiped Lorna's brow, and looked her in the eye.

"My lady... I dinna know the details of... ye and Laird Montgomery, but is it possible ye may be with child?"

Lorna stared at Bea a long moment, thinking back over the months. She'd not bled since making love to Jamie. That was at least three months prior. Pressing her fingers to her lips, a triumphant smile tugged.

"My lady?"

"Aye, Bea, I think I might be." She covered her lower abdomen with her hands. Her belly had just the slightest, ever so subtle, bulge. Not enough that she'd noticed before, and not enough that anyone would have taken note.

Inside her grew a child. Her and Jamie's child. A child born of love.

"Send Aunt Fiona to me," Lorna said.

"Let me dress ye first?" Bea asked.

Lorna nodded and let her maid fuss about her, fixing her hair and changing her gown, tidying up her room and then the woman gasped. "Ye need to break your fast! How could I have gone about this and that when ye needed to give that bairn sustenance?"

Lorna waved her hand in dismissal. "'Tis nothing so much as that. I just finished upending my belly. I needed a little time to quell it. But I find I am rather famished now."

"I'll go and have a tray sent up and then find your aunt."

"Thank ye."

While Bea left the room, Lorna couldn't stop staring at her belly in wonder. A secret smile curled her lips. It would seem her cloud of gray was finally lifting allowing a stream of perfect golden light to shine on her. She finally had a reason to go to Jamie that Magnus couldn't ignore. Finally a way they could be married that Magnus could not deny.

She was with child! Rubbing an excited hand over her belly, she glanced up at the ceiling and gave a prayer of thanks. Never had an unmarried, unbetrothed lady been so ecstatic for the fact.

"Ye're what?" Magnus bellowed, shaking the rafters above her head.

Lorna sat in his library, though she was antsy enough that at any moment she was likely to bounce right out of her chair. Beside her sat Aunt Fiona who'd supported her entirely, and broached the topic with Magnus.

"I am with child," Lorna repeated for what had to be the fifth time.

Magnus raked angry hands through his hair and stormed back and forth across his office like a cranky stallion about to kick anyone in his path.

"Montgomery's child," he stated.

Lorna nodded, no longer feeling the need to voice the fact.

"The bastard!"

"Magnus, if ye will please refrain from such language in the presence of ladies," Aunt Fiona scolded. Despite her frown at Magnus, each time her aunt looked Lorna's way, she smiled.

She'd confessed to Lorna that though she'd gone about things in a backward way, Fiona was indeed happy for her.

Magnus turned, his lips in a snarl and Lorna was quite certain whatever was about to come out of his mouth was not going to be nice. Time for her to intervene before their aunt—who'd supported her so wholly—got her feelings hurt.

Lorna stood, and walked around her brother's desk until she stood in front of him.

She grasped Magnus' hands in hers and stared into his eyes. "I know things have not turned out the way ye envisioned. That ye wanted more than anything never to see or hear Jamie's name again. But we love each other, brother. And we've created a life together. We deserve to be together and for our child to take his or her rightful place as heir to his seat."

When Magnus didn't respond, Lorna continued, "'Tis still a good match. An excellent match. Ye now have an ally that is on the royal council. Close with Wallace and the Bruce. What greater man could there be for me? He loves me Magnus, and he'll take care of me and the child. Please, I beg ye, let me marry him. If for nothing else than to reinstate my honor and make an honest woman of me."

Magnus' eyes softened at that. "Ye do deserve to have honor, for ye are one of the most honorable and courageous women I've ever met."

Lorna's smile widened. "Let me marry him."

Her brother's shoulders sagged, and then he tugged her in for a hug. "Our parents are rolling in their graves at what ye've done."

Aunt Fiona cleared her throat, and they both turned to see her sitting with a brow raised and that odd smile on her lips, like she held a great secret. "I beg to differ with ye, dear nephew. As I recall, ye were nicely warmed inside your mother's womb afore she and your father wed."

Magnus' mouth fell open and his arms dropped from around Lorna. "What? How could ye say such a thing."

Aunt Fiona shrugged daintily. "Because 'tis true."

Lorna started to laugh. She laughed so hard tears came to her eyes and she doubled over, causing both Fiona and Magnus to fuss over the child within her womb, each of them certain her laughter had to be doing the bairn harm.

But Lorna didn't care. She ran to the window, looked up at the beautiful summer sky and shouted, "Thank ye Father and Mother!"

Then she whipped around toward her brother. "Send a missive, for we leave at first light."

"My laird, a messenger has arrived to see ye."

"Send him in," Jamie said, staring at the stone wall of his office.

It would only be another return of the letter he'd sent Magnus, he was certain. The man never replied, only had his scrolls returned with a word from the messenger that his letters were to cease immediately. That didn't deter Jamie, but he was starting to wear down emotionally. He'd never stop wanting Lorna, never stop loving her, but he did wonder if they'd ever be given the chance to marry before Magnus was an old man.

The messenger was showed into his library and handed him the scroll. Jamie set it on his desk and waved the man away.

"My laird?"

He flicked his gaze back to the messenger who was covered in sweat and dirt for having ridden hard.

"Aye?" Jamie's tone came out gruff. Something that had started to happen far too often these days. He couldn't seem to shake off the anger, and only endless hours of work helped to stave his need to pummel Magnus to the ground.

"Laird Sutherland bade me tell ye the message is urgent."

At that, Jamie sat forward, shredding the wax seal. The man had actually written him back?

Jamie skimmed the letter once, disbelieving what he was seeing. He read it three more times before he completely understood.

Montgomery,

It seems your prayers have been answered, for not only did ye defile my innocent sister, but ye impregnated her. We shall arrive at Glasgow within a week's time. Be prepared to wed her immediately, else answer to me.

Let it be known, my agreement to the two of ye being joined in holy matrimony is not forgiveness for your sins, but I wish to restore honor to my sister's name, and see her happy.

Sutherland

Jamie leapt from his chair and bellowed a victory cry so loud it startled several birds that'd made their homes in the rafters.

Lorna and he would be wed! Lorna was with child. Such elation filled him that Jamie could barely contain himself. He ran to the window and glanced out to the courtyard below.

"Prepare, all of ye! For your new mistress comes soon!"

He gripped the messenger by the shoulders and shook him and then ran from his office in search of his housekeeper. Preparations needed to be made. Food for feasting obtained. Linens prepared.

He was to be a father!

By the time he reached the bottom of the stair, he pressed his hand to the wall, a sudden bout of dizziness coming over him.

"Are ye all right, brother?"

Ceana's footsteps were soft as she made her way over to him.

"Aye, perfect." But still the dizziness wouldn't pass.

He was to be a father… Lorna was with child. And she had so far to travel, and the roads were full of heathens.

He sat heavily on the stairs and looked up at Ceana, as beautiful as their mother had been.

"What's happened?" she asked.

"Magnus consented."

"Lorna is coming? Ye are to wed?" Ceana clapped her hands together a happy smile curling her lips. "Oh, how wonderful! We've a wedding to plan!"

"Aye, we do at that."

Ceana sat down beside him. "Why do ye not seem happy? I thought this was what ye wanted."

Jamie shook his head. "Aye, 'tis what I want. But I worry about her traveling so far with the bairn and the Sassenachs upon the road, and all the outlaws. Sutherland didn't mention how many guards he'd have sent with her."

"Wait," Ceana said. "Bairn? She already has a child? How long were ye dallying with her, brother?"

Jamie shook his head, a loony sort of laugh escaping his lips. "Nay, not a bairn yet out of the womb. She carries my child."

"Oh, I see." Ceana smiled all the more and tucked her arm around his at the elbow. "All will be well. Send your men out to clear the roads. Do ye know when she is coming?"

"The missive said a week."

"Plenty of time. We shall have your room redecorated, and a wedding prepared for her. Your Lorna shall not want for anything."

Jamie planted a kiss on his sister's head. "What would I do without ye?"

"Och, ye got along well enough without me, didna ye? I mean, look at the particulars—ye stole another man's bride, and got her with child, an act of which her brother witnessed, and ye came home still alive after the fact. A success, nay?"

Jamie laughed. "Ye tease me mercilessly."

"Aye, and I will until we are old and wrinkled, brother. Besides, the way I look at it is this—if ye hadna dallied with the Sutherland lass, I'd not have found my own love."

"MacKinnon."

"Aye, he is a dream to me."

"I'm sorry your first marriage was not so pleasing. If I'd known the man was a bastard I could have tried to put a stop to it."

Ceana shrugged and waved her hand in dismissal. "'Tis nay matter. If I'd not been married to him, I would have been married to someone else, who may still be alive, and then I never would have met Gabriel."

"Then I suppose in the end all of us do win."

"Aye. I canna wait to meet her."

"Ye will love her."

"I'm certain of it."

Jamie stood, his dizziness gone, and once again triumph and joy filled his blood. Damn, but he couldn't wait to hold his woman in his arms again.

CHAPTER TWENTY-THREE

*T*he ride to Dunrobin was treacherous and laboriously long. It seemed every five minutes Lorna had to stop to relieve herself, or vomit, or scarf down whatever food her brother stuffed into her waiting hands. She felt like an invalid, completely out of her own control. And yet, through it all, she was ecstatic. She'd go through any amount of discomfort in order to be with Jamie again.

Before they'd left, Aunt Fiona had promised that in a month's time, the vomiting would at least cease, but given her huge appetite before, that increase was unlikely to fade, and well, with a bairn sitting on her bladder, even if it was pint sized she didn't think her runs for relief would ebb either.

She'd hugged Ronan and Heather good bye, promising to visit come the spring after she'd recovered from giving birth, and begged them to tell Blane she loved him.

Magnus was ornery the entire ride, especially when they'd encountered a band of English knights. She'd stayed hidden in the woods while they dispatched of the men, quite easily. She smiled with pride, knowing that part of their success was due to the training Jamie had given them. But the encounter utterly troubled Magnus.

After that, they'd traveled through the night and slept during the day, a change that messed harshly with Lorna's countenance the first two days, after which she seemed to grow used to it.

But now they were nearly there, Magnus had let her stop at a trickling burn in order to wash up and change into a gown of light blue and a matching cloak. Within the hour, she would be in Jamie's arms again. Her heart leapt at the thought, and she turned grateful eyes on her brother.

"Thank ye, Magnus."

Magnus looked sternly at her, though for all his bluster, she knew that beneath, he was still her loving brother.

"Dinna thank me," he said through clenched teeth. "Ye already compromised yourself."

Lorna worked hard not to laugh at his attempts to scold her. He'd never condone aloud what had happened, but she knew he'd forgiven her some days before, maybe even weeks. She smiled and batted her lashes. "Ye will see one day, brother, that even though ye're Laird Sutherland, love will come up to catch ye in its grasp."

"I dinna think so."

Lorna prayed that one day Magnus would open his heart, for she couldn't imagine him living the rest of his life as hard as he'd lived the first twenty-nine. He had a lot of heart, a lot to give, if only he'd allow himself. More likely than not, a lass would have to steal away her brother's heart before he was aware he'd given it.

"We shall see," Lorna said. But when she noticed her brother was no longer beside her, panic welled in her chest.

She wrenched around in her saddle to see what kept him, the move alerting her that once more she needed to make use of a private bush. He'd stilled his horse and looked ready to bolt. Oh, nay, not on his life!

"Magnus..." Her tone held a warning note. One he'd better know meant she was about to completely explode.

He nudged his warhorse forward. Thank the saints, because it was too late to turn back now. She'd rather complete the journey on her own—and she would. Angel had a good amount of energy left in her to bolt forward from the wretched lot of them if it came down to it.

Besides, they were nearly upon Glasgow Castle. No doubt a scout had already returned word to Jamie of their approach. Her heart seized once more. She'd hold her bladder. It had been a lifetime since she'd seen Jamie. Zounds, but couldn't they ride any faster? Though she supposed riding faster would dirty her gown—and would probably not be good for the bairn. As it was, her muscles ached from their journey, and she was so exhausted she could sleep for a week if they'd let her. In a soft bed. With Jamie's arms wrapped around her.

Far in the distance, she could see the towers of Glasgow Castle rising above the forest.

"Magnus! There 'tis! That's the castle, is it not?"

"I believe so," he grumbled.

She frowned at him. While she'd found his foul mood to be quite comedic the majority of their journey, she could no longer abide it. Sometimes, it was necessary for a big grumpy grouch to be nice, no matter his sour feelings.

"Ye'd best quite your frowning. This is a happy day for me, no matter how ye feel about it. Show me some support, brother. I'd hate to remember one of the happiest days of my life as one of the worst for ye."

Magnus glanced over at her, apology in his eyes. "I'll try."

That was good enough for her. She smiled, then turned her gaze back to the crenellations she could barely make out above the trees and watched as they grew closer and closer. Butterflies flew and wiggled in her belly, and her breath came quick.

About an hour or so later—and a reluctant stop on her part to squat behind a bush—their horses' footsteps echoed joyously over the wooden bridge covering the moat at the castle. Each clop shouted their arrival and the triumph that Lorna felt at finally being given her wish. It was just after noon and the sun blazed in the sky, glinting off the shields of the men standing atop the main gate tower. She searched their faces, recognizing Toby who nodded in her direction.

Magnus raised his hand. "Laird Sutherland to see Montgomery."

The gate doors opened allowing them entrance. Lorna beamed at her new home and then spotted Jamie standing tall and proud in the center of the courtyard. Her breath lodged in her throat, stomach plummeted. His smile was glorious as he locked his gaze on hers. Then he turned to her brother and nodded.

"I didna think ye'd keep your word," Jamie said to Magnus as they entered the bailey.

He was just as handsome as Lorna remembered, if slightly altered, a reminder of how much time they'd spent apart. The summer sun had put streaks of auburn in his dark hair, and he'd grown a short beard. Jamie gave Magnus a wide, arrogant, grin before he turned to wink at Lorna, making her heart skip a beat.

Lorna couldn't help the squeal of delight at seeing him. Not waiting for anyone to help her dismount, she swung her leg over the side and jumped down from Angel. As soon as her feet hit the ground she was running. Meeting Jamie halfway, she leapt into his arms.

She kissed all over his face, ran her hands through his hair, and finally, at long last, their lips crashed together in a fiery kiss she might have been embarrassed to display in front of everyone, except for the fact that she was too overjoyed and filled with need to care. She was home! She was with Jamie!

Love flowed from every pore in her body, entangling with Jamie's own outpouring. They whispered words of love, of how much they'd missed each other, of how their prayers had been answered, of how they'd never leave each other's sides.

Behind her, Magnus growled, but she ignored him. She'd not let anything ruin her joyous reunion.

"We'll be on our way now," Magnus said gruffly, having not bothered to dismount.

Lorna turned around, a scowl on her face. "Ye would not stay to see me married?"

"Come, Sutherland. The priest is ready and a feast prepared. I would have ye here to give us your blessing, then ye can be on your way. But I warn ye, word is that the English are marching on Stirling. Wallace and his men have already deployed," Jamie said, and she squeezed his hand tighter for having offered his support.

"Och, I dinna care a fig about the English," Magnus said. But then his eyes caught hers and that look he'd given her so many times, the one that said he was sorry and cherished her crossed his countenance. "We will stay for the wedding, but not the feast. We must return to the Highlands."

Lorna wished he'd stay longer, but she was happy he would at least remain to see her wed.

"I'll have my cook pack your men a feast to go then," Jamie said.

Magnus grunted his approval.

A few grooms appeared at their sides. Magnus and his retainers dismounted allowing the grooms to take the horses to the stables to be brushed down, fed and watered.

Jamie whispered into her ear, "I have missed ye more than ye know. I thought I'd live forever mourning the loss of ye. I can hardly believe ye're here. I love ye so much."

"Oh, Jamie," she said. "I love ye more than life itself."

"Let's get married, love."

"Aye, let's do it now afore Magnus changes his mind," she giggled.

"Och, let him brood, he'll never be able to tear ye from my arms now."

Lorna giggled and squeezed Jamie tight around the waist, feeling the muscles ripple beneath her fingertips.

"Ye can divest yourselves of your weapons before entering the chapel," Jamie said, eyeing Magnus with suspicion. It wasn't a suggestion.

Magnus slowly grinned. "Ye think we came prepared to battle ye?"

"The thought did cross my mind. After all, I did—"

Lorna gasped, and whipped a warning gaze at Jamie. He was baiting her brother, the devil.

Magnus held up his hand. "Dinna say it. I already know what ye did to my sister. I was there if ye recall, and I gave ye more than a bloody lip, too. All that matters is ye intend to marry her and honor her. That ye'll take care of the babe ye created." He fingered the dirk at his side and his small targe shield, making Lorna wonder if her brother would try another challenge like he'd done at Dunrobin. "We are always prepared for an ambush, especially with the Sassenachs crawling all over the land."

Lorna breathed a sigh of relief. Magnus signaled his men and they divested themselves of their weapons, tossing them in a pile on the courtyard ground. Swords, axes, maces, dirks, and battered targes.

"Impressive," Jamie quipped.

"We are always thorough," Magnus said with an arrogant chuckle.

Lorna rolled her eyes at their immature displays of manly pride.

"Indeed. I will keep that in mind." Jamie stepped forward and offered Magnus his arm.

Magnus stared at Jamie's outstretched arm for the span of several agonizing heartbeats. She so wanted them to get along. She flicked her gaze up at Jamie and couldn't help the utter joy at finally being in Glasgow, and the smile that filled her face was full and genuine.

When Jamie moved forward she saw that Magnus had reached out his hand and grasped Jamie's forearm, shaking it in a show of respect and allegiance.

Lorna beamed at him, and for the first time in weeks, Magnus smiled. Without a second thought, she left Jamie's side for a second, to hug her brother tight.

"Thank ye, Magnus," she whispered.

"Och, dinna thank me, sister, I but wanted to see ye happy. 'Tis all I've ever really wanted." And then he was pushing her back toward Jamie, where she belonged.

She gripped her intended's hands, filled with excitement, and a little nausea.

"Let us go to the chapel," Magnus said gruffly.

"Aye, let us go," Jamie said, looking down at Lorna and kissing her once more with a fire that heated her blood and made her go weak in the knees.

In just a few moments time, she would be Lady Montgomery.

At last.

CHAPTER TWENTY-FOUR

*W*hile the rest of the Montgomery clan, council members, Wallace, Malcom, Ceana and MacKinnon, were dancing and feasting to their hearts contents, Jamie yearned for a feast of another kind. He could no longer wait to have his bride all to himself.

"Let's disappear," he whispered in her ear, gripping onto her hand.

Lorna smiled and nodded. They glanced around the room, and thinking that no one would notice them, they slowly headed toward the door of the great hall and the stairs.

"The Laird and Lady Montgomery wish to go to bed!" shouted Wallace, always vigilant and never missing a beat.

Jamie groaned. He knew what was coming next. They would try to lift them up into the air and carry them upstairs. They'd want a first-hand view of the consummation, but Jamie wasn't about to let that happen. Lorna was his and his alone.

He swept her up into his arms and ran for the door. They ducked through and then he took the stairs two at a time, barely noticing the extra weight of her in his arms. She giggled the whole way, and when they reached his chamber he shoved open the door and kicked it closed. Footsteps echoed on the stairs.

"They're relentless," he muttered. He set Lorna down and then barred the door. "But they'll not be allowed entry this night, or any other."

"Oh, how romantic," Lorna exclaimed behind him.

Jamie turned around to see what she was talking about, his eyes lighting on all the feminine, romantic touches.

"Stunning. Ceana has been busy," Jamie said.

Upon the table below the window that had been opened letting in a wonderful summer breeze and giving them a perfect view of the moon, was a jug of wine, two new goblets engraved with an L and a J, a platter of cheese, fruit and bread and another of sweets. The bed covers were pulled back, folded at the base of the bed and flower petals were strewn on the sheets. On either bedside table, was a bowl full of apples.

When Lorna caught sight of the apples she whirled around. "Did ye tell her?"

Jamie felt a sheepish smile touch his lips. "Ceana asked. It was an evening in which she was particularly filled with sorrow and we shared many intimate secrets."

Lorna nodded, not showing the least bit of upset about it, instead she displayed understanding. "I canna imagine being widowed at her age, even if the man was not right in the head. At least now she's found peace with MacKinnon." A bright smile covered her face. "A fact that has helped us greatly."

"Indeed it has." Jamie grinned and came forward wrapping his arms around Lorna and pulling her into his embrace.

"I've been waiting what seems like forever to hold ye in my arms."

Lorna slid her hands up his back, massaging along his spine as she pressed her face against his chest. "It felt like a lifetime. I still find myself looking at ye and disbelieving I'm here, and then it hits me and a shiver steals up my spine. Excitement beyond belief keeps my face in a forever smile."

"Och, love," Jamie said, slinging his arm around her shoulder. "I feel much the same way. These last months were torture. I find myself looking at ye every moment to be sure ye're really here." He placed a gentle kiss on her forehead. "Do ye want some wine?"

She looked up at him, her green-blue eyes suddenly clouded with desire. "Wine can wait, Jamie, but I dinna think that I can."

Out in the corridor, the crowd had finally made it to their door, and the hammering of fists and shouts for entrance came. Jamie was about to tell them all to bugger off when he heard Malcolm's voice booming for the lot of the rats to leave them be. Several grumbles were heard, a few bawdy taunts and then their retreating footsteps. Jamie and Lorna smiled at each other as they waited for the voices to recede and then finally, there was silence.

Taking a step away from him, Lorna untied the Montgomery sash from her waist that he'd given her during their wedding ceremony and dropped it on the chest that stood at the end of the bed.

"Are ye certain ye dinna need wine?"

Lorna laughed. "Are ye nervous, Jamie?"

"Nay, lass, not in the least."

"Neither am I, and as I said afore, wine can wait, but my body burns for ye." She tugged at the sleeve of her gown.

"Och, lass, I'm so glad ye said that, for mine does the same." And he was going to undress her this time.

Jamie stepped forward and turned Lorna around, swiping her long plait aside to place a heated kiss on the side of her neck. He breathed in her scent, always intoxicating.

"I love ye," he whispered, surprised at how much he really did. Never in his life had he thought he'd be where he was, and he was damn glad. There was no going back.

"I love ye, too," she said, reaching up to stroke the back of his head.

Jamie slowly undressed her, kissing her from head to toe and back again. Savoring the changes in her body, the slight swell of her belly, her fuller breasts, curvier hips. She was beautiful before, but carrying his bairn… He couldn't quite figure out what it was, other than the fact that they'd create a life inside her body that made him desire her all the more. On his knees he pressed his face her belly, kissed her there.

Lorna's abdomen trembled at his touch, and she ran her fingers through his hair, looking down at him with a mixture of love and longing.

She toyed with the ties of his *leine* shirt, and then went about undressing him much the same way. Kissing each of his knees, she worked her way up until she reached his engorged shaft. Jamie nearly choked when she took it in her grasp and gazed up at him with mischievous eyes. Then she was kissing him and his own eyes rolled into the back of his head.

Untrained, aye, she was, but it didn't matter, her velvet hot mouth was sweet heaven as she kissed, licked, sucked his turgid flesh. Ecstasy consumed him until he was on the verge of exploding. Jamie pulled her away, unwilling to let their encounter end there.

"Good God, lass, ye'll have me on my knees."

She quirked a brow. "Right where I want ye."

Jamie gave a teasing growl and then lifted her up into the air. She wrapped her legs around his waist, her arms around his neck, and the heat of her sex pressed to his throbbing cock. It was enough to make a man mad with need. He gritted his teeth and carried her to the bed, where they tumbled down onto the fragrant petals.

THIS COULD BE HEAVEN FOR ALL LORNA KNEW. A FEAST ON THE TABLE, flowers surrounding them, and the man she adored making sweet love to her.

For hours they explored, kissed, tickled, caressed. Never had they been able to just explore without a time limit. Always sneaking behind closed doors, alcoves, barns and gardens. Now they could savor one another, and not worry over whether they'd be interrupted. This was their time to worship each other. To give one another pleasure, and enjoy the bounty of such a glorious prize of having someone to love.

It was a dream come true, a miracle. How funny the world was, that as a child she'd been running from mayhem, and he'd come to swoop her up. When the time came for them both to seek a mate, once more he'd come along and swept her up. Only this time, she was ready and willing to be carried away.

As their bodies collided in sweet surrender, Lorna savored Jamie's touch, his whispered words of love and tenderness. She clung to him as he moved, rose her hips to meet his. Kissed him endlessly until they were both out of breath and then kissed him some more.

He showed her they could make love tenderly, cuddled together on their sides with her back to his chest. He kissed her shoulder, her neck, tugged at her ear, stroked her hip and then reached forward to slide his fingers through her folds until her body sang out with pleasure, and then he rolled her onto her back where he took her once more to the top of the earth and tossed her up into heaven.

And then she was over top of him, taking control of their lovemaking until Jamie was crying out her name with pleasure.

They feasted naked on cheese, bread, apples and watered wine, until Jamie licked a dribble of apple juice from Lorna's lips. The slightest provocation was all either of them needed before their bodies were once again on fire, and they explored making love in a chair. Then Jamie lifted her up and carried her back to the bed, still buried deep inside her.

Lorna commended him on his prowess and he answered in kind by showing her just how competent he was in the ways of pleasuring her with his mouth, hands and finally thrusting home until they both trembled, shivered and cried out their release.

Collapsing onto the bed, Jamie pulled Lorna into his arms, her back flush to his chest, his hands stroking the swell of her belly. Their breaths came quick, their bodies' slick with sweat.

"There's a little one of us in there," Jamie whispered, swirling his finger around her belly button.

"A little bit of both of us," Lorna said, rolling over, wanting to face him. Before she fell asleep she wanted to be able to gaze upon his face. "I've longed for this," she whispered, and then yawned, exhausted not only from their lengthy lovemaking, but the extensive journey and the overlong day.

Silver shafts of moonlight streamed in from the open window, as did a gentle breeze that cooled their overheated skin.

Her yawn prompted Jamie to do the same, and then they both laughed. "'Twas beautiful, just as ye are."

A sleepy smiled curled her lips. "This is beautiful—us together." She slipped her arm beneath his and around his back and a thigh over his, snuggling closer. "I know at some point ye'll have to go and fight with Wallace, but until then, I want to fall asleep each night seeing your face."

It was an inevitability, and one she'd known about from the beginning. Until then, she'd savor every moment they had together and pray for his safe return.

"And I want to wake each morn seeing your beautiful smile." He rubbed his nose against hers. "I'll never leave ye for long, and I'll dream of ye every night that I'm away."

Lorna leaned in for a tender kiss, once more struck with bountiful gratitude that she was here. She could still envision him running toward her as a child, much as he'd come toward her on the moors as a woman, and on the beach, and every place. He'd always been there for her, just as she'd always wanted him to be.

"My hero," she murmured.

And they fell blissfully asleep, curled in each other's arms, together at long last.

If you enjoyed **THE HIGHLANDER'S TEMPTATION,** *please spread the word by leaving a review on the site where you purchased your copy, or a reader site such as Goodreads or Shelfari! I love to hear from readers too, so drop me a line at* authorelizaknight@gmail.com *OR visit me on Facebook:* https://www.facebook.com/elizaknightauthor. *I'm also on Twitter:* @ElizaKnight. *If you'd like to receive my occasional newsletter, please sign up at* www.elizaknight.com
Many thanks!

MORE BOOKS BY ELIZA

Pirates of Britannia

Savage of the Sea
The Sea Devil
A Pirate's Bounty

The Stolen Bride Series

The Highlander's Temptation
The Highlander's Reward
The Highlander's Conquest
The Highlander's Lady
The Highlander's Warrior Bride
The Highlander's Triumph
The Highlander's Sin
Wild Highland Mistletoe (a Stolen Bride winter novella)
The Highlander's Charm (a Stolen Bride novella)
A Kilted Christmas Wish – a contemporary Holiday spin-off
The Highlander's Gift — coming soon as part of The Sutherland Legacy
spin-off series!

The Conquered Bride Series

Conquered by the Highlander
Seduced by the Laird
Taken by the Highlander (a Conquered bride novella)
Claimed by the Warrior
Stolen by the Laird
Protected by the Laird (a Conquered bride novella)
Guarded by the Warrior

The MacDougall Legacy Series

Laird of Shadows
Laird of Twilight
Laird of Darkness

The Thistles and Roses Series

Promise of a Knight
Eternally Bound
Breath from the Sea

The Highland Bound Series: (Erotic time-travel)

Behind the Plaid
Bared to the Laird
Dark Side of the Laird
Highlander's Touch
Highlander Undone
Highlander Unraveled

Wicked Women

Her Desperate Gamble
Seducing the Sheriff

Kiss Me, Cowboy

~

UNDER THE NAME E. KNIGHT

Tales From the Tudor Court

My Lady Viper
Prisoner of the Queen

Ancient Historical Fiction

A Day of Fire: a novel of Pompeii
A Year of Ravens: a novel of Boudica's Rebellion

ABOUT THE AUTHOR

Eliza Knight is an award-winning and *USA Today* bestselling indie author of over fifty sizzling historical romance and erotic romance. Under the name E. Knight, she pens rip-your-heart-out historical fiction. While not reading, writing or researching for her latest book, she chases after her three children. In her spare time (if there is such a thing…) she likes daydreaming, wine-tasting, traveling, hiking, staring at the stars, watching movies, shopping and visiting with family and friends. She lives atop a small mountain with her own knight in shining armor, three princesses and two very naughty puppies. Visit Eliza at http://www.elizaknight.comor her historical blog History Undressed: www.historyundressed.com. Sign up for her newsletter to get news about books, events, contests and sneak peaks! http://eepurl.com/CSFFD

facebook.com/elizaknightfiction

twitter.com/elizaknightauthor

instagram.com/elizaknighfiction

Made in the
USA
Monee, IL